Advance pr...

...I tore through
...with my breath held.
...able to travel the tube again
...out thinking about this novel...'

Sam Carrington

'*Tubing* is a cracking read with an
intriguing premise – as the twists racked up,
I found it impossible to put down'

Elizabeth Haynes

'A modern-day *Looking for Mr Goodbar*'

Fay Weldon

'Sharp, smart and deeply erotic, this intelligent
thriller offers surprises all the way to the end
of the line. Essential, compulsive reading'

Matt Thorne

Early reader reviews

'A very good read with plenty of twists and turns'

'Love love love this story. Read it all in one sitting'

'It gripped me from the first page and I loved
the twists in it. I have no hesitation in
recommending this book'

'A well written tale. I would definitely
read more by this author'

'A five-star read that will blow your mind'

'A sharp, original, erotic thriller
with numerous twists and turns'

'The book cracks along at a terrific pace and was
different enough from anything I've ever read before
for me to enjoy it'

'I read this book in a day… it is the perfect novel
for losing yourself in for a couple of hours.
And who knew the tube could be a setting
for more than a commute?!'

'This was an enthralling, mysterious novel that
kept you on your toes and made you second-guess
who you could trust'

TUBING

K.A. McKEAGNEY

RedDoor

Published by RedDoor
www.reddoorpublishing.com

The right of K.A. McKeagney to be identified as the author of
this Work has been asserted by her in accordance with sections
77 and 78 of the Copyright, Designs and Patents Act 1988

ISBN 978-1-910453-56-8

A CIP catalogue record for this book
is available from the British Library

Cover designer: Clare Connie Shepherd
www.clareconnieshepherd.com

Typesetting: WatchWord Editorial Services
www.watchwordeditorial.co.uk

Printed and bound by Nørhaven, Denmark

For Dan, my one constant

One

She stood with her back against the toilet door. She could see her reflection in the mirrored tiles on the back wall above the cistern. Mascara and eyeliner stained her cheeks. Her hair fared no better: a halo of frizz had formed around the crown, while the rest lay lank on her shoulders. Pressure built in her nose and throat until tears were rolling down her cheeks again.

'Polly?'

She held her breath.

'You in there?'

The door pushed against her back. She'd unwittingly picked a cubicle with no lock.

'Polly!'

It was Alicia. Polly had been in the toilet for the last half-hour while Alicia sat in the bar waiting for her.

The door pushed into her back again. She stood firm.

'Please leave me alone,' she whispered, barely audible, through gritted teeth.

They were in a bar on Chancery Lane. It was high-end – abstract art, thick glass-panelled walls and blue-tint lighting. They'd chosen a table at the back and ordered a jug of mojito to share. Polly hadn't been enjoying the evening. Not the fault of Alicia, her drinking companion – she was just too preoccupied with thoughts of what she wished she'd been doing.

Polly had only known Alicia for a couple of weeks. She was the new receptionist at work. The role suited her: she lifted the mood in the otherwise stagnant office. Polly would often find herself tittering behind her laptop while Alicia batted off advances from the mostly middle-aged men in the office using her quick wit dressed up in her South London accent. They flocked to her; she was impossible to miss. Today she was wearing a tight black pencil skirt and a neon-pink bustier top so small that every time she leant forward her breasts bubbled over.

'So, hon,' Alicia had said, after the third jug of cocktails had arrived, 'I've been chattin' for ages. How's you?'

She was right, she'd been talking solidly for the last few hours, but Polly didn't mind; she wasn't in the mood to talk. She was just entering the 'tired' phase of being drunk on an empty stomach. 'Fine,' she replied. She could have said more, but hoped she wouldn't have to.

'Just fine? There must be more going on than just *fine*.'

Polly looked at Alicia; she was beaming at her expectantly.

'Oh, you know, the usual…just the usual.' She tried to shrug her shoulders but her entire body felt like a dead weight.

'How's your fella? Oliver? That's his name, right?'

Polly gave a single nod.

'What does he do again?'

'Orthopaedic surgeon.'

'Sweet,' Alicia said, her eyes suddenly wide and shining. 'You bagged yourself a doctor – lucky lady. He got any cute doctor friends?'

Polly smiled, but didn't bother to answer.

'You guys been together long?'

'Three years to the day,' Polly replied with a snort.

'It's your anniversary? *Today*?'

Polly nodded.

'What the hell ya doin' here gettin' drunk with me?'

Polly slumped down deeper into her seat and started flicking the straw in her cocktail glass.

'Oh,' said Alicia.

'We never said we'd make a big deal of it,' said Polly, suddenly defensive. But she had been hopeful. Unfortunately, no big surprise had materialised. She'd seen Oliver briefly that morning. He'd left barely the impression of a kiss on her forehead as he ran out of the door, saying he was due in surgery all day and not to wait up.

'You wanna talk about it, hon?' Alicia asked.

Polly could feel tears pricking her eyes.

When they had first arrived at the bar, it'd been empty, but now several hours later it was packed. The noise of chatter and pounding minimal-techno was making her head hurt. She turned to look at the table next to them. It was swarming with City boys, all eagerly licking their lips, waiting for the slightest sign of encouragement. This was the last place she wanted to be. She needed to get out.

'I gotta go to the loo.' Her voice breaking, she grabbed her bag and got to her feet.

'Oh, hon, don't cry,' Alicia said, reaching forward. But Polly was already up.

'I'm OK,' she said, swallowing hard, trying to make the lump in her throat go away. 'I just need a minute.'

Polly had to fight her way through the crowd to get to the ladies' toilet. She was almost there when she heard someone call her name. She turned around.

'Polly? Oh, my God, it *is* you. What on earth are you doing here?'

It was Charlotte, Oliver's older sister.

Charlotte glided through the crowd as it parted for her. It was the way things were for Charlotte; she had the kind of poise that meant she floated everywhere. She looked beautiful, a crossover dark green dress wrapped her enviable figure, her make-up was perfect, and her soft blonde hair was swept up effortlessly away from her face. Polly couldn't help looking down at her own clothes. She winced when she realised she was wearing her trainers; she'd left her heels under her desk at work.

Charlotte leant over and air-kissed Polly on each cheek, blanketing her with a heavy, sweet scent. 'I didn't know you drank here,' she said, giving her a quick glance up and down. 'Can't imagine it being your sort of place.'

'I don't usually. Just came down for drinks after work.'

'Is Oliver here?' Charlotte said eagerly, looking round for her brother.

'No, just me and a friend from work,' Polly said sheepishly.

'Oh...' Charlotte looked confused. 'I thought you and Oliver were—'

'Charlotte!' someone shouted from behind, cutting them off. They both turned to see a guy in thick-rimmed glasses making a gesture to ask if she wanted another drink.

'Be there in a sec,' Charlotte called back in her sweetest voice, before turning back to Polly. 'Jesus, I can't wait to get out of this bloody place. Muggins here has once again been tasked with taking the visiting surgeons out to see the sights and sounds of London. I might put on a couple of stone and stop washing so they don't ask me again,' she said

4

sarcastically. 'Shame Oliver's not around,' she continued. 'He'd have them tied up in knots over the new diagnostic guidelines for arthroscopy to treat meniscal tears,' she finished with a chuckle, then stopped when she realised Polly hadn't got the joke.

At the mention of Oliver's name, Polly felt tears burning her eyes again.

Suddenly Charlotte paused. 'Did he...?' She grabbed Polly's left hand, gripping her fingers hard, then said, 'No, good.'

'What?' Polly said, pulling her hand away, shaking it after the unnecessarily hard squeeze.

'Nothing. I have to go.' And Charlotte was gone, the crowd parting for her as it had before.

Polly pushed her way through to the ladies', tears streaming down her face.

She listened carefully, waiting to hear Alicia leave. When she was sure she'd gone, she slowly started bouncing the back of her head against the toilet door. It made a satisfying clunk with every hit. Polly knew what she needed to do to make herself feel better. She turned round, lifted the toilet seat and vomited. She didn't need to put her fingers down her throat – she'd been doing it on demand since she was fourteen.

She emerged from the toilets twenty minutes later. The table she and Alicia had occupied had been taken over by the City boys. They'd managed to ensnare several pretty young things and were busy scheming on them. Alicia was nowhere to be seen. Polly headed straight for the door.

Once outside, she checked the time on her phone. 12.23 a.m. Three minutes until the last tube home. There were five missed calls on her phone and the voicemail icon throbbed angrily in the corner of the screen. She chose to ignore it. She dived across the busy main road and into Holborn tube station.

As she ran through the station to the platform she could hear the train doors beeping, ready to close. She flew down the last few steps and rounded the corner. There was no way she was going to make it. But then, seemingly out of nowhere, someone ran on ahead of her and managed to get an arm and a leg through the doors, forcing them to bounce open again. She jumped in after him.

The train was busy, the last one of the night always was. There were no seats free, so she made her way to the smaller, less crowded vestibule at the end. The carriage was stifling. The weather in London was unseasonably warm for June and the heat from the day was still trapped underground, making it humid and sticky. Polly leant back on the cool metal archway of the doorframe. She closed her eyes, too drunk to keep them open any longer.

She occupied herself with thoughts of food. She needed comfort – bread slathered in soft butter and nutty chocolate spread. She could almost taste the salty-sweet goo in her mouth. She decided to stop at the all-night corner shop on the way home and get a baguette, if not a sliced white loaf. Also a pint of full-cream milk to wash it down with – and some laxatives, if they had any.

The train jerked to a halt at the next station. More late-night revellers pushed their way into the carriage, pressing Polly further back. She begrudgingly opened her eyes and reasserted her bit of space in the corner.

It was then that she noticed him.

From the reflection in the train's darkened window she could see that he was staring at her. At first she thought it was a trick of the light, a reflection of a reflection, making it seem as though he was looking at her. But, as she slowly turned her head to the side, his followed, until they were both facing one another.

She had no idea how long he'd been watching her. He made no motion to look away or hide the fact that he was staring. He just stood there, perfectly still and serious, his eyes like hooks in her. She stared back, stunned for a moment, then looked behind her to try to figure out what could possibly have provoked such a reaction. There was nothing. When she turned back he was still staring.

Polly was struck by how incredibly beautiful he was. His face looked as if it had been carved of stone, it was so striking and perfectly symmetrical. His high cheekbones and brow caught the light, making his dark brown eyes almost black. His skin was lightly tanned and his thick, sun-kissed hair was pushed back away from his face in waves. He almost didn't look real; there wasn't a crease, wrinkle or blemish on him – he was flawless. Neither one of them moved, both remaining perfectly still, facing one another, but something was happening between them. Polly had no idea what, but it hijacked her senses. She could still hear the rattle of the train and the low hum of chatter, but everything was out of focus; there was only him.

They stayed like that for several seconds, until Polly's brain caught up and she looked away. Despite her coyness, she couldn't help letting her eyes trail down his faultless body until they reached the floor.

As the train pulled out of the station, he slowly moved forward towards her. Polly looked around at the other commuters. No one was looking at them. Most were unwillingly drawn to a commotion in the main vestibule, where a group of girls were talking and squealing loudly in Italian, while two guys strutted round them like peacocks.

He stopped just before their bodies touched. They lingered millimetres from one another, eyes locked. She held her breath until she felt the palms of his hands gently come into contact with hers. His touch was so slight it was almost non-existent, like a fine powder. His hands slipped into hers, slowly interlocking with her fingers.

He continued to hold her gaze, only breaking it for a second to look down at her mouth. He pressed his lips together, as though imagining what it would feel like to kiss her. She saw his Adam's apple bob as he swallowed hard. Without thinking, she slowly moved closer.

When their lips met, the soft resistance fired every nerve-ending in her body. She closed her eyes as they slowly started to kiss – softly at first, then gradually he started pushing into her mouth. He let go of her hands and slipped his arms around her waist. Her entire body shivered. He pulled her in closer so their bodies had full contact. She could feel something hard digging into her hip. He took several careful steps forward, forcing her back until she felt the metal doorway behind her. The pressure on her lips began to lessen, signalling the end of their kiss. She opened her eyes. His features had softened and there was the start of a smile on his face, a mischievous smile.

He watched her carefully as he moved his hands downwards. They stopped just above the curve of her buttocks. She didn't want him to stop there. He read the look and started moving down further, until he reached the tops of her thighs. Again he stopped. He looked at her. She slowly nodded her head.

Suddenly there was urgency in his movement. His hands ran up under her skirt and on to her naked thighs. Her skin puckered instantly, every hair on her body standing on end. The tips of his fingers pressed deep into her flesh as they climbed up between her legs. Her breath caught as he slipped his hand into her knickers. He pressed and gently pinched, teasing, before sliding his fingers deep inside her. She groaned as he pushed harder and deeper, the knot in her abdomen growing as he slid his fingers back and forth. He worked faster and faster, applying more pressure with each movement.

As the blackness of the tube tunnel outside was replaced by the bright lights of Oxford Circus tube station Polly let out a small cry, unable to stop herself, every part of her body alive and open, flooded with sensation. She gripped on to him until the feeling passed, then opened her eyes. He was smiling at her. She suddenly remembered where she was and looked round, embarrassed. No one appeared to have noticed. She quickly straightened her clothes.

He leant in close to her, his smooth perfection brushing the side of her face. He whispered, 'Meet me again.' It made her heart flutter.

'Wh-what do you mean?' she stammered, still reeling from the intimacy.

But she didn't get an answer. He was already on his way to the open carriage doors. She watched as he got off the train and sauntered down the platform.

She prayed he would look back. He didn't.

Two

Polly slowly drifted into consciousness. She was in bed. Daylight seeped through the flimsy window blinds illuminating her eyelids. They felt heavy and sticky, a sure sign that she'd forgotten to take off her make-up before going to bed. She cursed herself, imagining the spidery trails left all over her pillow.

She desperately wanted more sleep, but her throat was raw and her head ached. She lay crumpled on her left side; her crushed arm and shoulder throbbed painfully. She carefully rolled over, trying to uncurl her spine and release her arm in one motion. With her eyes still sealed shut, she twisted round and groped at the bedside table for a glass of water. Her hand scurried round, identifying objects by touch – lamp base, mobile phone, splayed paperback of *The Woman in White*, lip balm, hairband with a nest of rogue hairs attached, tube of twenty-four-hour moisturiser – but no water. She pulled her arm back in under the duvet. As she did so, she felt skin brush against skin as the top of her arm touched her breast. She slid her hands down her body, working her way down until she felt a towel wrapped around her waist. Why wasn't she wearing her pyjamas?

She lay there feeling sorry for herself, trying to piece together why she was naked, dying of thirst, with a full face of make-up and a head that felt as though it had been dropped on the floor.

She could hear Oliver clattering about in the kitchen. She tried to call out to ask him to get her a drink but her throat was so dry she could hardly get any sound out – a papery, barely audible croak was all she managed. Then the memory hit her – the train, him, his face slowly moving towards hers. Her eyelids snapped open instantly and every muscle in her body went rigid.

'Morning, Pol,' said Oliver pushing the door open with his foot. He was wearing a pair of boxers with a gaping fly, and holding two cups of tea.

She lay perfectly still, a Kung-Fu grip on the edges of the duvet.

'You OK?' he asked cocking his head back.

She released the duvet. 'Fine,' she said. A nerve under her left eye twitched incessantly, as if it was trying to give her up.

'You don't look it.' He set the mugs on the bedside table and sat down next to her.

'Yeah,' she said vaguely. 'Too much to drink last night, I think.'

As soon as she'd arrived home the previous night she'd gone straight to the drinks cupboard in the kitchen and poured herself a large whisky. She hated whisky, but it was all she could find. Oliver had various open bottles; he considered himself a bit of a connoisseur. She'd downed the glass, then poured herself another one, the soothing warmth quickly engulfing her.

She subtly rearranged her towel under the duvet, pulling it up over her chest and securing it as best she could, then sat up. He passed her a mug. It was the one she'd bought him as a present when they first moved in together. It had a picture

11

of Kenneth Williams dressed in scrubs and the caption 'Ooh, Matron!' underneath. He'd bought her a pair of antique emerald and ruby-studded drop earrings.

She sipped tentatively, watching enviously as Oliver drained his mug of piping-hot tea. She was convinced his mouth was lined with asbestos. 'Ah, yes,' he gasped loudly at the refreshment. 'And what did you get up to last night?'

'A drink. Alicia from work,' Polly said, still trying to get the evening's events straight in her mind.

Oliver pulled a face. 'What were you doing hanging out with the little black pixie?'

She glared at him.

'I'm just joking, but you have to admit she's a funny little thing.' He had met the receptionist briefly when he met Polly at the office after work one evening. They'd exchanged five words at most. 'Did you go anywhere nice?' he continued.

She couldn't think clearly. At that very moment the feeling of the stranger's hands clawing up her thighs to her knickers flashed through her mind.

'Earth to Polly,' Oliver said, waving a hand in front of her face when she didn't answer.

'I'm sorry, what?' she said, trying to catch up with the conversation.

'Last night – where did you go for a drink?'

'Oh, some new bar on Chancery Lane,' she replied, unable to remember the name of the place. She was trying desperately to act normal, but couldn't bring herself to look at him.

'Must have been a heavy one: you were all over the place when you got in.'

Her head snapped up to look at him. She had no memory of having seen him when she got home last night. 'I don't remember. Did I get you up?'

'No, I just heard you.'

She couldn't help letting out a small sigh of relief.

'You were banging about in the bathroom for ages,' he continued. 'It was a mess when I went in there this morning, your clothes all over the place and a massive puddle in the middle of the floor.'

She vaguely recalled attempting to take a shower before going to bed. It had felt too weird sliding in next to Oliver after having been with someone else. She'd stripped off hastily, giving no care to her dry-clean-only skirt and hand-wash-only top. In the shower she'd tried to wash herself, but as soon as the jet of water had touched the tops of her thighs and gone between her legs she was tingling again. She hadn't been able to resist allowing her fingers to gently work their way in. She'd closed her eyes, remembering his face, and lost her grip on the shower head, spraying water everywhere, drenching the tiny bathroom.

'Oh,' she said, lost in thought.

It took several seconds for her to realise that Oliver had gone quiet. He was watching her, a serious look on his face.

'What?' she said, suddenly frightened that he could see inside her brain and was reliving the memory with her.

'I tried to call you last night. Did you get my messages?'

'No ... well, yeah, but not until late,' she said, remembering the five missed calls. She hadn't listened to any of the messages yet.

'I arranged for us to go out for dinner.'

'What?' said Polly. 'But you said you were on call.'

'I know I did.' He looked down at the duvet sheepishly and began picking at a tiny piece of fluff. 'I was trying to be romantic, surprise you.'

Polly looked at him, surprised. 'But you said not to wait up.'

'I know,' he said, looking annoyed. 'But I wanted to ... Oh, forget it.' He pulled away.

'You wanted to what?' Polly asked.

'It doesn't matter; it was nothing.'

'No, tell me.'

'I organised a surprise dinner, but you didn't answer your phone, so I couldn't get in touch with you. Serves me right, I guess.'

With thoughts of last night still running in her head, Polly closed her eyes and started massaging the bridge of her nose with her thumb and index finger.

'Don't get upset, Pol,' said Oliver moving in close and putting his arm around her. 'It's my fault, I should have told you about it, or at least said I was planning a surprise.'

She opened her eyes and looked at him. He gave her a half-hearted smile. Guilt crawled all over her; she wanted to make it all better. She leant over and kissed him. He responded, but as soon as her tongue ventured forward his lips clamped shut. She persisted, letting her towel fall away and pressing herself into him. He pulled away from her. 'Steady, Pol,' he said.

'Why?' she asked, her lips moving down his cheek then on to his neck.

'We need to get ready for work, and ... you're not washed or anything.'

'It doesn't matter.' She gently started nibbling at his earlobe.

'No. Come on, now.' He started pushing her away.

She stopped and looked up at him.

'Good girl,' he said, then got up and went into the bathroom.

Polly lay back down on the bed. She heard him turn the shower on. She couldn't remember the last time they'd had sex. When they had first started going out, things had been fine, kind of. But, since they'd moved in together, a blanket of contented domesticity had settled over him. Maybe he was nesting. The thought filled Polly with horror. Polly and Oliver had met on a blind date – they hadn't been set up together, the blind date had actually been with a guy called Ben. He was the brother of a girl she went to uni with. The date had been a disaster from beginning to end. Ben was late. She'd sat in the restaurant awkwardly for forty-five minutes. When he finally turned up, he was wearing a T-shirt and jeans. Polly had made an effort, in a short black dress and heels, and she felt horribly overdressed – she knew it the second she walked into the restaurant. She'd thought with a name like The Royal it would be a posh place, but most of the people were in casual gear, slouched around in mismatching chairs and tables. When Ben got to the table, he had looked her up and down and said, 'Like, wow,' sarcastically, before leaning forward to kiss her on the cheek. Polly nervously overshot her head as she bent forward, and he ended up kissing her ear.

Their conversation was stilted from the start. They would either talk over the top of one another or sit in long silences when neither could think of what to say. Polly drank far too much wine and, having barely touched her meal, ended up getting pissed. But not a good pissed. The atmosphere between them made her feel nervy and cynical. She kept coming out with things that she didn't really think or mean. Ben seemed to enjoy this and spent the rest of the evening questioning everything she said, tying her up in knots.

Just as the bill came, he excused himself, saying he needed to use the toilet. Polly, feeling ridiculously paranoid, thought he might have done a bunk, leaving her to pay. After a couple of minutes she got up from the table to look for him. She found him still in the restaurant, just by the toilets. She ducked back round the corner just before he saw her. He was on his mobile. She couldn't help listening to the conversation.

'What the fuck were you thinking? She's a nightmare.' Pause. 'I'm not being mean. She's sat at the table pissed as a fart. And the bill's just turned up. She barely took a mouthful of her food and no doubt she expects me to pay for it. I fucking hate ana girls.' Pause. 'Sis, of course she's anorexic, or a puker. Either that or she's got some kind of wasting disease. Hey, wait a minute, you haven't set me up with a terminally ill chick, have you?' Then he laughed, a loud, raucous laugh.

Polly didn't listen to any more. She went back to the table, grabbed her coat and left in tears.

As she reached for the door handle, an arm had nipped round and pulled it open for her. 'Let me get that for you.'

Polly looked up. It was Oliver.

'Oh,' he said, noticing the tears streaking down her face. 'Are you OK?'

'Fine,' she muttered as she moved past him.

'Are you sure?'

Something in his voice made her stop. He sounded so concerned. She looked back up at him and her bottom lip started to quiver uncontrollably.

'Hey, Polly, what's going on? Where are you going?' Ben's voice had come booming from behind them.

'I gotta get out of here,' Polly muttered.

Oliver took one look at Ben then gently guided her out of the restaurant and on to the pavement. 'Fancy getting a coffee somewhere?' he asked.

She nodded, unable to speak for fear of the avalanche of tears that were about to fall.

Oliver wasn't Polly's usual type. He was blond, for a start, and big. He'd played rugby as a prop forward until his knees had given out a few years before. He had the stocky build for it, but, since he'd stopped playing, most of his muscle had turned to fat. But it suited him: he was comfortable in his skin, and it was difficult to imagine him any other way. He was older than her by almost nine years. When he mentioned he was a surgeon, she was instantly on edge, waiting for him to start patronising her, but he didn't. He was charming and funny and gentle. She told him what had happened on her blind date, all but the bit about Ben saying she was anorexic. Oliver said he wanted to take her on a proper date. She accepted.

She heard Oliver turn off the shower and the clatter of curtain rings as he got out. She slowly sat up and re-secured the towel around herself. It was then that she noticed the four deep fingertip marks near the top of her right thigh. They already had purply-yellow rings around the edges. She placed her fingers over each one and pressed down. They were tender to touch. She closed her eyes. *Who was he?* She was suddenly tingling all over again.

'Shower's free.'

She opened her eyes to see Oliver standing at the bedroom door, and quickly pulled down the towel to hide her bruises.

'It's almost eight,' he said.

She didn't answer. She should be leaving for work in fifteen minutes. She moved to get up, but had to stop for a second: she felt woozy and her head ached worse than ever. Eventually, she shakily got to her feet and plodded towards Oliver, still standing at the door. He tapped her on the bum as she walked past; she shot him a sour look.

When she got to the bathroom, it was a mess. Her clothes were strewn everywhere and soaked through. Oliver had left it exactly as he'd found it and, from the looks of it, used her skirt as a bath mat.

Three

Polly got to work half an hour late. It took her ages to get ready and leave the house – the connection between her brain and her body kept malfunctioning.

She got the tube to work as usual. As soon as she got on, she couldn't help having a quick check around to see if *he* was there. He wasn't, of course.

Polly made up one half of the legal department for a newspaper called the *London Voice*. The other half was James, a barrister who only came in one day a week as a favour to the paper's owner, Lionel. Polly's job was to keep on top of the filing and other admin bits until James could make it in. She had no legal training, and had only got the job because Oliver had pulled a few strings – his parents knew someone who knew someone.

Working for a London paper wasn't really living up to her expectations. She'd had visions of being in the hubbub of a busy press office, breaking news all around her, an experienced journalist spotting some hidden talent in her and taking her under their wing. In reality, the *London Voice* was a free paper with a non-existent readership on the brink of collapse. The only reason it had survived its first year was because Lionel kept pumping his own money into it. She'd thought about looking for other jobs, but didn't want to appear ungrateful, especially after Oliver's parents had pulled strings for her. She decided to bide her time. The only staff journalist on the paper, Ron, was hardly the archetypal shit-hot journalist; his latest big break had been to do with council housing benefit fraud. She'd started carrying round a notebook with her, to write down feature ideas to pitch to Lionel. She was waiting until the right moment presented itself; she already had three pages of possibilities.

The good thing about having a hangover was that it distracted her from all other thoughts. She spent the morning hiding behind her laptop, focusing solely on the task at hand and keeping movement to a minimum. Alicia emailed several times, asking what had happened to her last night. She ignored the emails. From where Polly was sitting she could see Alicia was busy tied to the phones. She felt bad enough about Oliver; she didn't want someone else giving her grief.

By lunchtime, Polly was beginning to feel human again. Her stomach felt hollow and painfully empty. She usually went to an organic deli off Tottenham Court Road for lunch – they had a range of OK-sized salads that were under four hundred calories – but today she needed something with more sustenance. She reckoned she must have lost at least a pound from not eating yesterday evening or having any breakfast – she deserved a treat.

There was a small café across the road from her office. She'd never been into it before, although she walked past it nearly every day. The menu board outside peddled thick-cut sandwiches, pasties and fry-ups – the promise of stodge was impossible to resist.

It was a small, dank place with chequered tablecloths and tomato-shaped ketchup bottles. It smelt of chips and dirty grill pans. The sandwich counter was busy, but she only had to wait a couple of minutes to be served. She ordered a white baguette with cheese, ham, tomato and extra mayonnaise. Her tastebuds prickled as she watched the stubby-fingered waitress prepare it through the glass counter. She knew she'd be bloated and have a carb-hangover later, but her body demanded salt and starch. She picked up a bottle of sparkling water from the fridge and paid.

As she turned to leave, she spotted Alicia seated opposite the counter. She'd spread herself out across an entire table, reading a magazine and suckling at a can of Diet Coke. Polly couldn't believe she'd missed her when she was queuing. As soon as she saw her, she put her head down and quickly walked to the door; she wanted nothing more than to go back to the privacy of her desk and devour her baguette. She was just pulling the door open ready to leave when she heard Alicia's husky voice calling her name.

She was tempted to carry on and pretend she hadn't heard, but a woman with a pushchair coming in forced her to pause and then back up. Polly looked across, forcing on a smile.

Alicia beckoned.

Polly reluctantly went over. Alicia pulled out a chair as she approached. 'Hey, hon, how's it goin'?' she said as Polly sat in the chair next to her. 'I emailed you a couple of times this morning, didn't you see?'

'I've been really busy today, haven't been checking my mails,' Polly replied, forcing herself to maintain eye contact – she'd read somewhere that liars always looked away.

Alicia folded up her magazine so Polly could put her lunch down. 'Just wanted to check you were OK after last night. What happened?'

'What do you mean?' replied Polly, looking down at Alicia's plate. It had the remnants of fried eggs, chips and a reconstituted meat patty on it.

'You went to the loo and then totally disappeared.'

'Oh, yeah. I wasn't feeling great so I went home.'

'I wish you'd said somethin', lady. I came looking for you. I was worried.'

'Oh,' said Polly. She felt bad. 'Sorry.'

'No worries, just glad you're OK.'

Polly looked down at her baguette and bit her lip. Her stomach rumbled painfully. She couldn't wait any longer. She tore off the wrapping and took a large mouthful. She let out a small groan as the flavour brought her mouth back to life.

Alicia chuckled.

'What?' said Polly, suddenly self-conscious, putting her baguette back down.

'Nothing, just good to see you enjoyin' your food.'

Polly hated eating in front of other people, especially other women. She imagined they were working out how many calories and grams of fat she was consuming, compared to how many she should be having.

'Don't let me stop you,' said Alicia encouragingly.

Polly tentatively picked up her baguette again and took a small bite.

It wasn't long before Alicia was in full flow. Polly did her best to follow what she was saying, but the food was so good she couldn't concentrate on anything else. She didn't think Alicia had noticed; she seemed content with the occasional nod and 'yep'.

When Alicia suddenly stopped, Polly looked up at her.

'You're not with it today, are you?' the receptionist said.

'Huh?' Polly replied, trying to rewind the last couple of seconds' conversation in her mind. 'What makes you say that?'

'You've not listened to a word I've said.'

Polly blushed; she felt embarrassed at being caught out, and even worse for letting it show. 'I'm sorry,' she said, putting the last of her baguette down. 'I didn't get to bed till late last night and I've been feeling rough all morning.'

'Trouble on the tube, eh?' Alicia asked, coolly raising her left eyebrow.

'What?' snapped Polly. There was something in her tone that caught Polly's attention. It was so considered and deliberate.

'The tube … you said you didn't get home till late …'

'What about it?' she demanded.

'Whoa, girl, it was just a question.' Alicia put her hands up defensively. 'Fuck, something must have happened, though.'

Polly stared at her, trying to decide if she was just being paranoid. She turned it over in her mind for several seconds before choosing to test the water.

'I … um …' She hesitated for a second, suddenly unsure of where this conversation would lead. 'There were these two people on the tube …'

'Yeah?'

'They were kind of … you know …'

'What?'

'In the corner of the carriage …' Polly trailed off. She watched Alicia's reaction carefully.

'Come on, out with it, lady.' Alicia was getting impatient.

'You know … doing things two people shouldn't be doing together in public.'

'Fuckin'?' Alicia asked, her eyes lighting up.

'No, just touching each other, stuff like that.'

'What?' Her voice went all high-pitched and screechy. 'You never got a bit frisky on the tube on the way home before? Bitta grindin', bitta teasin', till ya get home and…' She kissed her teeth and rolled her tongue.

'No, no, this was different. They didn't know each other. Well, that's what it looked like to me,' Polly finished, quickly correcting herself.

'Really?' said Alicia, moving closer. 'So, what happened?'

'They were both just kind of standing there, then he walked up to her and started kissing her and touching her, but it was so weird because they didn't say a word to one another.'

'Saucy,' said Alicia.

They sat in silence for several seconds, Polly unsure how to continue the conversation. Then Alicia started up again, telling her about some American reality TV show about drag queens that she just *had* to watch.

'Afternoon, ladies.' The voice interrupted them from behind. They both turned to see Jas with a takeaway in hand. Jas was the tech guy who worked in their building. Polly spoke to him from time to time. She wasn't really sure what he did – something to do with servers and backends. He had his own small office a couple of floors up from hers.

'I couldn't help overhearing your conversation.' He pointed to the queue snaking along the sandwich counter. 'I thought I'd come and enlighten you both.'

'Excuse me, private chat,' replied Alicia, annoyed at being cut off mid-sentence.

'Sorry,' said Jas sheepishly. 'Just heard you mention the tube thing, is all.'

'What do you mean?' asked Polly, immediately intrigued.

Jas pulled out a chair and sat down. Even though he was talking to Polly, he couldn't keep his eyes off Alicia. She, on the other hand, was looking away, irritated.

'Meeting strangers on the tube and, you know … doing stuff with them. I done it.' A wide grin spread across his face when Alicia slowly turned to look at him, her head cocked back slightly.

'Really?' asked Polly. 'Are you serious?'

'Yeah,' said Jas, 'damn straight.'

'Sure, sure,' Alicia said sarcastically.

Polly stared at him, disbelieving. 'What tube line were you on?' she asked.

'I think it was Central … yeah, yeah, it was the Central Line,' he said, nodding nonchalantly.

'What time was it?' Polly pressed on.

'What is this? Twenty Questions or summink?'

'No,' replied Alicia, 'I think she's just trying to catch you out because you're full of shit.' She turned to look at Polly, exhaling through her nose loudly. 'Can you believe this guy?'

'So how many times have you done it?' Polly was trying to keep the conversation going. She had butterflies in her stomach.

'Couple of times.'

Alicia tutted and rolled her eyes.

'So how does it happen?' Polly pressed on. 'I mean, how do you know who's up for it?'

'It's an arranged thing. People set up meetings on certain trains at certain times, then one dude gives a signal to the other and they just go at it,' he replied. 'It's called tubing.'

Four

'Tubing.'

The word spun round and round in Polly's brain before it finally popped out of her mouth. She cleared her throat and quickly looked around to check if anyone had noticed – no one paid her any attention.

Since talking to Jas, she'd been desperate to get back to work and on her laptop. But when she got to the office James was sitting at the desk behind hers, working through the backlog of paperwork she'd left for him. He had a clear view of her screen.

She slumped down at her desk and spent the rest of the afternoon pretending to work. She opened up a document and spent a lot of time scrolling up and down and zooming in and out, but not actually doing anything. Eventually, she zoned out, letting her mind wander to the sound of tapping keys and the low murmur of voices.

She thought about *him* – the guy from the train. It was the first time she'd gone through the events properly since it happened. She indulged herself, letting her mind run through every second of the encounter. Every time she imagined him touching her, her stomach would flutter so hard she could barely stand it. She could almost feel his fingers on her, inside her. She still couldn't believe it had happened, it seemed like a dream, but it was real. She lifted up her skirt to look at the four deep fingertip marks on her thigh. But then in the next instant she felt appalled at herself. What had she been thinking? He was a total stranger; she'd been so intimate with him. What if someone had seen them? But her fingers kept finding the fingertip bruises. She pushed down on them, gently at first, then harder and harder. The pain took her breath away.

At four, James finally left. As soon as she heard his briefcase snap shut, she was instantly alive and free of the apathy that had settled over her all afternoon. She was on Google before he was out of the door, curiosity getting the better of her.

She searched using the term 'tubing' first. She waded through several pages of places to ride and rent tubes – big rubber rings to float down rivers on. After about seven pages she decided it was pointless, so clicked back and changed her search terms to 'sex tube trains'. Several YouTube pages came up among an array of porn sites. The videos claimed to show people having sex on trains, but she couldn't make out who she was supposed to be looking at, let alone what they were doing. Initially she forgot to turn off the sound on her laptop. She jumped out of her skin when she pressed *Play* and sex groans blasted the office. A few heads turned but no one said anything. She figured most of them were probably looking at porn themselves anyway.

She went back to the search results to check out a couple of news stories. One was about a couple having oral sex on a train and then getting charged for lighting up cigarettes afterwards. The next was about an adult movie that had been made using mobile phones while half a dozen people went at it on a busy Russian commuter train.

She didn't realise it was after five until most people in the office had already left. She was struck by the silence. She looked around at the empty desks. She'd never seen it this deserted before. The sunny weather had encouraged everyone to leave on time.

She was back at Google contemplating a new set of search terms when she heard Alicia's voice. 'Working late tonight, hon?'

Her fingers froze instantly. She hadn't realised she was still in the office.

'I've just a few bits to do before tomorrow,' Polly lied without looking up, trying to make it clear she was busy.

'Well, make sure you're not here too late,' Alicia said, gathering up her bags. 'None of us is paid enough to be doing overtime in this place.'

Alicia took forever to get out the door. First she dropped her handbag, then she couldn't find her pass key, then her mobile rang and she talked for ten minutes through the half-opened office door. Polly was forced to eavesdrop. She was cooing to some guy, facing Polly and pulling expressions at her as though somehow trying to invite her into the conversation. Finally she left, fluttering her gel nails behind her.

Polly decided to search for 'sex underground' this time. Big mistake. It brought up nothing but masochism sites. She changed it to 'sex London Underground' – more YouTube pages of people apparently having sex on trains, but nothing convincing or of any use.

She sat for ages trying to think of other words to describe it. She couldn't believe 'tubing' hadn't brought anything up. She tried searching for it again, just to make sure she hadn't missed anything.

At half-past six the office cleaners arrived. They tutted loudly as they tried to clean around her. She decided to give up.

She got home at 7.15, tired, frustrated and in a foul mood. Oliver was in. He was making dinner, some chicken and pasta thing. She'd planned to collapse in front of the TV but, as soon as she walked in, he started fussing and trying to bulk out the sauce so she could have some too. She told him she didn't want any – after her pig-out at lunch, she was only allowing herself a small bowl of cereal for dinner – but he insisted.

Sometimes it felt as if food was an obsession for him: three hearty meals a day without fail – even if he got up at two in the afternoon, he'd still fit in all three. He made such a ritual of it, and always dragged her into it. She felt like one of his patients. After they'd been together for a couple of months he started mentioning that he thought she was too skinny and that she needed to feed her body properly. At first she found it endearing: he enveloped her in his care and concern. But since they'd moved in together a year ago she'd put on over half a stone, and his constant concern was beginning to grate. Most nights Polly was happy with cereal or a piece of toast, but he'd put a stop to all that. She was beginning to think he was a feeder, using food as some kind of sex substitute.

Just as they sat down to eat, her mobile rang. Polly jumped up to get it from her bag. For an insane moment she thought it might be *him* – maybe he'd got her number somehow.

'Leave it, Pol,' Oliver said.

'It might be important,' she replied. By the time she got to it her heart was racing in anticipation.

It was her dad.

Sighing she took the call anyway. At least it got her away from the huge pile of carbs Oliver had just placed in front of her. The smell was making her mouth water.

They made small talk about the hot weather and her job. After a few minutes he got round to the reason for his call. She didn't need to be told; Polly had known the reason the second his name came up on the screen.

'Now I don't want you to get upset, love, but I've bad news. It's your mother.'

Polly wasn't about to get upset; she received a phone call like this about once a month.

'She's in a bad way.'

'Uh-huh,' said Polly.

'The doctor said not to worry, but, oh ... ' He trailed off.

As a child, Polly had accepted her mother's illnesses as the norm; she'd never known any different. But as she got older she started to notice small inconsistencies. One day her mother would claim that her left leg was so stiff she couldn't move it, but the next day it would be her right. Or she'd say that she'd had crippling back pain all morning and hadn't been able to move from her bed, yet Polly had seen her out in the garden smoking. She had mentioned it to her dad once. He'd told her that her mother's condition was like that – unpredictable – and could change from one moment to the next.

'If we could just get a diagnosis, you know? Maybe this time ... We all need to try and stay positive.'

Neither of them spoke for several seconds.

Eventually her father said, 'Well, she's comfortable now and the doctor's coming back to see her tomorrow. Says he'll refer her to another specialist.'

He sounded drained. Her dad was well into his seventies, twenty years his wife's senior. Retirement had never really happened for him; he'd gone from engineer to carer. She wanted to comfort him, she knew he was genuinely worried, but she couldn't bring herself to acknowledge her mother's ridiculous behaviour.

'Are you OK, Dad?'

'Me? I'm fine, fit as a fiddle.' She imagined him puffing and panting, doing a jig, just to prove it. 'Maybe you could come home for a visit. She'd like that.'

Polly knew her mother wouldn't be fussed either way.

Just then she heard a click on the line. She wondered if her mother was listening in on the call from the phone upstairs. She probably was.

'I'm busy with work at the moment.'

'I'm sure they'd understand if you told them your mother's not well.'

'I don't know.' She desperately wanted to finish the call. She looked over at Oliver shovelling forkfuls of pasta into his mouth. 'I'd better go, Dad, Oliver's put dinner out.'

'Well have a think about it and let me know.'

'I will.'

'Oh, before you go, maybe you should give me your work number, you know, just in case the worst … well, just in case I need you in a hurry.'

'Just use my mobile.'

'I can't always get through to you on that thing.' Despite his years as an engineer, her dad couldn't get used to the concept of communication without wires. She'd tried to explain it several times, but he told her it wasn't for him.

To get off the phone, she gave him the number, then said goodbye.

Oliver had cleared his plate by the time she sat back down at the table. She took a couple of forkfuls from her plate and left the rest – it was cold.

Five

Polly spent the next couple of days at work scouring the internet for any mention of tubing. She couldn't help herself: the experience had been so intense she could do nothing but think about it. She knew James wouldn't be back in for at least a week, so she didn't even have to pretend to work. She felt exasperated. She tried every search engine, forum, blog and social networking site she could think of. There was nothing, not a single reference to tubing. It made no sense. Surely, if it existed, there'd be mention of it on the internet?

She briefly considered mentioning it on Facebook to see if any of her friends knew. But Oliver might see, so instead she updated her status to 'fed up'.

Since she had moved to London, Facebook had become a lifeline for Polly. It seemed the older she got, the harder it was to make decent friends. She'd left everyone she knew back home or in Bristol where she went to uni. Oliver's friends were nice enough, but they were much older than her and all had high-powered jobs as doctors or barristers. She had very little in common with them. Whenever she spoke to them, she felt as if she were having a conversation with someone's parents.

She had a couple of new friend requests on Facebook, one from a girl she'd gone to school with who she'd barely spoken to, and another from some guy she thought she recognised from her literary criticism class at uni. She accepted both; it didn't really matter if she knew them or not, only another 144 until she hit a thousand.

On Friday, against her better judgment, she went up to the seventh floor to talk to Jas.

'Hey, Polly,' he said as she hesitantly made her way into his office.

Polly looked around the room. She'd never actually been in his office before, only ducked her head round the door. It was tiny, and from the big square porcelain sink at the far end she guessed it had once been a broom cupboard. It was crammed with bits of circuitry and dismantled hard drives. Even the sink had a couple of devices precariously balanced on the edge. A musty smell filled the air, like a teenage boy's bedroom first thing in the morning. She thought it was probably coming from the sink or the overflowing bin on the floor, or it could have been from the green-grey growths on the plates and cups that littered every surface. She spotted a mug she'd lost a couple of months ago. The handle was missing.

They made small talk for a while, then she told him she was having a problem with her keyboard – a squeaky spacebar. He told her he couldn't help – he was only contracted to deal with network issues, not hardware. She already knew that. At that point, Polly almost chickened out. She started walking out of the door, then stopped and turned back. 'Actually, Jas, you know that thing you were talking about the other day at lunch…'

'Hmm?' he said absently returning to his computer. The screen reflected lines of code in the lenses of his glasses. 'What thing?'

'The tubing thing,' replied Polly embarrassed.

A wide, toothy grin broke on his face. 'Yes, what about it?' he said, pretending to work.

'I was just wondering how you found out about it.' Her fingers picked at the flakes of loose paint on the doorframe.

'Why, Polly, you've never struck me as that type of girl,' he said, looking up to face her.

'No, no,' she said, 'I'm not looking for me, it's for a friend.' She winced as she said it.

Jas's expression suddenly changed: his eyes grew so wide, she thought they were going to pop out of their sockets and roll across the desk. 'No...' he said. 'It's not Alicia, is it?'

Polly thought for a second. Should she? Then she slowly nodded.

Jas erupted from his chair, bouncing up and down with excitement. 'She is fucking filthy – I knew she was.'

'Jas, Jas!' Polly exclaimed, trying to calm him down. 'This is just between us, right? I promised I wouldn't say anything.'

'We're safe,' he replied, his eyes glazed in the midst of a fantasy.

'So?' said Polly. 'How did you find out about it?'

'What? Oh, yeah. I was doing an... ahem...' he looked up at her sheepishly '...an online chat thing.'

Polly looked back at him confused.

'You know what I mean, right?' he continued.

She had no idea what he was talking about.

'OK, OK, I was in a sex chat room,' he admitted, his face flushing slightly. 'Some dudes were talking about it.'

'But how did you get involved? Arrange a hook-up?'

He was still for a second, then swivelled his chair round and stood up. 'Sit down, Polly,' he said, pulling a spare chair up to his desk.

She sat. Then he sat.

'I'm going to be honest with you, just like you've been with me about Alicia. We can trust each other, right?'

'Of course.' Polly could feel the butterflies in her stomach.

'I've never actually done it…' Then he added quickly, 'Tubing, I mean.'

The butterflies dive-bombed to the pit of her gut. 'Oh.' It was hard to hide her disappointment.

They were both silent, neither able to look the other in the eye. Then Polly said, 'Well, what did they say about it in this chat room?'

'OMG, it was total filth. This guy started—'

'No, no, not that,' Polly cut him off. 'I mean, about how they met. If they were strangers, how did they know who to approach?'

'No idea. I googled it, but couldn't find anything. I think it's a secret thing – only people in the know are allowed in, not mere mortals like you and me, Polly.' He laughed. Polly didn't. 'That, or…' He trailed off.

'Or what?'

'You know what blokes are like. It's probably a load of shit.'

'No, it's definitely not…' She stopped herself.

Jas looked surprised. 'You what? Polly? Tell, tell.'

'Nothing, nothing,' she said hastily, backing out of his office.

She left him shaking his head in disbelief. 'Polly!' he said. 'Alicia's one thing, but you…' She darted down the stairs.

She went home that evening feeling depressed. It got the weekend off to a bad start. Oliver kept asking her what was wrong, which made her feel worse – not only had she cheated on him, but she was in a foul mood because she couldn't figure out how to do it again. The more elusive tubing became, the more she wanted it. They were supposed to have dinner with a group of Oliver's friends on Saturday night. She couldn't bear it, so faked a migraine and spent the evening alone in the flat eating chocolate and cheese, and watching Baz Luhrmann's *Romeo + Juliet*. She knew every line.

She reeled between elation at the memory of what had happened, and a kind of despair over the loss of it. The entire encounter had probably only lasted four minutes at the most. She'd only seen him and known him for four minutes. But she'd never felt anything like it; the experience had been so raw and exhilarating. She had to see him, she just *had* to. She felt consumed by the memory, consumed by him. In moments of lucidity she could see how ridiculous she was being, but the feelings overwhelmed her and she could think of nothing but him and how he'd touched her and how the other people on the train had been around them, standing right next to them, not seeing them, no idea what was happening right under their noses.

On Sunday she felt rotten. She'd overindulged and now had a migraine for real. She spent most of the day in bed feeling miserable.

By Monday, the fingertip bruises on her thighs had almost gone. Only four barely distinguishable yellow marks remained.

When she pressed on them, she felt nothing. All hopes of finding him were fading.

Six

Polly scrunched her face up in disgust.

'Stop it,' she said.

She heard the words before she realised she'd said them out loud. The couple sitting across from her looked up and exchanged glances.

She smiled weakly, then quickly turned to look out of the window.

She was on a bus. Two weeks had passed since the tubing incident and she knew nothing more. She was doing her best to forget all about it; she'd wound herself up in knots with it and it was going nowhere. She'd decided to stop taking the tube. But the more she told herself to stop thinking about it, the more frequently the flashbacks came, each with a little more detail added until it had become the full-length porn version that had just popped into her head.

She'd been thinking about something else entirely, working out what she needed to take to the dry cleaners, when out of nowhere she had been struck by an image of herself completely naked on a tube train. *He* was fully clothed. He sidled up behind her, running his hands up and down the bare flesh of her back, turned her round and bent her forward, placing her hands on the seat in front. The train was packed with people, but no one appeared to notice them. He undid his trousers, letting them fall to the floor, and then fucked her from behind. She was slippery with sweat, moaning as he pummelled into her harder and harder.

It was filthy. But there was nothing she could do to stop it – the more she tried, the worse the fantasies got.

The couple sitting opposite got off a few stops later. She turned front again. She gently massaged her aching neck until it eased.

The couple had left their newspaper behind on the seat. Polly leant forward and picked it up. She had at least another fifteen minutes until she got to Holborn. Getting the bus to work every day was becoming a pain – it took half an hour longer than the tube.

She flicked through the paper. There was nothing of interest. She stopped on a story about a farmer who got his arm trapped in a tractor and cut it off with his own penknife, and one about a woman who jumped in front of a tube train at King's Cross, decapitating herself in the process. She liked the gruesome stories.

She was almost done with the paper when she noticed a feature about a new dating site. It had been set up for men and women who wanted to hook up with people they spotted out and about in London. There was an interview with the couple who'd started the site. The girl had been sitting opposite the guy on a bus in Shoreditch. They'd smiled at one another and he'd even waved goodbye when she got off at her stop. At the centre of the feature was a picture of her getting off the bus and him waving to re-enact the scene. The girl had really regretted not talking to him, so had started a social media campaign to find him. She'd posted details everywhere: of the bus they were on, what time, description of him, description of her – she even had a hashtag going.

The hashtag bit caught Polly's attention. She pulled out her phone and typed #Tubing into the search, but only found herself scrolling through yet more pictures of people riding huge rubber rings down rapids and snowy mountains.

'Urghh,' she said aloud.

Her stop was just coming up. She got to her feet and stomped off the bus. She was so preoccupied, she didn't see the black cab hurtling towards her as she crossed the road. She got a mouthful of abuse from the driver as he swerved round her. She barely looked up from her phone.

Once in the office, she dumped her bag down next to her desk and crumpled into her chair. She sat for several minutes before opening her laptop and typing '#TubingLondon'. It brought up a couple of twitter posts, mostly pictures of crowded stations or service messages. A map of the London Underground also came up. She stared at the names of the stations, then went back to the search and typed '#TubingHolborn'.

She found what she was looking for immediately. The first post was from yesterday.

Male hook up with male. Central Line. Holborn westbound train. Third carriage. 7 p.m. tonight. Wear green top. #TubingHolborn

One user had liked the post. She clicked on their username: @terri127re. It took her to a blank profile.

There followed other posts from earlier in the month. She clicked on the first handle; again it took her to a blank profile. She clicked on the next – again a blank profile. All the profiles were blank.

She typed '#TubingLeicesterSquare'. The first post was from today.

> *male hook up female. northern line leicester*
> *square southbound. last carriage 11pm.*
> *#TubingLeicesterSquare*

She clicked on the handle: @can852ran. There was no picture or any other information. The profile had only just been set up that month.

Seven

Polly was sitting in a pub in Maida Vale. She snuck a look at the time on her mobile. It was 10.22 p.m. – just over half an hour to go. It would take her at least that to get to Leicester Square from where she was. She drummed her fingers nervously on the table.

She was waiting for Charlotte to come back from the bar. Ever since Polly and Oliver had started going out, his sister had been insisting they meet up for monthly suppers, just the two of them. Charlotte said it was because she wanted them to get to know one another better, but it was a thin disguise for the regular grilling Polly received.

She couldn't believe it when she'd flicked through her diary that afternoon and seen the dinner date with Charlotte pencilled in. 'Of all the fucking days,' she'd muttered to herself. She had spent an hour building up the courage to call and cancel. She'd chickened out three times, hanging up before the first ring. It had occurred to her that maybe the dinner was a sign meant to bring her to her senses. In the end she had decided that was nonsense and finally let the phone ring long enough for Charlotte to answer. In a nervous voice, she'd told Charlotte she needed to work late so couldn't make it. Charlotte had refused to accept her excuse, and had told her she'd be waiting for her at the restaurant as arranged. There was no arguing with Charlotte.

Polly had arrived at the pub an hour late. She couldn't quite believe it when she got there and Charlotte was still there waiting; she'd been hoping she'd have given up and gone home. There was a dribble of red wine left in her glass and a look of disappointment on her face.

Charlotte had chosen a table right at the back, even though there were empty ones next to the full-length frontage that opened up on to the bustling pavement. The air was stifling this far back. Polly had picked up the menu from the table and used it to fan herself. Charlotte had immediately plucked it out of her hand and returned it to the table.

Charlotte had been adamant that Polly order a main course, even though she only wanted a starter. In the end, Polly had relented and ordered a chicken Caesar salad with the dressing on the side. Charlotte had ordered steak and chunky chips. When their food arrived, Charlotte had wolfed hers down at speed. Polly's dish arrived drenched in dressing. She'd spent most of the meal carefully dissecting the salad, hunting for dry leaves, while enviously watching Charlotte pop each forkful of rare meat and ketchup into her mouth. She couldn't understand how Charlotte managed to stay so thin despite having the diet of a teenager. She should have been fat and spotty, with all the grease and sugar she consumed, but she was like a china doll, with her porcelain complexion and delicate features. She'd been single ever since Polly had known her, something she couldn't fathom. There were always men buzzing round, but she never seemed interested.

'Here we go.' Charlotte was back from the bar. She put the drinks down on the table. Polly didn't register her return.

'Polly,' Charlotte said in a shrill voice.

'Huh? Oh, thanks,' said Polly when she saw the drink in front of her. She'd asked for a Diet Coke. She'd already had a couple of glasses of wine and wanted to keep a semi-clear head for later. She took a sip; it wasn't diet.

'So, tell me about work,' said Charlotte, getting comfortable in her seat again. 'Oliver tells me the job is going well.'

'Yeah, it's great,' she replied. She could feel the minutes slipping by. She needed to come up with a quick excuse and get going.

'And Oliver's flat – everything OK there?'

She always referred to it as *Oliver's* flat; it was a gentle reminder.

'Fine,' Polly replied, the tips of her fingers playing with the cold condensation running down the side of her glass.

'Did Oliver mention I managed to get theatre tickets for Friday? Good seats too – we're in the Royal Circle.'

'Right,' replied Polly absently.

Charlotte turned her head until she was looking at her sideways like an inquisitive cat.

'Is everything OK, Polly?' she asked. 'You don't seem at all with it this evening.'

Polly seized her chance. 'Actually, Charlotte, I'm not feeling that great.' She dithered for a moment – time of the month or diarrhoea? 'Time of the month.' It was a lie; Polly couldn't remember the last time she'd had a period.

'I have some painkillers.' Charlotte picked up her handbag and unzipped it. From across the table, Polly could see it was immaculately packed and organised. She went straight to the buttoned-down secret pocket at the back and extracted two ibuprofen.

'Been drinking.' Polly shrugged. 'Shouldn't really.'

'You'll be fine,' Charlotte said, shoving the tablets at her.

'I really don't like to,' she replied. 'I think I'll just go home. You don't mind, do you?'

Polly was glad she'd chosen period pains over the runs. Charlotte, like all the other members of her family, was a surgeon, so had no time for trivial ailments – they dealt in real illness. She could see how much even a complaint of period pains was irritating her.

Charlotte looked at Polly for a long time before speaking. 'Are you sure you're feeling unwell, Polly?'

'What do you mean?'

'I don't know … you seem different, and you've dressed up a bit. I never normally see you looking like this.'

Polly instantly regretted keeping her heels on and doing her make-up in the toilets at work before she left. She'd even hitched up her skirt a bit and unbuttoned her top as much as she thought she could get away with.

'I don't know what you're talking about,' Polly said as boldly as she could. 'I always dress like this.'

'Really?' asked Charlotte suspiciously. 'Looks to me like you're planning on going somewhere else tonight.'

'No,' Polly snapped back.

They sat in silence. Polly was too scared to say anything else.

Eventually Charlotte said, 'I have to go now anyway, I'm in surgery early tomorrow morning.'

Polly was out of there like a shot.

Outside the pub, she checked the time – it was 10.40. She walked quickly to the end of the road, then started running once she was sure the pub and Charlotte were out of sight. Her run only lasted thirty seconds, until she bent her ankle over the side of her heel. She limped the rest of the way to the tube station.

Luckily a train was just pulling in when she got to the platform. By 10.50 she was at Piccadilly Circus. But at that point her luck ran out – signalling problems meant the Piccadilly Line wasn't running. After a mad hobble along Coventry Street, she got to Leicester Square.

Once through the barriers, she quickly made her way down the escalator to the southbound platform of the Northern Line. It was busy with late-night drinkers and tourists. She looked up at the board – a train was due to arrive in one minute. That was too early, the message had said 11 p.m. The one after was due in three minutes, which would make it 11.01 p.m., about right.

Now her rush was over, her heartbeat caught up with her and she realised she was sweating. She collapsed on a bench and used her hand to fan herself.

A warm gust of air signalled the next train's arrival. Most of the people on the platform moved forward to get on it. Polly watched the few that hung back. One of them must be here for the meeting. There were two guys huddled together chatting, a family of tourists, and a young woman on her own, gazing into space. Despite her vacant stare, she seemed nervous, constantly tapping and flicking the strap of the bag hung across her chest. It must be her.

Polly couldn't take her eyes off her. She was pretty, in a mousey kind of way. She had long, straight brown hair and a heavily made-up face. It was obvious she didn't usually wear make-up – the colours didn't suit her and she'd used too much or too little in all the wrong places. She was wearing a flimsy black sleeveless dress with pull ties at either side of her waist, and a pair of black-heeled ankle boots. It was a strange outfit. The boots weren't meant for show; they should have been hidden under a pair of jeans or trousers. She didn't have any tights on, either, so a milky expanse of skin was visible.

The loud click-clack of kitten heels coming from the other direction interrupted Polly's thoughts. She turned to see a tall blonde walking on to the platform. She was wearing a tight red dress and cropped leather jacket. She turned right and made her way towards Mousey and the end of the platform. She was alone. Polly was suddenly unsure. Perhaps it wasn't Mousey – maybe it was the blonde? They were both standing at the end of the platform. Polly stood up, watching both of them, trying to figure it out.

The train broke through the darkness of the tunnel and came to rest in the station. The doors beeped, then opened. Within seconds, disembarking passengers were flooding on to the platform. Both women stepped up, ready to board the same carriage. Polly followed. But then Mousey suddenly sidestepped and went for the end carriage. Polly suddenly remembered the message: the last carriage. She tried to catch up and lunged through the doors nearest just as they started closing. She hadn't made it into the same carriage as Mousey, she was in the one behind, but there was a small windowed door adjoining them that she could see through.

It was quiet this far up on the train – most people had boarded in the middle. A woman with several bags was sitting on the side bench next to the windowed door. Polly climbed over her mound of shopping to get a clear view of Mousey. The woman begrudgingly rearranged her bags so Polly could pass. Now in place, Polly looked on as Mousey pulled the strap of her bag over her head and put it down on the floor beside her. She watched and waited.

The train set off into the tunnel.

From where Polly was standing, Mousey's carriage looked empty except for a small group of twenty-somethings talking excitedly down the far end. Mousey moved deeper into the corner, sliding her back along the clear plastic divider to the archway of the door. Her eyes flicked about nervously, then they suddenly stopped and fixed dead ahead.

A man slowly came into view. He must have already been on the train where Polly couldn't see him. She could only see the back of his head. He kept walking forward until he was right up against Mousey. She watched as his tanned hand ran up her milky-white thigh. Mousey leant back and moved her legs apart. She closed her eyes as his hand pushed up further, pulling her skirt with it. Polly moved closer into the window and caught a glimpse of her naked crotch.

Mousey dropped her head back as his hand began to touch her intimately. He brought his other hand up to her throat and pressed flat against it, pushing down hard. Her eyes were closed and her mouth wide open. Polly watched as her mouth changed shape, forming silent words and sounds; she imagined she could hear them through the noisy rattles and clatter of the train. He ran his hand from her neck down to her breast, taking the small mound into his grip and squeezing it hard. She reacted, her face flushing and her cheeks puffing air in and out. Polly bit down hard on her own lip as she watched.

Abruptly, the man swung her round so he was against the arch and she was now in front. It was *him*. Startled, Polly immediately ducked down under the window, ending up crouched on the floor of the train. The woman with the shopping grunted irritably as she kicked over one of her bags. Polly had completely forgotten she was there. 'Sorry, sorry,' she said, diving across to pick it up.

'Leave it,' the woman commanded. She bent down to sort it out herself.

Polly stayed squatting for several seconds. She couldn't believe it was *him*.

She stood up, careful to avoid the window. The woman on the bench eyed her suspiciously. Polly ignored her and edged closer to the window. When she was sure that he wasn't looking in her direction, she moved back into her original spot. She could see what was happening from the speed at which Mousey's arm was moving.

Polly was struck by their audacity. She looked over at the group of people still down the far end of the carriage. They were engrossed in conversation, totally unaware of what was going on. It seemed unlikely that they would see anything even if they did look over – a view of his back at best – but she was still amazed.

When Polly looked back, his head immediately swung to the side. For a second Polly thought he'd seen her. She shrank back from the window, keeping them both just in view. Mousey was still tossing him off. He lifted his hand up and put it on top of her head and slowly began pushing her downwards. She responded, dropping to her knees. Her head began moving backwards and forwards. He looked down at her and started thrusting his cock into her mouth viciously. She responded by moving her head back and forth faster and faster. He plunged in one last time and all the tension drained from his body. Mousey turned immediately and spat on the floor. She got to her feet and pushed him in the chest. Polly couldn't tell if she was annoyed with him or just being playful. He smiled, using only the left side of his mouth, then he quickly turned to the doors to get off the train. As he stepped down on to the platform, he zipped up his flies.

Polly stood stunned for a few moments. The sound of the beeping doors brought her back to her senses and she jumped out after him.

She followed.

She tried to keep her distance, but hung back a little too long on the platform and nearly lost him when he went down a side tunnel, avoiding the main railway station. She had no idea where she was until she saw a sign for Waterloo station. By the time she caught sight of him again he was at the top of the escalators. She had to run all the way up, barging past dawdlers as she went. When she reached the top, she screeched to a halt. He was standing just up ahead. She ducked behind one of the tiled pillars near the guards' station. He was having trouble getting through the barrier. The guard was examining his pass. He gave it back and pointed to another barrier. He swiped his card again; this time the gate opened and he walked through. She waited until he was around the corner before fumbling for her own card and following him through the exit.

He didn't waste any time – he was already running across the road by the time Polly was out of the station. She tried to follow, but the cars kept coming. She ran to the lights, impatiently punching the button at the crossing with her thumb while she watched him walk down past the Old Vic and into The Cut. The lights changed to amber and she shot across the road.

She'd been to The Cut a couple of times before. It was a pedestrianised street that ran along the railway arches. It'd been recently redeveloped, and each archway now housed a swanky bar or restaurant.

He went into a darkly lit bar playing loud samba music. She waited at the door as he made his way down to the tiny bar at the back and ordered himself a drink. She watched as he sat down on a stool and took a swig from the bottle, her heart hammering in her chest.

It was a Tuesday, so the place was quiet. Polly sat down at one of the darkened side tables near the entrance. She couldn't take her eyes off him, terrified that she might lose him again.

She was deep in thought when a waitress approached. 'Drink?' she asked listlessly.

Polly looked up blankly.

'Do you want something to drink?' the waitress repeated slowly and deliberately.

'Umm – vodka,' Polly replied. 'Double,' she added curtly.

The waitress walked off towards the bar.

She returned a few moments later, carrying a tumbler on a silver tray. She placed it on the table. As soon as her back was turned, Polly picked it up and downed it in one. It tasted disgusting, but had the desired effect, topping up the alcohol she'd had earlier, immediately deadening her nerves.

She stayed put. She kept telling herself to get up and go to him, but each time she bottled it and just kept sitting there.

He was on his second beer when she decided it was now or never. She picked up her bag and quickly walked towards the back bar. The throbbing samba beats were deafening as she made her way past the empty dance floor. She shakily sat down on the stool next to him.

He was looking in the opposite direction so she assumed he hadn't noticed her. She stared at him. A single spotlight lit his face from above, making him look like a statue.

He nonchalantly turned round to look at her.

'You like what you saw?' he asked, facing forward again.

She couldn't speak. He knew. He'd seen her watching him on the train.

'Of course you did, otherwise you wouldn't have followed me,' he said, not waiting for her to answer, draining his bottle of beer.

They sat in silence. He seemed perfectly comfortable. Polly was in agony. She had no idea what to say, and was beginning to wonder what the hell she was doing.

The barman came over to them. 'More drinks?' he asked.

'Another beer. And she'll have a double shot,' he said turning to her. 'Like a gin? Or vodka?'

She stared back at him.

'Yeah.' He was smiling now. 'Vodka.'

When the barman's back was turned he leant in close to face her, 'So which are you? A watcher or a doer? You've done both now.'

She didn't answer. She could feel the warmth of his body and smell the scent on his skin.

'I think I'd like you to be in on the action,' he continued. 'I was hoping you'd find me.'

An enormous grin broke across her face; she couldn't help it. 'Me too,' she murmured, totally lost in his black eyes.

The bartender came back with their drinks. He picked up his beer and took a mouthful. Polly tried to pick her glass up, but was shaking so much most of it spilt all over her hand and on to the bar.

'Let's do it again,' he said.

She nodded automatically.

He pulled his phone out of his pocket ready to take down her number. There was no hesitation: she told him immediately.

He slipped his phone back in his pocket. 'I gotta go.'

And with that he was gone.

Polly sat at the bar bewildered. Had that really just happened? Had she really just found *him*? She took a large gulp of her drink. It still tasted foul, but she needed it.

She reached into her bag to check her phone. The time was 12.29. She'd missed the last tube. Usually the thought of having to get several buses home this late at night would have made her want to cry, but not tonight. Her mind was racing, and she needed the long journey home to try and settle.

'Hey, you gonna pay the bill?' the barman shouted as she turned to leave.

She spun round. He pushed a silver dish with a receipt on it towards her.

'Sorry,' she said, embarrassed that she'd forgotten to pay for the drink she ordered when she first arrived. She picked up the bill, lifting it close to her face to read it in the dim lighting. The total was printed in bold at the bottom. It said she owed £44.

'Excuse me,' she said to the barman, who now had his back to her and was reorganising the spirits neatly displayed on the shelving behind. The wall was made up entirely of mirrors. She hadn't noticed before. 'I think you've given me the wrong bill,' she said.

He snatched it from her hand then lifted it up close to his face. 'Nah,' he said. 'Three beers and two double vodkas. That's what you both had, right?'

Eight

The text message came two days later. It read:

> *tottenham court road*
> *central line westbound*
> *tomorrow 17.49*
> *4th carriage*
> *dress slutty*
> *no underwear*

Polly was sitting at work. When she read the message her heart started pounding.

'Ready, Polly?' Lionel was standing in front of her desk, peering down at her through his reading glasses.

'Huh?' she said without looking up, her eyes glued to the phone.

'Prayers. It's three.'

She squinted up at him, her vision fuzzy from having stared at the screen so long. Lionel's big head beamed at her. He reminded her of a Labrador; all that was missing were the black pads around his mouth and a lolling tongue hanging out the side.

'I'm sorry, Lionel,' she said. She looked at her laptop. A calendar reminder had popped up fifteen minutes ago, announcing the weekly update meeting, or 'Prayers', as Lionel liked to call it. 'I'll just grab my stuff.' She picked up her notebook and pen, carrying them in one hand, her mobile phone still attached to the other.

She followed him into his office. The room was hot and stuffy. The hot weather still hadn't broken and the humidity in the city was becoming unbearable. Unlike the rest of the building, Lionel's office had no air-conditioning, a result of poorly planned partition walls. All he had was an old desk fan on his filing cabinet that had minimal effect. Someone had done the unthinkable and opened a window. Notepads and bits of paper wafted vigorously in an attempt to make use of the fresh air.

There was only one chair free next to the door. Polly tipped it up on its side in an attempt to shut the door behind her, but she was so flustered she couldn't manage it. Lionel jumped up to help. He noticed her trembling hands and gave her an encouraging smile.

It was the first time Polly had been to one of these meetings. James usually gave an update on the legal department's activities, but he was busy today and had asked Polly to step in. She'd been chuffed – it was her chance to pitch some of her feature ideas. She'd sketched out a few ideas in her notebook on Monday and had meant to write them up later, but with everything that had happened over the past few days she'd completely forgotten to finish it off, let alone sort out the legal department update.

Lionel kicked off the meeting. She tried to concentrate and follow what he was saying, but after the first sentence she lost him. Her stomach churned at the thought of tomorrow evening. She couldn't believe he'd texted. Her phone had barely left her hand yesterday. She'd longed for this message to arrive but, now it was here, she suddenly felt sick, a mix of nerves and excitement.

'Polly … Polly … hello,' Lionel was waving at her from his desk. She looked up. Everyone in the room had turned to look at her. 'Can we have your update now?'

She stared back blankly, then, when she registered what was going on, said, 'Of course.' She picked up the notepad in her lap and rifled through it for her notes. They weren't there. She had the wrong pad. She tried to remember what she'd written down earlier in the week, but she couldn't think straight.

'I … uh … um …' She looked around at the expectant faces. There was silence; no one was offering anything. She could feel her cheeks burning. Eventually in a very small voice she managed, 'I'm going to be sick,' then got out of her chair and turned to run. She wrestled with the door handle before finally wrenching it open. As soon as she was out, she dashed to the ladies'. She heard Alicia call after her from the reception desk as she rushed past. 'You OK, hon?' She ignored her, slamming the door shut then flicking the lock.

She put the toilet lid down and sat on it. The bathroom was cool and silent. She had a thin film of sweat over her face. She allowed it to dry in the cold air. After a couple of minutes her legs became restless and forced her on to her feet. She started pacing on the spot.

'What are you doing?' she whispered to herself. 'Why are you fucking everything up, Polly?' she said a little louder.

She stopped and started to shake herself vigorously, her arms flailing and her head nodding. When she finally stopped, her hair had fallen loose in front of her face. She tugged at the band holding her ponytail. It pinched strands of hair, pulling at her scalp. She pulled harder, yanking the band free. The relief was immense as her hair fell around her shoulders.

There was a knock at the door. Polly stopped perfectly still and held her breath.

'Hon, are you OK?' There was a pause. 'Hon, it's me.'

Polly exhaled loudly, relieved it was only Alicia and not Lionel or someone else from the meeting.

'I'm fine,' shouted Polly through the door.

'Can I come in?'

No! thought Polly – she wanted to scream it through the door. She needed some time on her own.

'You've been in there a while,' Alicia continued when Polly didn't answer. 'Lionel wants me to check you're OK.'

'Fuck,' she whispered through clenched teeth. She reluctantly went to the door and unlocked it. What did she think she was doing anyway, hiding in the toilets? Pathetic.

Alicia immediately pushed the door open, shoving Polly out of the way, then slammed it shut and locked it behind her. 'So, what's going on, lady?' she asked with genuine concern. She was standing so close that her breasts were squashing into her, and Polly could smell strawberry liquorice laces on her breath. She instantly took a step back.

'Nothing, I just wasn't feeling very well,' Polly replied.

Alicia made her way over to the window and yanked it open, then pulled out a lighter and packet of cigarettes from her pocket. 'They all think you're pregnant.'

'They what?' Polly said, exasperated.

'You're a woman in her twenties who runs out the room shouting you're gonna be sick – what do you expect?' She paused for a second, cigarette hanging on her lip and lighter poised. 'You ain't, are you?'

'Of course not!' Polly's voice echoed round the airy bathroom.

Alicia lit her cigarette and inhaled deeply.

Polly stared at her. 'Are you sure you should be doing that in here?'

'Who's gonna know? We're the only two that ever use this toilet. Are you gonna grass me up?'

'No.' Polly had a flashback to school days smoking weed behind the chemistry labs. 'What about Janice?'

Janice was the accounts lady.

Alicia sucked her teeth loudly. 'Janice never comes in here. I don't reckon she does bodily functions – *far too common*,' she said, putting on a posh voice for the last bit. Polly couldn't help laughing.

'Want one?' Alicia held out the packet of cigarettes.

Polly had given up smoking shortly after meeting Oliver – his patronising glances were far more effective than gum or patches. She thought for a second, then said, 'Yeah.' The first drag made her feel light-headed.

They smoked in silence next to the open window. Slowly Polly's shoulders dropped back down and the tension drained from her body.

'So what's up?' asked Alicia.

Polly was sorely tempted to tell her everything. She hadn't felt this kind of concern from another woman in ages. 'Just stuff,' she replied, using the toe of her shoe to work free a loose floor tile.

'You are hard work, girl, you don't give nothin' away,' Alicia said, frustrated.

Polly looked up from beneath the hair that had fallen in front of her face.

'I get it,' Alicia said. 'Man trouble, right?'

Polly slowly nodded.

'Oliver?'

Polly shook her head.

'Someone else?' Alicia raised her expertly drawn left eyebrow.

Polly nodded again.

Alicia turned and stubbed her cigarette out on the red brick of the window recess before throwing it out. Polly followed suit. Alicia waved her hands around in an attempt to waft the smoke away. 'How old are you, Polly?'

'Twenty-eight.'

'Wow, you work fast – you're moved in and settled down with your guy already.'

'Well, sort of.'

'You do live together, right?'

'Yeah.'

'Sleeping in the same bed and all, not roomies or nothin'?'

'Of course.'

'Then I hate to break it to you, hon, but you are officially settled down and living with a guy.'

Silence.

'How old is Oliver?' Alicia continued after a few moments.

'Thirty-seven.'

'Oh, I get it. *He's* settling down, not you.'

'No, not necessarily, I just—'

'So why are you messin' with some other guy?' Alicia interrupted.

Polly stayed silent.

'I'm not judgin' you or nothin'. There's nothin' wrong with settling down, if that's what you want. Is it what you want?'

'Yes,' Polly replied quietly.

'Could you be any less enthusiastic?' Alicia laughed.

'I do want to be with him,' Polly said assertively. 'We have our problems, but doesn't everyone?'

'Depends what they are.'

Polly sucked in her cheek and bit down on the fleshy inner part while she thought about it. 'OK. Sometimes I'm not sure how *into me* Oliver really is.'

'What do you mean?'

'He's always really affectionate and telling me he loves me and I totally believe him, but he's just not very good at showing it.'

'Huh?'

'Well, it's just that we don't always … you know … he's not always keen to show me, like … physically how he feels.'

'You mean like sexwise?'

Polly wondered if such a word existed. 'Yeah,' she replied, 'sexwise.'

'Hmm,' said Alicia, pausing to think. 'If there are a hundred guys on the earth who are right for Polly, what number would you say Oliver is?'

'I don't get you.'

'Say for every person in the world there are only a hundred other people who are right for them, like number one is the most perfect guy ever and number twenty-five is still pretty good, but there might be things that aren't quite right. Where's Oliver?'

'Well he'd be pretty high up there because he's a great guy and —'

'Just give me a number.'

Polly considered it for a moment. 'I'd say nine.'

'That's pretty good,' replied Alicia. 'So, I'll ask again, why are you messin' around with this other guy?'

Polly stayed quiet.

'Like I said, I'm not judging you,' said Alicia putting her hands up as if to surrender. 'You wanta know what I think?'

Polly nodded.

'Oliver sounds like a great guy, but a pretty damn important part is missing.'

'What's that?' asked Polly.

'Passion – that "fuck me right now" feeling – you get me? Sex isn't everything … well, it is to me …' She laughed her raucous dirty laugh then continued. 'If there's no sex, then you *are* just roomies. You know what I'm saying?'

'Yeah, but you can't have that all the time. We've been together for three years. Things calm down.'

'Did you *ever* have that feeling with him?'

'Well, sort of – I mean …' She couldn't lie. She'd fallen for Oliver's compassion and his kindness, rather than …

'Anyway, why can't you feel like that all the time? It's not just men who get to feel horny, you know. Fuck, I'm horny all the time and I ain't gonna apologise for it. You shouldn't neither.'

Polly shrank back a little.

'Don't you be embarrassed about this shit,' Alicia said defiantly. 'If your guy isn't into it, then that's his problem, not yours.' She paused. 'You know what, Polly? I think Ollie's got you all wrapped up with a cute little bow on the box already.'

Polly looked confused.

'I mean, it's like this – take me, everyone thinks I'm this little black girl from *Sarf London*, I've heard it too many fuckin' times to mention. I'm a triple whammy – not only am I black, but I'm female and I got a big arse and titties to boot. So that's me in a nutshell – the world has put me neatly in my box. We all do it – people are easier to handle that way. Problem is that once you're in the box, it's real easy to start believing it yourself, that you are only these things. No offence, hon, but I'm betting Ollie's got you in a little box all of your own and this guy has come along and lifted the lid.'

Polly could feel tears stinging.

'I don't want to upset you or nothing, but you need to know that you are the boss of you. No one else can make decisions for you and you shouldn't be looking to no one to do it for you. It's not about what Oliver wants or what Facebook or frickin' TV thinks – it's you. If it don't feel right, then it's not right, but if something feels good then it is good – own it. Own your own happiness and pleasure.'

Nine

The next morning Polly got up and showered at seven-thirty as usual. She dressed in a fitted black high-waisted skirt and a sleeveless purple linen shirt with a tie detail around the neck. She carefully tucked the shirt into her skirt, making sure it was pulled in tight and didn't bag over – when it bagged it made her look bloated. Last night's weather forecast had said it would be hot and humid again, but she went back into the bedroom to get her black cardigan just in case. She hesitated for a second before opening the wardrobe and wondered if all this was really necessary. She decided it was, grabbed her cardigan and then gently clicked the wardrobe door shut. Oliver fidgeted, kicking the duvet up and rolling on to his back. She looked over at him. The hair on one side of his head lay perfectly flat while the rest stuck up wildly, and his cheek had deep creases in it from the pillowcase. She stayed very still until she heard the slow, regular whistling of air leaving his nostrils again.

In the bathroom, she did her face – a light brush of mascara and a squeeze of liquid blusher on each cheek. She rummaged through the jewellery box she kept on top of the bathroom cabinet, unable to decide what would go with her outfit. Eventually, she slipped on her carved wooden bracelet and the delicate gold chain with a round, hollow pendant that Oliver had given her for Christmas. She struggled with the catch. She contemplated waking him and asking him to fasten it for her, it would give weight to her alibi, but in the end she decided it would be overkill. After a dozen attempts she finally hooked it herself.

She looked in the mirror and took a deep breath. Her stomach fluttered again. She shook it off and got on with her hair. She ran her fingers through it to get rid of the last of the tangles, then pinned up the front with a couple of grips.

At 8.20 she pulled on her trainers. She picked up her two bags – a small leather handbag which had her purse, keys, phone, travel pass and other essential bits, and her canvas tote bag that held her book, heels, cardigan and umbrella. She pulled the door shut behind her, and then gave it two hefty shoves to make sure it was definitely locked.

Once outside, she turned left and made her way towards Shepherd's Bush tube station, her regular route. She'd given up on the bus; there was no avoiding the tube any more. The builders working on the site across the road were already on their morning tea break. They were lined up on bricks and planks, basking in the sunshine. Polly got three wolf-whistles, one more than usual. She saw the young mother who lived two doors down with her brood. She was trying to squeeze them all into her tiny car. There were little arms and legs kicking and screaming all over the place. Polly smiled at her, but got no response. The woman just stared back blankly, as if her brain were still asleep.

She turned right into the alleyway at the end of her road. It was a short cut she'd only recently discovered. It took her straight up to the main road, bypassing the junction. When she got there, the guy at the corner shop was already setting out the flower and newspaper stands. He was well ahead this morning. As usual, he was overseen by his father standing solemnly at the shop door. He was using a pen lid to scratch an itch just under the front of his turban.

After that, she didn't recognise anyone – they all merged into the faceless mass of Londoners.

When Polly had first moved to London, she'd been overawed by the hustle and bustle of the city and found it exhausting just being here. She'd grown up in a small village surrounded by green fields and wide-open spaces. She never appreciated it until she moved away. In London noise seemed to attack from all angles, and at first she'd struggled with the seemingly endless bodies ducking and diving in front of her. She wasn't used to the darkness, either. The huge buildings cast shadows over her everywhere she went, so even when the sun was out the air still felt cold. She found herself constantly crossing the road chasing the sunny spots. The first time she walked over Waterloo Bridge, it felt as though she had just come out of a long dark tunnel, but was then straight back into it on the other side.

Having lived in London for several years now, she was used to its rhythm. There was a pattern that everyone unconsciously followed, a dance that no one needed to be taught. It made sure things moved along smoothly. Londoners knew how to criss-cross effortlessly, pre-empting one another's movements.

Five minutes after leaving the flat, Polly got to Shepherd's Bush tube station. But she didn't go in as she should have done. She didn't make her way down to the Central Line. She didn't fight her way on to a train to Holborn then make the short walk to the office at the other side. She wasn't going to work.

Instead, she ducked into a quiet coffee shop round the corner. She ordered a small soya latte and sat down at a table out of view from the front windows. Her plan was to stay there until Oliver went to work, then go back home and wait for evening.

Her coffee sat on the table in front of her, getting cold. She didn't normally drink coffee, it made her feel rotten an hour or so afterwards, but she needed something, and it was too early for alcohol. She waited to call Lionel at the office before taking a sip – she was trying to preserve the morning croakiness of her voice. By twenty to nine, she decided it was time. Running out of yesterday's meeting came in handy – Lionel was full of concern and understanding. He wished her well, and told her to take it easy and not rush back to work. Once she'd hung up, she guzzled down the coffee.

Oliver was scheduled for the late shift at the hospital so she knew he wouldn't be leaving the flat until at least ten-thirty. At eleven she decided it was safe to go home.

Back at the flat, she slumped on the sofa, still wearing her trainers and with both bags slung over her shoulder. She stayed like that, staring into space and thinking – comfortable in her discomfort.

When Polly was twelve, she had made a plan. She wanted to be engaged for two years before getting married at twenty-eight, then have her first kid at thirty. She wanted at least three children – four if there was time. According to her plan she wasn't far off track. But the older she got, the more the dream was becoming a nightmare. When she was little, she'd tried to picture what it would be like to be grown-up and living with a boyfriend. She had imagined a woman who was mature and self-assured, in control of her own life. In reality she felt exactly the same as she did as a child, just a lot more insecure. There had been no transformation into this mythical grown-up. She wasn't there yet. She might never be there.

She couldn't help wondering if tubing really even counted as cheating? She knew it did, but it wasn't as if she was in love with the guy and planning to run off with him; they'd barely spoken. It momentarily crossed her mind that maybe even it was Oliver's fault: he wasn't interested so she'd had to go to someone else.

She went round and round in circles. She prayed for an epiphany or some great revelation – no such luck. The only thing she kept coming back to was what Alicia had said – *if something feels good then it is good – own it. Deny yourself nothin'*.

Just after midday, Polly managed to get off the sofa. She changed out of her work clothes and put on a pair of leggings and a T-shirt. She watched TV for a bit, then tried to read, but she couldn't settle. She logged on to Oliver's laptop to check Facebook. There was nothing of much interest. She flicked around a couple of other sites then gave up.

She went into the bedroom and lay down for a sleep. It didn't take long for her to drift off. Sleep had always been her solace; it gave everything a new sheen, took away all the crap. Today was no exception, and when the alarm on her phone went off at four, she jumped up out of bed feeling full of energy. She was ready.

Polly strode into a busy Tottenham Court Road tube station – rush hour. She felt giddy, partly with excitement, partly because of the three shots of whisky she'd downed before leaving the flat. She made her way down the escalator, holding on tight to the moving handrail. She was wearing her red satin stiletto heels. They'd cost a fortune, but she was wooed by the five-inch, steel-tipped heels. She rarely wore them; despite the satin finish the peep-toe front strap felt as if it cut right to the bones of her toes. But on occasions such as this she was willing to endure the pain.

The end of the escalator caught her unawares, and she had to use the people around her for support until she made it to the wall. Commuters huffed and puffed as she got in their way. She felt an irresistible urge to giggle. She felt so filthy, all these people around her going about their usual boring business, whilst she walked amongst them on her way to meet *him*. She could feel the material of her skirt brushing her naked buttocks.

She continued down the walkway, staying close to the wall just in case. Her steel-tipped heels echoed loudly along the tiled floor, drawing backward glances from several men. She made her way down the steep staircase that led out on to the westbound platform, revelling in the sound of her heels clanging on the metal runners.

On the sixth step, the shoes became her undoing. She stumbled, but managed to grab on to the handrail, hoisting herself up just before her bum hit the stair. A torrent of people pushed past her, rushing for the train that had just pulled in. She heard a couple of sniggers and a few commuters turned back to look up at her. Polly stayed put until they'd gone. Only then did she realise that the back of her skirt had ridden up when she tripped and her naked buttocks were on display. As she stood up straight and wrenched down her skirt, she felt like crying. She squeezed her eyes shut, hoping the feeling would pass.

'You're OK, Polly, you're OK.' Her voice echoed in the empty stairwell. The sound was soothing and made her feel a bit calmer. Her voice was a lot more assured than she felt inside. She brushed herself down, took a deep breath and continued on, albeit with a little less spring in her step.

The platform was busy and noisy. She checked the time on the board – 5.47 p.m. Her heart started to pound. She walked down the platform behind the crowd that had just come off the train and were now making their way to the exit. Her ankles gave the odd wobble, protesting her heels. She kept her mind focused and busy on the task at hand. She stopped three-quarters of the way down the platform, she reckoned this would be about where the fourth carriage would stop.

She slowly turned around and made her way to the back wall. She leant against the tiles – they felt cool against the flush of her body. She watched as tourists, shoppers and people on their way home from work trickled in slowly, filling up the platform again.

The sound of electric 'eels' racing down the train tracks made her jump. A strong rush of warm wind lifted her skirt. She quickly moved her hands to keep it down, checking around her to see if anyone had seen, but no one had noticed. The warm wind over her naked thighs and buttocks teased her. She was suddenly tingling all over; she couldn't wait to see *him* again, feel his hands on her body. She closed her eyes for a moment, completely losing herself in the memory.

When she opened them again, her reflection stared back at her in the carriage window that had stopped directly in front. She'd been worried about bumping into someone she knew, but she barely recognised herself. He'd said to look slutty, and she'd done her best. She'd scrunch-dried her hair into big wavy curls. Her hair was naturally curly, but she usually straightened it. She was a little out of practice and had used too much mousse, and, looking at it now, had ended up with beauty queen hair. She'd gone to town on her make-up too. Her eyes were rimmed with thick black eyeliner and her lashes long and gloopy with mascara. Her cheeks had a sheen of pink blush, and her lips were a glossy cherry red.

She scanned down the train then moved to the double doors at the centre of the fourth carriage. The train doors beeped, then opened in front of her. She took a deep breath then pushed her way in through the mass of bodies tightly packed together in the busy carriage.

People were squashed in the vestibule and in lines between the seats. Polly squeezed her way into a tiny gap by the door and looked for something to hold on to. The heat was almost unbearable and the air was thick and rank. She gripped on to a handrail at the back of a seat. Her hands felt slippery with sweat. The doors of the train beeped again and then shut.

The train pulled off into the tunnel. Polly had no idea what to do next, so she stayed where she was. She bristled with excitement.

She waited.

And waited.

Nothing happened.

By the time the train got to the next stop, she was still standing there, waiting. She tried to look for *him*, but there were too many heads and newspapers in the way for her to see any further than the faces directly in front of her. She managed to push her way round so she was facing the other way, but still couldn't see him. A woman next to her tutted and the guy opposite gave her a filthy look for upsetting his newspaper arrangement. She glared back. She was starting to panic.

'Where is he?' she muttered to herself. No one acknowledged she'd spoken, she barely noticed herself.

It occurred to her that she might be on the wrong train. She unzipped her handbag and groped inside for her mobile. As soon as she found it, she felt hot hands on each of her thighs and a body press in behind her. She stopped dead, dropping her phone back into her bag. She turned to look, but his head darted forward, pressing against her cheek so she couldn't.

'Don't,' he whispered. 'Keep looking straight ahead.'

His voice was so quiet she could barely hear him. His breath tickled her ear, bringing back memories of the last time. She began to tremble. As he pulled away, she felt thick stubble brush against her cheek and she could smell his aftershave.

She leant her body back into his. There were commuters packed tightly in around them so all that was visible were their heads. Nobody knew about his hands quickly moving under her skirt and on to her hipbones. They felt coarse against her smooth skin.

He wasted no time moving downwards to her crotch. His hands came together in a V-shape from her hips until his fingers met her tight, wiry curls. He kept going until he reached the soft folds. He slid two fingers either side of her clitoris, making his way to the slippery wetness. He pushed both fingers inside. It took her by surprise and she gasped. He immediately withdrew his fingers and started massaging her smooth inner fleshiness.

Polly tried desperately to keep herself composed. She kept glancing at the people around her to see if they'd noticed. They were all lost in their own worlds, listening to music or buried in the screens of their phones or newspapers.

She tried to stay as still as possible so not to draw attention to herself, but he kept applying more pressure and force, pulling her deeper and deeper into her core. She teetered on the edge. She bit down on the inside of her lip until she tasted blood.

Then suddenly he stopped. She felt his damp fingers trail along the tops of her thighs as he moved behind on to her buttocks. He rubbed and squeezed handfuls of flesh, the tips of his fingers bruising her. He moved to the centre and into her crevice. He used both hands to pull apart her buttocks. He pushed and probed, trying to find a way in. It burnt when his finger finally penetrated. It felt like nothing she had ever experienced before. The sensation grew more intense the further he pushed inside. She opened her mouth and let out a small cry.

Several commuters turned round to look at her. She could see their disgruntled expressions, but she felt powerless to do anything about it.

Before she knew what was happening, he clamped both hands around her arms and pulled her backwards. She couldn't keep up so she ended up being dragged into the corner. The crowd reacted to the kerfuffle passively, rearranging themselves as a collective, flicking open their newspapers again and turning their backs to her.

Once he had her in the corner, he lifted her so she was on her feet again, then quickly turned so she was facing the blackened window, completely obscuring her from view. He pushed her up against the window and pulled up her skirt. He grabbed one of her hands, pulled it behind her and stuffed it into his already opened flies. She gripped the shaft of his penis and squeezed as she ran her hand up to the tip. Her fingers lingered on the head, gently stroking. He jerked her hand down roughly. She did as she was instructed and started rubbing him back and forth harder. She felt his stubbly face against her cheek as he dropped down towards her.

'Rougher,' he whispered.

They mimicked one another's movements in their secret corner. She could feel his sweat dripping on to the back of her neck and his stifled moans grew louder with each breath.

As the train careened into the next station, he bit down on to her neck and ejaculated. He pulled away, her body still trembling. She opened her eyes and took a few deep breaths before turning to face him. She felt coy and excited at the same time. She wanted some of the intimate closeness they'd had together the last time.

But when she saw his face her smile faded.

She lifted her hand up to her mouth in horror.

It wasn't *him*. She'd never seen the man standing before her – he was a total stranger.

He leered back at her, then nonchalantly got off the tube.

Ten

Polly turned the key in the front door as quietly as she could. All the way home she'd been praying that Oliver would be out, but the thin strip of light coming from under the door told her otherwise. As she carefully pushed the door open, she could hear the sound of sizzling. He was cooking, *again* – it smelt like sausages and onions. Once inside, she carefully closed the door so the lock only made a small clicking sound, rather than allowing it to slam shut as she usually did. She turned as quietly as she could and crept to the bedroom.

'Hey, Pol,' said Oliver, poking his head round from the kitchen. The lounge door was open, so he could see straight through to the hallway and caught her mid-tiptoe.

She froze.

'I thought I'd make us a quick supper before we go out.' He smiled at her, his face flushed and red from the heat of the kitchen.

'Right,' she said. She dithered over what to do – make a run for it to the bedroom, or walk into the lounge and get it over with? In the end she decided to stay put.

He continued smiling at her through the open doorway. When she didn't move, his brow furrowed. 'What are you doing?' he asked.

'What do you mean?'

'Why are you just standing there? Come here.'

He moved towards her, his arms outstretched ready for a cuddle.

She didn't move. He couldn't see the state of her in the darkened hallway. She knew that as soon as she stepped into the light he would see how filthy she was.

When Polly had turned around on the train and seen the stranger behind her, she'd been mortified. She'd thought it had been *him* touching her – that she'd been touching *him*.

This guy was in his late forties, neatly dressed in a grey suit and black tie. He was tanned, with a shaved head. She could see from the pattern of stubble on his scalp that he was balding. In any other situation she probably would have thought that he was OK-looking for an older guy, but after what they'd just done together he made her skin crawl. His mouth was open and breathless, he had bubbles of spittle in the corners, and his forehead and top lip were beaded with sweat. She couldn't believe how stupid she'd been. From the first moment he laid his hands on her, she had known something wasn't right. The way he touched her wasn't the same as before: he was much rougher, he even smelt different, and the way he had pushed his finger inside her from behind... she couldn't bear to think about it. She wondered how he even knew to pick her out, but then she figured she was the only one on the train dressed like a slut. Suddenly the whole thing seemed like total lunacy. What had she been thinking? She felt disgusted with herself.

Worse still, in the confusion, she hadn't been able to get to the train doors before they closed. She'd suffered the indignity of being squashed among the other commuters, not knowing who'd seen what. Most of them had ignored her, for which she was thankful. A few stared at her, unsure what had happened but knowing something had. Time stood still in those three minutes it had taken to get to the next stop at Lancaster Gate.

As soon as the doors opened, Polly was through them like a shot, almost falling over her heels.

Once outside, she had crossed the road to Hyde Park. She didn't know what to do or where to go, so just wandered aimlessly. Her feet ached with every step. She kicked off her shoes and walked barefoot on the grass. She'd read somewhere that walking barefoot cleansed your aura – it couldn't make things any worse. The flawless blue skies of the last couple of days were suddenly gone. The park was gloomy and overcast, and the air ripe and heavy.

She came across a green hut that had been made into a café/kiosk. Her mouth felt dry and sticky, so she stopped for a bottle of water. She turned to walk away then stopped and decided to get some cigarettes. The guy behind the counter wasn't expecting her to turn back. She caught him leaning over the counter, leering at her. She looked down at herself; she'd forgotten how she was dressed. She got her cigarettes and matches and marched off.

It started drizzling so she stood under a tree to shelter. She could have stayed under the kiosk awnings, but couldn't stand the thought of people seeing her. She lit a cigarette. She hoped that this guilty secret would eclipse all the others. She chain-smoked as the rain poured down. And she cried, a lot.

By the time the rain stopped, she was marooned on her own small island of grass. She should be getting home. She blew her nose on a leaf and wiped her face on her shoulder. She negotiated the enormous puddle barefoot. Her feet squelched in the muddy ground. It was much deeper than she expected, and the water came halfway up her calves. It felt nice at the time, but, as soon as she put her shoes on, the grit irritated the soles of her feet and got between her toes.

Now, standing in the darkened hallway dressed like a whore with her bare legs caked in mud, her hair stringy and plastered against her head, and make-up streaked down her face, she couldn't move.

Eventually Oliver moved forward, turning the hallway light on as he approached. 'Wow,' he said as soon as she was illuminated. 'What have you been up to?'

She didn't say anything.

'I know you like to make fashion statements, but jeez…this is too far!' He laughed and moved closer. 'Is that mud?'

Tears began to slip out, and before she knew it she was in full flood.

'Polly… Oh, Polly. What's wrong, darling?'

He moved towards her and encircled her with his arms. Polly stayed rigid with her arms firmly down by her sides. He smelt of clean washing and home cooking. She wanted to hug him back, but she couldn't. Instead she leant her forehead on his shoulder and let her dirty tears soak into his T-shirt.

She knew she'd have to explain herself. Her mind raced, trying to think of something before he asked again, but her head felt heavy and fuzzy from smoking half a packet of cigarettes.

Before she had time to come up with anything, he pulled back to look at her face.

'What happened? Are you OK?' There was nothing but love and concern in his voice.

'I'm OK. I…erm…it was just…' She couldn't finish. Tears choked her.

'Did something happen at work? On your way home?'

She nodded, grasping on to anything she could.

'Tell me.' He sounded so worried.

She took a couple of deep breaths, stalling for time. She suddenly remembered an incident she'd seen when she first moved to London. An old lady had been hit by a bike as she crossed the road. It was the strangest thing, watching her flying through the air like a kite caught up in the spokes.

'I got run over by a bike.'

'You what?'

'I was crossing the road, and I didn't see him coming, and I sort of lost my balance and got dragged along with him.'

'A motorbike?'

'No, a bicycle.'

'A bicycle?' He looked confused for a moment before breaking into a smile then laughing.

She tried to laugh along, but ended up crying again.

'Oh, silly Polly,' he said, trying to control his laughter. He hugged her close again, enfolding her head in his chest. She could have stayed there forever. 'When did it happen? Straight after work?' The bass of his voice boomed through his chest into her ears.

'Yeah…erm…no.' She suddenly remembered the time. 'I went for a walk in a park after work. It was on my way back from there.'

'A walk?' he said, pulling back to look at her.

'Yeah, thought I'd get some fresh air, clear my head.' She tried to make it sound bright and breezy.

He didn't say anything, just continued to look at her. She imagined he was studying her face for clues.

She was forced to carry on, 'You know … things at work are tough with James being out so much, and when I spoke to Dad the other night about Mum …' She started crying again.

Oliver leant back over the kitchen counter and grabbed a piece of kitchen roll. She couldn't imagine what she looked like, big black tears and sticky snot everywhere. He put his hands on each of her shoulders. She blew her nose. It was good to get it all out.

'Is that why you've been cheating?'

He said it so offhandedly she almost missed it. She looked up at him, thinking she'd misheard.

'What?'

He was gripping her a little tighter now. It was comfortable, but firm – she wasn't going anywhere.

'Because you're feeling stressed and upset?'

Her heart started pounding. 'What do you mean?' The words barely came out.

'I can smell it on you.'

Her entire body was instantly rigid. Could he smell him on her? His touch? His aftershave? She remembered the damp, sticky patch on the back of her skirt; she'd felt it when she was on her way home. She was horrified to find it, and, though she managed to wipe most of it off, it had marked. Was the pungent smell of him coming from her skirt? Or the hand she used to wipe it away? Or was it her? Could Oliver smell her familiar scent? Were her own sticky fluids giving her away?

'You've been smoking. You stink of cigarettes. I thought you'd stopped all that nonsense.'

She could have dropped down dead.

'Oh … yeah,' she said weakly, 'sorry.'

He gave her that look. She hated that look. Then he let go and walked into the kitchen. 'Go and get yourself cleaned up. Dinner's almost ready, then we've got to get going.'

'What? Get going where?'

'To the theatre. Charlotte got tickets. She said she told you about it when you had dinner together the other night,' he said from the kitchen.

Polly vaguely remembered Charlotte saying something about the theatre, but she'd been far too distracted at the time to take it on board. There was no way she was going anywhere tonight.

'I'm not feeling great, Oliver. I think I'll just have a bath and go to bed.'

'Don't be silly. She's paid for the tickets already,' he said. She could hear him in the kitchen moving pots around and getting plates out.

This was the last thing she needed.

'I'm really not up to it.'

He popped his head round from the kitchen. 'Come on, go and get changed, dinner's almost ready.'

'I don't want any dinner!' She wanted to be alone. She couldn't cope with getting dressed up and pretending everything was OK for the rest of the evening.

'It'll make you feel better. I made your favourite – sausage and mash.'

It wasn't Polly's favourite meal at all, it was Oliver's.

'No, I'm just going to have a bath then go to bed.'

'Polly, we've got tickets.'

She was beginning to get annoyed. 'I don't care.' She felt so uncomfortable in her clothes and her feet were throbbing.

He opened his mouth to speak, but just a 'pah' sound came out, as though he couldn't believe how unreasonable she was being. He shook his head. 'Let's just sit down and eat,' he said, then he turned away, as if dismissing her childishness.

'No,' she shouted, 'I'm not going!'

He turned back. He looked genuinely hurt. 'Pol...'

'I don't want dinner. You didn't make it for me, you made it for yourself. And I'm not going out with you and your sister again. Hasn't she got any of her own friends to go out with?'

Her voice was high-pitched and screechy. It sounded horrible in the high-ceilinged room. Oliver looked at her in disbelief. She'd never lost it in front of him before. He struggled for words.

She reached out and grabbed the handle of the lounge door and slammed it shut.

Polly sat in the bath until the steaming water turned cold. When she had first got in, the hot water had stung like crazy where he'd pushed into her arse. It made her wince.

From the bathroom she heard Oliver on his phone to Charlotte. He told her that Polly had had an accident on her way home and they wouldn't be able to make it to the theatre. From his answer she could tell that Charlotte was annoyed. He apologised profusely and told her that he needed to stay home and look after her. Polly prayed that she'd persuade him to go, but he kept insisting that he needed to stay. 'Honestly, Charlotte, I've never seen her so upset.' Eventually Charlotte let him off the phone.

He knocked on the bathroom door to tell her. She ignored him. He tried to open the door, but she'd locked it. He soon got the message and left her alone.

When she finally got out of the bath, she looked at herself in the full-length mirror on the wall. She stood naked while water beaded down her body. The bruises on her thigh had completely disappeared now. She turned around and looked behind her at her reflection. She could see fresh red marks on her buttocks where the other guy had pinched into her flesh, and she noticed a small bite mark on her neck.

She faced front again and carefully examined the rest of her body. Her collarbones stuck out sharply on each shoulder, and the hollow where they met in the middle was more pronounced than usual. The bathroom light caught the xylophone of ribs that ran from under her neck to her breasts. She touched each one in turn then moved on to the scar high up on her abdomen. Her fingers pushed and prodded the thickened mound of skin. There was a time when she could have put her finger right through it into her stomach. When they first took the feeding peg out, the hole didn't scab over right away and she had found it impossible to leave it alone. The tender skin around it had itched and prickled, enticing her fingers to play. She'd peeled off dressing after dressing despite constant reprimands. She'd known what she was doing; it would heal eventually. Her body was littered with similar scars.

She knew she'd lost a couple of pounds over the last few weeks. When she was in the clinic she was banned from using weighing scales so developed a new method. She spent hours carefully studying her body, getting to know the look and feel of certain bones and areas. Her hips and collarbones were the best indicators; her ribs and spine were pretty good too. She always knew she was in danger when her knee joints and elbows became too prominent: the doctors had warned her dad to look out for these in particular.

After her bath she changed into a pair of clean pyjamas and went to bed. She desperately wanted sleep, but it wouldn't come. For the first time her safety mechanism failed her. Her body felt agitated and fidgety. Even the muscles around her eyes wouldn't relax. They kept flickering, making it impossible to keep her lids closed. She considered getting up, but there was nowhere to go in Oliver's small one-bedroom flat.

Just after midnight, Oliver came to bed. She always went to bed before he did. Usually he'd snuggle up to her back when he got in. It always made her feel safe just as she was drifting off to sleep. But he didn't tonight. She could just about make him out in the dark. He lay facing the wall at the edge of the bed. It wasn't long before his loud, squeaky nostrils started up. Usually his snoring irritated her, but tonight she used the sound to try to pretend it was just like any other night.

Eventually sleep came, but only for a few hours. Before she knew it, she was awake again. Her throat felt dry, and her nose was blocked from crying so much earlier. She lay there for a while, but with each breath her throat felt more and more raw. She reached out for her glass of water on the bedside table, but there was no glass. She remembered her argument with Oliver and how she'd stormed out – she hadn't brought a drink to bed.

As much as she didn't want to, she had to get up. She pulled back the duvet and tried to push herself up into a sitting position. But her body wouldn't work; her muscles felt like dead weights. Even her eyelids, which had insisted on continuously flickering earlier, refused to budge. She was starting to panic, getting thirstier and thirstier. With all her strength she pushed herself up and flopped her feet to the floor. She hoped they would miraculously spring to life and carry her into the kitchen, but they didn't. She ended up sprawled in a heap next to the bed. She lay there for a while, commanding her eyes to open, but they wouldn't budge. Soon she gave up and propped herself on all fours and crawled blindly to the bedroom door. It was cold and gritty on the wooden floorboards. She navigated her way to the door. Once there, she lifted herself up to reach the handle. As she moved her arms upwards, they brushed against the smooth skin of her breasts. Her eyes snapped open and she looked down. She was naked.

'Why am I naked?' she said aloud. Her voice sounded bassless and sinister in the dark, as if it hadn't come from her...

Suddenly, she was awake. She could feel the warmth and softness of the duvet around her. She shuddered, shaking off the dream she'd just had. She was thirsty. She reached out to the bedside table for her glass of water. It wasn't there, of course.

She felt so tired and could barely open her eyes. She used her fingers to pry one open, but her eyeball remained rolled back in her head, refusing to focus. With a huge amount of effort she pushed herself up and dropped her feet to the floor. Her legs held her this time, but they felt so weak that she decided to let herself slowly go down on to her knees then forward until she was on all fours. She started crawling around the bed to the door. In her dream, she'd neglected to include the chest of drawers by the wall, parallel to the end of the bed. She smacked head-first into it. Cursing, she reversed out and went around. Once at the door, she reached up to click the handle open and crawled into the hallway.

It was freezing by the front door. A draught was coming from the gap underneath. She shivered in the cold and rubbed each arm in turn. She was relieved to find that she was fully clothed in her pyjamas. She gave a snort of laughter. As she crawled into the lounge, she noticed a dim light coming from the kitchen. She knew immediately that the cooker hood light was on. Then she heard the tap running. Someone was in there. She quickly hauled herself up on to her feet, using the doorframe.

'Oliver?' Her voice sounded very small.

No answer. She ran her hand along the lounge wall until she reached the archway into the kitchen. He was standing with his back to her by the sink in his boxer shorts. She stood in the opening.

'What are you doing up?' she asked.

He paid her no attention. She watched as he knocked his head back, draining a glass of water.

'Oliver?'

Nothing.

'Oliver, are you ignoring me?'

No answer. He didn't even move; there wasn't even the slightest flicker or tension in his body to show that he knew she was there.

'Is it because of earlier? Is that why you're not talking to me?'

Still nothing.

'Look, I'm sorry I lost it. It was just a really shitty day.'

She walked over to him and slipped her arms around his waist from behind. He felt warm, and she shivered against him. She held him tight, burying her face into his back. He didn't respond. She could smell something familiar on him, an aftershave, but it wasn't the one he usually wore. In fact he didn't really feel like Oliver at all. His body was harder and less rounded, and his back felt hairy and greasy. She started to pull away.

Suddenly he turned and grabbed her by the arm.

'Don't look at me,' he spat.

It was the stranger from the train earlier.

She gasped, lurching up in bed, her eyes wide open this time. She could hear Oliver inhaling and exhaling loudly next to her. She was freezing – cold sweat ran down the side of her face and neck. She took a couple of deep breaths then lay back down. The bed sheets felt damp and her pyjamas were saturated. She lay in her cold discomfort, desperate to get up and change, but completely unable to move.

Eleven

After her nightmare Polly barely slept. She couldn't quite believe what she'd got involved in. She spent the rest of the night staring at the ceiling, waiting for Oliver to wake up.

As soon as she heard him stirring she sat up and leant over so she could watch for when his eyes opened. She startled him, looming over him – not the best start.

'What are you doing?' he asked.

'Waiting.'

'For what?'

'For you to wake up so I can tell you I'm sorry.'

'Oh, yeah,' he said, turning away from her.

'Please don't be cross with me. I was a total bitch, I know.'

She forced herself on to him, clambering over his body so they were facing one another, then ducking under his arms so that he was cuddling her even if he didn't want to. After a couple of seconds he gave in and squeezed her tight. It felt like the safest place on earth.

In the hours she had been lying awake she'd decided that her flirtation with excitement or intrigue or what-ever it had been was over. She had no intention of telling anyone what had been going on; she could barely get her own head around it, let alone try to explain it to someone else.

The next message arrived the following evening.

Her phone was in her handbag in the hall. It was set to silent. She didn't hear the gentle drum as her phone vibrated against the hallway floor, and she didn't see the glow from the open mouth of her handbag as the brightly lit display flashed on and then off again. At the moment the message arrived, Polly was cuddled up to Oliver on the sofa while he watched the cricket. She hated cricket, but after everything that had happened she just wanted to stay close to him. He was surprised by her interest, but took great delight in explaining the action to her. The message sat there for the rest of the night, innocuously waiting for her to find it.

She finally saw it on her way to work in the midst of negotiating a busy pavement and thinking about dinner. She had decided to make Oliver a fancy meal that evening, maybe lamb or something with sea bass. She wasn't much of a cook, but she was sure she could figure something out. There was a nice little deli not far from work on Conduit Street; she'd get most of the ingredients there during her lunch break. Anything else she needed, she could pick up from the supermarket on her way home.

But her plans were quickly forgotten when she looked at her phone to check the time. She stopped dead.

fancy doing it again? tomorrow 19.15, leicester square, piccadilly line, train heading to hammersmith. c u at last double doors

People started pushing past her angrily, trying to get round the pile-up she'd caused behind her. It took her ages to realise. When she finally did, she moved out of the way to an empty doorway and just stood there staring at the message. She didn't know what to do. Her thumb hovered over the Delete button for a while, then she moved it away to see what time it had arrived. It had been sent Sunday at 9.57 p.m. She checked the number it had come from. It was different from the last one.

She read the message over and over. What the hell was she involved in? Had her number been randomly given out to anyone who wanted it? Was she being rented out as some kind of slut for men to fuck on trains? Maybe that had been the point of the first guy, like a pimp testing her out. The thought filled her with horror. She wanted to throw the phone to the ground and smash it to pieces.

By the time she got to work, she was raging. She stormed up to her desk and threw herself down in the chair. The more she thought about it, the angrier she got. She couldn't believe she'd been blindly dragged into some kind of prostitution ring.

She got very little work done that morning, despite having a deadline to meet for James. She couldn't focus. Her work phone rang several times, but she didn't want to speak to anyone, so she just let it ring. Eventually, Lionel shouted through his office door, 'Will somebody answer that bloody phone!' and she was forced to pick it up. It was her dad. She'd known giving him her work number was a mistake.

'Hi, Dad,' she said, after he'd bumbled through his introduction without realising it was her on the end of the line.

'Polly? Is that you?' he said when he finally realised.

'Yes, it's me.'

'They've given you your own phone?'

'Yes, I have my own phone at work.'

'Well, that's grand.' He sounded genuinely proud of her.

Silence. She didn't say anything. There was no reason to ask why he was calling; she often received a follow-up call when her mother had had one of her turns. She slumped down in her chair and dropped her head forward until it was almost touching the desk.

After about five seconds, he said, 'I just wanted to let you know that your mother's much better now.'

'Right.'

'She's a lot more comfortable.'

'Uh-huh.' Polly couldn't keep the contempt out of her voice.

Pause.

'I thought we'd have heard from you before now, love, you know, about coming back for a visit. You said you'd think about it.'

'Yeah, I know,' she said, 'I've been meaning to call, but I've been busy with work and…'

'Oh, I'm sure you have, love. I know you, you work so hard – too hard sometimes,' he said. 'But it's important. I think it would really cheer her up. She gets very depressed, especially now she's in the chair.'

Polly shuddered. In the past few years her mother had started using a wheelchair. On her last visit home, Polly had twice caught her out of it. The first time had been when she was bringing her a cup of tea (her dad had asked her to). As she'd pushed open the lounge door her mother had seemed to slump and her chair had started wheeling backwards, as if she'd sat back down too hard. On the second occasion, Polly had found her in the garden lying on the patio with her chair tipped up on its side opposite her. Polly couldn't fathom how she could have fallen out on a completely flat surface with her going one way and the chair the other.

She picked up her pen and started clicking it furiously. It was all she could do to keep herself in check.

'It'd do you good, be a nice wee break for you away from London. Why don't you bring Oliver with you too? We'd love to meet him.'

The thought of taking Oliver home to meet her parents made Polly feel physically sick. She came from a picturesque village in Dorset, but the bungalow her parents lived in had been moulded from concrete in the 1970s. It came complete with a car port and dining hatch. Oliver knew the village well – he had gone to a public school a few miles away in Somerset. He thought she'd grown up in one of the large stone-clad cottages with beautiful low beams and a pretty walled garden. It was his assumption – she hadn't bothered to correct him.

'Well, think about it, love,' her father said when she didn't reply.

She felt bad: she knew it was her dad who wanted to see her, not her mother. She hadn't seen him for a couple of months now. The last time had been when he'd come to London to visit, something he did from time to time. She much preferred it that way. 'You got any free time to come and see me?' she asked hopefully. 'We could go to that steakhouse you like.'

'I'd love to, darling,' he replied, 'but I'm not sure your mother will be able to make it. She'd find the journey too difficult.'

Polly crossed her fingers. Here's hoping, she thought.

'Well, why don't you just come?'

After a short pause he said, 'OK, that would be grand.'

They made arrangements to meet for lunch on Thursday the week after next, then said their goodbyes.

Polly was left feeling lousy. She was pleased to be seeing her dad, but with him came her mother and all her baggage, even when she wasn't around. Just hearing about it made her feel bad.

She looked at the time – 11.48 – not even lunchtime yet.

'Fucking crap-hole morning,' she muttered to herself.

She contemplated putting her head through her computer screen or making a chain of paperclips to hang herself with.

Just then her mobile sprang to life, juddering across the table. She picked it up. It was a message from her phone provider announcing a new method of pissing money away with them. She pressed down on the Delete button angrily and made a mental note to call them later and tell them to fuck off. Once that message was cleared, the list of other messages appeared. She clicked on the one she'd received last night. She read through the details of the meeting again. Who the fuck did he think he was, treating her like some kind of whore?

It was then that she decided – she would go to the meeting tonight and tell whoever it was exactly what she thought of them.

Twelve

The last set of double doors on the tube train opened and there he was, leaning against the metal handrail, waiting for her. It was *him* – the guy who'd started it all off that first night. There were no games this time, no hiding among the crowds or appearing as if from nowhere. The carriage was almost empty – there were no places to hide. He smiled coolly and moved forward to greet her as if they were old friends.

Her day hadn't improved much during the afternoon; she was livid by the time she saw him. She walked straight up to him and slapped him hard across the face. He put his hand to his cheek, taken aback. Polly was as shocked as he was; she had had no idea she had been going to hit him. She stepped back, not knowing what to do with herself.

His surprise didn't last long. He grabbed her by the wrist and pulled her arm up behind her back, twisting her round in the process. It happened in a blur; all that registered was the pain. She held her breath, scared that the slightest movement would make her arm twist up higher.

He pushed her towards the train doors ready to march her off. A guy sitting close to them looked up at them from behind his paper, shock written across his face when he realised what was happening. He hesitated for a moment, then stood up. 'Hey, what are you doing, mate?'

'Sit down,' *he* replied firmly. He used his free hand to throw his fist out towards the other guy's face. It made him jump and flop back down into his seat. Other passengers in the carriage looked over. The train doors started beeping ready to close. Still holding on to Polly's arm, he pushed her forward and out the door before it slammed shut.

Out on the empty platform, he kept hold of her. He hustled her through the corridor towards the exit. Just before they reached the opening to the escalators, he ducked them into a small side corridor. He loosened his grip, allowing her to untwist her arm, and then moved in front of her and grabbed her hand as if he were pulling her along by a lead. She scuttled behind him until she lost her footing and fell to the floor. He didn't let go of her; she ended up being dragged along until they reached the dead end.

There were no strip lights this far down in the narrow corridor. The area wasn't meant for the public, so it only had a dull emergency light next to a chute cut into the wall. It gave out a sickly yellow glow. From the smell, she guessed it was a rubbish store. She saw black bags piled up next to the chute. She scrambled up to her feet.

The second she was up, he grabbed her by the neck and slammed her against the wall. She was up on her tiptoes instantly, trying to relieve the pressure on the front of her throat.

'Why the fuck did you do that?' he said, his face only inches from hers. The puff of each word made her jump.

She stood there silently, her entire body trembling in tight little movements.

When she didn't answer he let go and turned his back on her. He put his palms on the opposite wall and leant into it as if he were holding it up.

Polly slid down until her feet were flat on the floor again.

The two of them stayed like that for what seemed like an eternity, the air between them brooding. Polly didn't know what to do. She should leave, but she didn't.

When he finally turned round to face her again, he was much calmer.

'Why did you slap me?'

'I … er … don't … I was angry.' Her voice came out shrill and erratic. She couldn't think clearly enough to make a full sentence. She could just about make out his eyes staring at her in the dim light.

'Why?'

'Because of what happened the other day on the train.'

'But I wasn't even there.'

'I know,' she said quietly.

'Oh, I get it. Did you think you were meeting me?'

She didn't answer.

'Tubing is a game,' he said moving in closer and placing his hands either side of her head so she was boxed in. 'It's uncomplicated, no-strings-attached sex.'

She suddenly felt stupid and embarrassed, especially in front of him. A game clearly not for the likes of her, she thought. She stared at the floor, wishing she could disappear.

He moved in closer to her and gently lifted her chin with his hand until she was looking up at him.

'Do you want to play?'

He was so close to her now that she could feel his breath on her face and the heat from his body. She couldn't answer. They both stayed perfectly still while the tension grew between them. Without any warning he lunged forward and squashed his lips into hers. He pushed so hard that she could feel his cheeks pressing against her face.

His hands were everywhere, running up and down her body and pawing at her clothes. Sensation ran from the tip of her head, through her chest, to the fluttering in her stomach. He pushed her against the wall harder until he had her pinned exactly where he wanted her. She heard him fumbling with his belt buckle. He kicked at her feet until she moved her legs apart, then roughly pulled at the button of her trousers and unzipped her fly. She knew what was coming next. It suddenly felt as if everything was happening too fast. His hands were in her trousers, pulling them down, then slipping into the band of her knickers.

What about everything she'd decided the other night? What about Oliver? She pulled away from his lips, moving her head to the side, trying to catch her breath. She inhaled deeply, and the stink of the bins caught in her throat.

'No,' she said pulling away.

He ignored her and carried on pushing his hand down between her legs.

'Please stop,' she continued.

He didn't stop.

'No,' she shouted, and pushed him away.

This time he stopped immediately and took a step back. 'Fine,' he said, lifting his hands up as if to dismiss her.

They stood facing one another. She quickly pulled up her trousers and wrapped her arms around herself.

He looked at her. 'What is your problem?' he asked.

She didn't answer.

'You're wasting my time,' he said after a couple of seconds. Then he did up his trousers and turned to walk away, shaking his head.

Polly panicked. She didn't want him to leave. Every logical thought in her brain told her to let him go. But she couldn't. She felt very scared – not of him or what he would do to her; of what she was about to do.

She reached out to stop him. He turned back and stared at her for several seconds, then roughly pushed her by the shoulders up against the wall. At first she thought he was pushing her away, but then he moved in, grabbing her buttocks and pulling her forward so that the top part of her back was leaning on the wall and her hips were jutting out.

He moved slowly and deliberately this time. There was no rush in his movements; there was no need for urgency – he had her. He started undoing the buttons on her shirt, carefully loosening each one, then lazily moving to the next. She watched his fingers at work, her chest heaving under the strain of her breath. He remained calm and composed, as if he were carrying out a menial task. When he finished he pushed open her shirt and yanked down the cups of her bra, revealing her breasts. Every hair on her body stood on end waiting for him to lay his hands on her. But he didn't, he just looked at her.

Eventually he reached out his hand and ran his finger very slowly from the top of her right collarbone to the left. His finger ran back to the middle and down her breastbone, languidly stroking over each rib in a zigzag until he brushed over her scar and reached her belly button. Then he stood back and stared. He never once looked at her face, just intently studied her body.

Then he bent down in front of her and very slowly pulled her trousers down inch by inch. Her fists were clenched down by her sides. The excited feeling in her stomach had turned into an ache that spread down to her crotch. She was in agony. He was punishing her, making her wait. When her trousers were all the way down, he lifted out first her left foot then her right. He then slowly moved back up to her crotch, his face so close she could feel his hot breath on her thighs. He let his hands run up over the tops of her legs and on to her hips. He gripped the protruding bones, his fingers moving to her buttocks and digging into her flesh before letting his hands rise up and encircle her waist. It made her gasp, he squeezed so tight. Then without warning he pulled her knickers down roughly. She yelped in surprise.

He stood back against the opposite wall and stared at her. She stayed as still as she could, naked except for the shirt still hanging open around her shoulders and bra now fallen to her waist. She watched him as he ran his hand through his hair, leaving it on his neck. He looked at her for a long time, admiring his work. She trembled uncontrollably; the wait was unbearable. Then he very slowly undid his trousers as he stepped back towards her. He stood pressed against her for a few more seconds then grabbed underneath each buttock and hoisted her up. She felt her buttocks bang against the cold wall tiles. Her legs gripped around him and he was inside her. He lifted her up higher so he could push into her harder. She cried out in relief.

He thrust into her deeper and deeper. She wanted to scream, let everything pour out. All the clutter and indecision dissolved from her mind until she thought of nothing but him and the pure lust she felt for him.

She could feel his tongue run up over her neck to her ear.

'You so tiny, so tight,' he whispered breathlessly. His hands moved to her protruding hipbones and gripped them again, forcing them back so he could push into her deeper. 'I feel like I could break you, like I could break your tiny pelvis.'

She could barely keep herself upright, the sensation overwhelming her.

Then suddenly she heard voices. In her haze, she thought she'd imagined it. She looked to her left towards the bright light of the main corridor. The darkness of the passageway they were in made her feel as though she was spying through a telescope. A man in a pinstriped suit with a briefcase rushed past. He took small, quick steps, like a cat in a fast walk.

The voices grew louder. She saw a couple, arm in arm, march past. She caught a snippet of the woman's voice. In its rise and fall she said something about going for dinner on Friday. Then another couple went past, then a woman, then another. More and more faces flooded by. Polly was having difficulty keeping track as he rocked into her harder and harder. She glanced down at him. He was watching them too.

The noise of the people passing grew louder. When she looked back again, there was a crowd standing by the entrance of their passageway. They all faced forward, bunched up in a bottleneck, queuing for the escalator. They were so close she could hear their footsteps as they edged forward, the tinny treble coming from headphones, even the rustle of a newspaper. All the while, he continued thrusting into her. She couldn't take her eyes off them. She concentrated hard, trying to keep the waves of pressure from coming. The crowd began to dwindle. She started moaning when she couldn't hold off any longer. A woman at the end of the queue stopped and looked down into the corridor. Her eyes searched through the darkness and settled on Polly. She bent down and took a tentative step forward. From the way she moved it was clear that she couldn't really see what was happening, but her eyes had found Polly and remained fixed. Polly looked down at him to see if he'd noticed. He was staring back at the woman. His breathing was getting heavier and heavier as he pounded into her. Someone knocked into the woman from behind and she saw that the queue in front of her had moved. She gave one last look and then walked on.

Every muscle in Polly's body contracted and then released. She flopped forward and collapsed on to him. He gave one last thrust and ejaculated inside her. They stood leaning against one another, breathless, neither ready nor able to move.

After a long while, he let go and she leant back on to the wall. He bent down and pulled his trousers up. She heard the clunk of his belt being buckled. She was still naked; she didn't care.

He moved towards her and cupped her face in his hands. He pressed his mouth against her lips, pushing in hard to kiss her, then said, 'I'll be in touch.'

She watched him walk back to the brightly lit corridor. It occurred to her that he didn't know her name and she didn't know his. She considered shouting it to him, but she knew that wouldn't be part of the game.

Thirteen

Polly was hooked. She didn't see *him* again for two and a half weeks. In the meantime she met up with two other men.

She set up a fake account on Twitter using a randomly made-up name, @44oro. A few days later, she found a meeting on a Victoria Line train in rush hour for that evening. It was from a male looking to meet up with a female. It hadn't been responded to yet, so she liked it.

The guy was late fifties, she guessed. His hair was almost totally white. He had a deep tan and a smart, pampered look. He wore a light grey suit. She could tell from looking at it that it was quality, a mixture of pure wool and silk. It fitted perfectly, even though he was quite short – it wasn't off-the-peg. For a moment she thought of Oliver; he had the same expensive tastes – unless he got to pick the lining himself he wasn't interested. Solid gold cufflinks held together pinstriped sleeves. The shirt was impeccably pressed and had the sharp newness of freshly opened packaging.

She hadn't worked out exactly how she'd find him in the carriage stated in the tweet, but she needn't have worried: his eyes were on her the instant she boarded the train. He beckoned her over with a nod. She hesitated, looking around at the handful of commuters already on board, but she knew it was him. When she looked back, he smiled at her. It was enough to make her go to him. Up close his face was marked with age, but he was handsome.

He took control immediately, putting his hands on her hips and swivelling her round so her back was to him. He gently guided her through the vestibule until they were in the corner behind a couple chatting.

It was just past six p.m. on a Tuesday. The train was outside central London so was only partly full. He whispered in a thick Italian accent, 'Let's wait until it's a little busier, shall we?' There weren't enough bodies on board to conceal themselves behind.

Polly nodded without turning to look at him. Her eyes glazed over as she stared dead ahead and waited. He gripped her tightly around her waist. She'd been nervous about the meeting all day, but now the moment was here and she was in his arms she suddenly felt very calm.

As the tube train travelled deep into central London, more and more people piled on at each stop. She felt bodies push in close, their heat pinching the air. A young guy with floppy hair and glasses accidentally stood on Polly's foot. She didn't look up, just heard a mumbled apology. She was too preoccupied with what was about to happen.

He started slowly, gently stroking her stomach, his hands moving in a circular motion. She let him take his time. She was determined not to lose control and give herself away as she had last time. She groaned inwardly when he slid his fingers under her shirt and on to her nipple. He pinched it, teasing and twisting until it was hard.

His other hand moved down under the waistband of her skirt then worked its way into her knickers. Polly almost buckled as he pressed between her legs, his fingers massaging applying more and more pressure. The pleasure was almost excruciating, the intensity too much. She tried to pull away, but his fingers followed.

She looked at the commuters around her, as she trembled, trying to stay in control. They were right in the corner of the carriage, facing front. No one noticed them except for the guy with the floppy hair and glasses; he was staring directly at her. She hadn't realised how close he was. He must have felt the bumps and thrusts from the Italian's arm. She gave a shaky apologetic smile back, but at that moment his fingers pressed so deeply she could do nothing to stop her mouth opening wide.

The young guy's face broke into a wide leer, his mouth dropped open slightly. He was watching.

Polly quickly turned round to face her Italian partner. He looked surprised, and a little put out. 'Don't face me, darling,' he said. 'Turn around.'

'Someone's watching,' she said, swallowing hard.

'That's part of the fun, no?' He exhaled heavily. 'Enjoy it.'

She turned back. The young guy was still there, watching her, waiting for the performance to resume. She couldn't do it; she couldn't carry on.

She turned back again. 'I can't,' she said.

He frowned at her, clearly annoyed. 'In that case…' He briskly pulled her round so she now had her back in the corner. He put his hands on her shoulders and tried to push her down. She resisted at first, but soon relented and let her back slide against the metal of the doorframe. She felt relieved to be hidden beneath the sea of bodies. He fumbled with his flies and pulled out his erect cock, thrusting it forward into her face. She obliged, but not with her mouth; she took it in her hand instead. It didn't take long for him to ejaculate.

As soon as he was done, he pulled her up by her arms. The young guy had moved in closer and was watching when she emerged from beneath the crowd. He had the same dirty leer on his face.

The Italian guy smiled at her politely, 'Lovely to meet you,' he said as the train came to a halt at the next station. He bowed slightly and then left.

The watcher winked at her and followed him out of the same door.

The second meeting took place a week later. This time she put out her own tweet.

Female hook up with male. Bakerloo Line.
Paddington southbound. Second carriage. 6.30
tonight. #TubingPaddington

She nearly missed the train. When she got there, the ticket hall was packed. Only one barrier was open; the rest had been closed to prevent overcrowding. She was forced to wait in line as the crowd very slowly filtered through. A large clock on the wall to her right ticked away the seconds. By the time she got to the front she was having palpitations. She lost her cool with an old guy who kept running his pass over the sensor to no avail. She huffed and puffed behind him. Eventually she slammed her hand down on the metal gate and shouted, 'You need to top up, you fucking moron.'

He looked up at her, shocked, 'You'll have to wait your—' he started.

'I don't have time for this,' she shouted, and pushed him out of the way.

Once through the barrier, she turned back to look at him. He was still there, repeatedly swiping his card on the reader.

The escalators to the platforms were no better. The queue was at a complete standstill on both sides. Polly tried to push past, but it was no use. The train was due in a matter of seconds. She stood at the back of the line, shaking with frustration, as the crowd moved very slowly forward.

When she got to the platform the train was still there. She ran at it and managed to get herself through the doors before they slammed shut.

Once inside, she spent a couple of seconds in the corner getting herself straight before looking for him.

She found the wrong guy first. She put on her sexiest pout, beckoning the stranger over. At first, when he ignored her, she thought they were playing a game. She winked at him and threw her head back, signalling to him. But she soon realised her mistake when the guy stared back, confused, then turned round in an attempt to work out what she was looking at.

'Bugger,' she muttered under her breath, then quickly turned, scanning the rest of the carriage.

The right guy was further down the carriage. She knew it was him immediately by the way he was smiling at her. He was very different – much younger, about the same age as Polly, which surprised her. He was wearing ripped jeans and a T-shirt, but she could tell he had money – his clothes were a bit too clean and the rips too exact. He had deep dimples on each cheek, and soft brown eyes that exuded warmth. He was cute. She couldn't help smiling back at him.

As they made their way towards one another through the busy carriage, neither of them could drop the stupid grins from their faces. When they finally met, he grabbed hold of her hand and just stared at her. After a while, her cheeks began to ache.

They stayed holding hands for several stops. Polly was beginning to wonder what was going on. She'd worn her mauve mini skirt with the zip all the way up the front specially – she'd thought he'd have gone straight for it. Then it dawned on her: he was new to this. A shiver of excitement prickled up her spine. She grabbed his hand and made her way to the corner at the end of the carriage. She sat him on the raised padded bench seat then pushed up against him and started to kiss him. They kissed like teenagers, coy at first, then becoming more frenzied. He tasted of mint.

The other passengers paid them no attention, too busy on their phones or with newspapers held aloft in front of their faces. Even if someone had noticed, no one would have guessed they didn't know one another; they looked nothing more than a pair of overzealous students. He made no attempt to touch her, other than to put his arms around her, pulling her closer. His tongue probed deep into her mouth and gave no sign of letting up.

After a minute or so, she started getting annoyed. She pulled away and looked at him squarely, tilting her head downwards. She wasn't exactly sure what she was trying to say, but from his lack of response nor did he. He stared back like a lovestruck teenager. She pushed her body close into his then ran her hand to the waistband of his jeans and on to his flies. His head dropped down, his mouth landing close to her ear. She angled her body in front of his so it acted as a screen against any prying eyes. She heard a gasp and his breath catch as she undid his fly and slipped her hand inside.

His penis was already hard. She gripped hold of it and began to rub him back and forth. She pulled up the zip on the front of her skirt so that it opened up wide, then grabbed on to his other hand and pushed it towards her crotch. His hand went a little way up her leg, but as soon as she let go he stopped. Annoyed, she grabbed on to it again and pushed it further up. He obliged, but again, as soon as she let go, he stopped.

She could tell from his breathing that he was almost done; he was panting loudly. His hand dropped away from her thigh altogether. She looked up at him. His cheeks were bright red and he had his eyes closed. She might as well not even have been there. She felt warm liquid ooze over her fingers and he went flaccid. He nuzzled his head into her neck. She dropped her hand away and they just stood there until the train entered the next station, her propping him up on her shoulder.

When they arrived, he said, 'Thanks, that was great.' He had an enormous smile on his face.

'Sure, no problem,' she replied.

He leant in and kissed her cheek, then followed the crowd of the train.

She stood in the corner for several seconds stunned.

'Sure, no problem,' she said again to herself. What a fucking stupid thing to say, she thought, like she'd just held open a door for him or picked up some change he'd dropped on the floor.

Fourteen

The last tubing meeting left Polly feeling a little uncertain. She couldn't lie to herself any more: it wasn't tubing she wanted, it was *him*. She found herself thinking about him all the time. She relived their first encounter and the moments they'd spent together in the tube station over and over. She longed for him, an ache in the pit of her belly that spread down to the tops of her thighs. At night, in the space between awake and sleeping, she could almost feel his hands on her, smell him, taste him. Her hand would automatically run down her body to between her legs. She would clench her thighs tightly together, allowing her fingers to slowly work their way in, massaging, then pushing back and forth inside herself until she came.

When the next message came, she knew it was from him. She could barely contain her excitement.

> *free tonight? central line, notting hill gate, 9pm – I've missed you*

'Polly, I can't seem to find the T&Cs. Where are they?'

It was James. He'd arrived in the office unexpectedly at nine that morning. Polly had got in at ten. He'd swiftly pulled her aside for a quiet word about her tardiness – her day had been shrinking, with her turning up later and leaving earlier.

The T&Cs was a document that set out the rules of business for the newspaper. Recently there'd been trouble over one of the clauses and someone was trying to sue them. James had managed to calm the situation and avoid a costly lawsuit. Polly was supposed to have amended the document last week so that it wouldn't happen again. She hadn't. She'd done a lot of daydreaming since James had last been in, but no actual work. It was hard to concentrate with *him* in her life.

'I saved it in the file,' she replied, knowing full well she hadn't.

'Are you sure, Polly?' James looked at her suspiciously. 'The file name in the folder hasn't changed.'

'Oh, I must have forgotten to change it, but I made all the amends.'

The more she lied, the easier it got. Initially she'd suffered the usual gut wrench, but after a while a certain confidence developed and the lies began pouring out with ease.

The problem was that she hadn't been listening properly when James had told her what changes to make to the document, so she'd been stuck as to how to make them. She promised herself that as soon as he left she'd dig out the notes she did have and sort it – no one would be any the wiser.

James left at one p.m. Polly had just opened the T&Cs document ready to try to fix it when she suddenly remembered what day it was – she was supposed to have met her dad at twelve-thirty.

She rushed to the restaurant and found him still sitting there in a booth on his own.

'Hi, Dad,' she said, wiping sweat from her brow: the humidity outside was oppressive. 'I'm so sorry, something came up at work; I couldn't get away.'

There was an empty coffee cup sat on the table in front of him. 'That's OK, love,' he said, smiling. He got up to hug her. 'My little girl with her big-city job. Come here.'

For a moment she lost herself; she felt as if she were eight years old again and had just got all her spellings right. Her dad was a burly Irishman who didn't just hug, he gave big bear hugs, squeezing her so tight as if trying to amalgamate them. 'I've missed you, love,' he whispered into her ear.

'I've missed you too, Dad,' she replied, suddenly realising just how much.

He pulled back to look at her. 'How are you?' he said, his face suddenly stern as he looked her up and down. 'Everything OK?'

She panicked: there was no hiding anything from him; he'd been through the doctors, psychologists and clinic with her.

'I've just been working too hard,' she replied, avoiding his eyes. She knew he'd noticed that she'd lost weight. They sat down at the table and he picked up the menu.

'What do you fancy?' he asked as he put on his glasses and started scanning down the list of dishes.

She didn't want to eat. She was too excited about her meeting later; her stomach was too full of butterflies to bother with food. Also, she didn't want to be bloated. She was tempted to lie and say she'd already eaten, but there was no way her dad would stand for that. In the end she opted for a starter.

'You'll need more than that, Polly,' he said. 'Pick a main too.'

'I don't want one,' she replied.

They were in danger of descending into their usual argument. The tension was broken by the appearance of the waiter who took their order, but the atmosphere remained once he'd gone.

'So, what's going on at work?' her dad asked, trying to lighten the mood.

'Not much,' Polly replied sullenly.

They looked at one another silently.

'Love, don't be like this,' he said. 'I just worry about you is all. I've seen how much you can hurt yourself, I don't want you to do it again.'

'I'm not,' replied Polly.

He reached over and took her hand across the table. 'I just want my girl to be happy and healthy.'

'I am, Dad.' It was true: over the past few weeks she'd felt so much better. 'You don't need to worry about me, I can take care of myself.'

'I know you can, but worrying about your daughter is part of a father's remit, I'm afraid, no matter what age you are. You'll see when you have kids of your own.'

But not part of my mother's remit, thought Polly.

Since Polly was fourteen she'd known exactly what her mother thought of her. Before then she'd known there was something wrong, but hadn't known what. It wasn't anything her mother had said or done, it was more the things she didn't say or do. Polly couldn't remember ever being touched by her, not a kiss or a hug, not even a pat on her hand. She was like a robot, programmed with all the right commands, but cold and completely blank inside where Polly was concerned. When Polly was young, she'd sometimes catch her mother staring at her. She'd be playing with her toys or reading a book, and she'd look up to see her mother watching, lip curled and a sour look on her face.

It was on a Tuesday afternoon shortly after her fourteenth birthday that she had discovered the whole truth.

Her dad had taken her mother to a hospital appointment. It was the first time Polly had been allowed to stay home alone. Usually she was dragged along, forced to sit in sparse, disinfected waiting rooms. She had been giddy with excitement when the front door finally slammed shut and her dad's Ford reversed out the driveway. She didn't know what to do with herself. She wandered around the house from room to room. Her parents slept in separate bedrooms; Polly couldn't remember a time when they hadn't, something to do with her mother's illness. She rarely went into her mother's room. Now, all alone in the house, she couldn't resist it. She went upstairs and slowly pushed open the door.

It was in perfect order, the bed neatly made, the surfaces polished, everything where it should be. Polly stood in the doorway for several minutes, daring herself to go in. When she took her first step over the threshold, her heart was racing. She wasn't looking for anything in particular, she was just looking. At first she didn't touch anything, but, the longer she stayed, the more assured she became. Before long, she'd gone from picking up the odd trinket to rifling through her drawers and wardrobe.

It was in the back of the wardrobe that she discovered the truth. In a large shoe box she found several exercise books. At first, Polly thought they were hers; they were exactly like the ones she used at school. She was momentarily touched by the thought that her mother had her old schoolbooks as keepsakes. But, when she opened them, it wasn't her handwriting she found, they were full of her mother's scribblings.

They weren't diaries as such, they were rants. Her mother had spewed her anger and hatred on to page after page. Polly had known her mother was unhappy, but she hadn't realised the extent of her misery. Whenever Polly thought back to this moment, she wished she'd packed all the books away again and left, but how could she? How could anybody? She read every word.

The food arrived and Polly's dad eagerly tucked in. Polly pushed her own food around her plate pretending to eat. Her dad watched disapprovingly. She tried to distract him by asking about the garden and what was going on in the church, but to no avail. In the end she ate it, but, as soon as she'd finished, she went straight to the ladies and puked it up.

When she got back to the table, the plates had been cleared and there was an envelope on her place mat.

'Just a little something for you,' her dad said, patting it, as she sat down.

She knew what it was immediately.

'Dad, you don't have to.'

'I know, I know, but I want to. Buy yourself something frivolous, have some fun with it.'

She opened the envelope. There were two sets of four £20 notes, each with a fifth folded around them. The Queen's head, as always, facing up on the right. 'Thanks, Dad,' she said, getting up to hug him.

She wished she *could* use it on something frivolous, but she had an outstanding credit card bill with interest that was mounting by the second. The cash would help fill a small part of the hole she'd managed to get herself into. Her parents weren't rich, definitely not by Oliver's standards, but her dad was generous with what he did have. Polly was extremely grateful.

Her father paid the bill and they said their goodbyes before Polly rushed back to work.

Fifteen

Polly got back to the office at three p.m. Her plan was to get on with the T&Cs document, but she was too excited about her meeting later to work. She texted Oliver to tell him that she was going out with Alicia after work – women's talk – he wouldn't want to know any more than that. She wished she could go home and change, but didn't want to have to lie to Oliver's face. She was wearing a floral dress cinched in at the waist by a wide brown leather belt and a pair of gladiator sandals – cute, but far from sexy. At least she'd brought her make-up bag with her.

After work she spent forty-five minutes in the toilets doing her face and backcombing her hair. She was pleased with the end result – cutesy, but naughty. It was just before six when she walked out of the front door of her office building. The warmth hit her as soon as she left the lobby. The humidity had cooled and the weather was now glorious. Her skin puckered the instant the sun touched her. She closed her eyes for a moment, letting the heat defrost her insides.

Three hours to kill.

She decided to walk up to Regent's Park. She stopped in a supermarket on the way. Her intention was to buy a small bottle of rosé to accompany her on her walk, but she ended up buying two miniature vodkas and ten cigarettes as well.

She entered the park through Portland Place. Once inside, she downed one of the miniatures before unscrewing the bottle of wine and dropping in the straw she'd nabbed from the shop counter. She lit a cigarette and drew deeply. She instantly felt light-headed. She sat on a bench, savouring the moment.

The park hadn't fared well in the unrelenting hot weather. The usually lush green grass was badly scorched. All that was left was an expanse of uncomfortable-looking hay. It hadn't deterred the scantily dressed couples and tourists frolicking in the early evening sun – the park was packed. The good weather always brought out too much skin. Polly couldn't believe how brazen people could be. You'd think in central London you'd get a better calibre of sunbather.

Her straw gurgled. She gave the bottle a shake; it was empty. She leant across the bench and chucked it in the bin. A poster on the lamp post opposite caught her eye. It was for the park's open-air theatre. A showing of *Romeo and Juliet* was on at seven-thirty tonight. A 'sold out' sign was plastered right across the middle of it. Polly couldn't believe they were showing *Romeo and Juliet* tonight of all nights. She checked the time on her phone; it was just gone seven. She quickly gathered herself together and got going.

The theatre was well signposted, so it didn't take her long to find. As she approached, the smell of barbecue made her stomach growl. Through the iron turnstile next to the box office she could see a huge spit roast on a carousel. A man in chef whites carved thick slices of pork on to paper plates and dished them out to the eager queue next to him. The sight of the juicy meat and the thick, smoky smell made her mouth awash with drool. She turned away; now was not the time to be thinking about food.

She distracted herself by looking at the black and white photographs of the cast hung along the box office wall. She looked at each one carefully. Romeo wasn't quite as she imagined him. He was short, with curly blond hair. The Nurse wasn't right either, a tall, slender black woman. Juliet was suitably thin and beautiful – she didn't spend long looking at her pictures.

The tannoy overhead announced that it was time for the audience to take their seats, the performance was about to start. Polly desperately wanted to see some of the play. The theatre was hidden behind a wall of eight-foot-high evergreens. They circled the entire stage and auditorium. She nonchalantly walked round to the left, away from the box office, to look for a way through. She knew she was heading in the right direction from the murmurings and occasional bursts of laughter from the audience. She kept going, sure she'd find a gap in the undergrowth to spy through. But the hedge grew thicker and thicker the further she went. She pushed on through, despite branches pulling at her clothes and entangling in her hair. She suddenly felt a sharp sting on the back of her neck, then another on her arm. A cloud of midges were swarming her. She quickly retreated, her arms shooting out around her, trying to shoo them away.

She stood back and looked around, frustrated. She wanted to see! It was a sign, stumbling across a showing of *Romeo and Juliet* on her way to meet *him*. She had to see. Then she noticed the corner of what looked like a bench poking out of the trees further down. She sized it up. If she stood on it she could probably just about see the stage. A hushed silence spread around the audience ready for the start of the play. She quickly made her way over to the bench and climbed on to it, grappling with branches for support.

'Hey, what you doing?'

She jumped, nearly falling backwards off the bench.

The voice was hidden in the bushes. Polly climbed down and started backing away.

'Hey, lady, where you going?' The accent was thick Glaswegian.

A man in a full-length dirty brown coat and no shoes emerged from the bushes. He moved so slowly, it looked as if he was morphing out of the greenery.

'I'm just going,' Polly replied, continuing to back away.

'I didn't mean to frighten you, girly. I just didn't want you clambering all over my beid.' He pointed to the bench.

Polly nearly gagged when the smell of him hit her, and again when she saw the state of his hair. It was completely matted with dirt and grease, so much so that it looked like a piece of plastic melted on to the side of his head.

'You trying to see the play for free?' he said with a cheeky smile and a wink. There were three black teardrops tattooed just below the corner of his left eye.

'No,' she said defensively.

'Looked like it to me.'

'I was just passing—'

'Och, I don't care, girly. You like old Shakey, do ya? Star-crossed lovers an' all?'

'Yes,' she replied, not really knowing why she answered.

'Forbidden love. Ach…' He paused, momentarily lost in thought.

For some reason Polly stopped.

'It's what got me in this state in the first place,' he went on, lifting his hands to indicate his appearance.

'Really?' Polly asked, genuinely interested.

'Uh-huh. I was married once, you know, had me a house and some bairns. But then I met a wee girl and fell in love… About your age, she was. A right bonnie lass.' He paused, losing himself again. 'Couldae been perfect, but "never was there a story of more woe…"'

Normally Polly would have made her excuses and left as soon as some old tramp started telling her his life story, but the alcohol had kicked in and she was intrigued. 'What happened?'

'We upped sticks and moved to London to be together. I left everything behind me – the wife, kids, job. But then we get here and she meets some new fella and tells me to feck off. Broke my bleedin' heart. Thought I were gonnae die. Didnae have nowhere to live, couldnae go back to Scotland, couldnae get a job, ended up here.' He shrugged

'That's so sad.'

'Maybe, maybe not. At first I was so feckin' mad, I couldnae believe it, after everything I'd given up for her. The thought of her with some other fella ate me insides. I couldn't do nothing 'cept get shitfaced – I can always get shitfaced,' he said with a wry smile. 'But then, you know what happened?'

'What?' Polly was hanging off his every word.

'It occurred to me that life's nae worth livin' if you dinnae jump every now an' then. If I hadnae gone with her, I'd'a spent the rest of my days wondering what wouldae happened, you know? What's worse – the pain o' havin' your heart broke, or never havin' loved enough to get it broke in the first place?'

Polly was transfixed.

'I may not have much,' he continued, 'but I still got it all up here, 'steadnae balls down there.' He jabbed his index finger at his temple then down into his groin.

'Yeah,' Polly replied slowly nodding her head in agreement.

He gave her a big cheesy grin. The few teeth he did have were black, and bloodstained around the gum. He thought for a moment, then said, 'Come over here, I got something to show you, girly.'

He turned round and took a few steps towards the trees before leaning forward slightly to fiddle with something. Polly eagerly followed.

She was standing directly behind him when he turned round.

'Get some of this, girly,' he shouted.

He'd opened up his trousers and had his penis and balls hanging out of his fly.

'Go on, suck it,' he said.

Polly turned and left.

Sixteen

At any other time in her life the incident with the tramp would have unsettled Polly, but not now. It made her more determined than ever. She chose to ignore his little indiscretion right before she left. He had a point. She wanted *him*, she knew that; why hold herself back? The connection between them was like nothing she'd ever felt with anyone before. The very thought of him made the ache in the pit of her tummy grow and grow unbearably.

She had butterflies when she entered Notting Hill Gate tube station. She waited near the mouth of the tunnel so she could see which carriage he was in as the train rushed past. She found him in the very last one. The train was empty this far back. He was the only person in the carriage.

He grabbed her the second she boarded. He pushed her up against the clear panel next to the seats and started clawing at her top. He nuzzled into her neck then used his tongue to lick up over her jaw to her mouth. He kissed her hard. His mouth was cool and fresh and his lips juicy, like biting into a ripe peach. She momentarily surrendered herself, her hands slipping on to his waist then running up the sides of his body pulling him closer. She'd been longing for this moment, everything about it felt right. But then she stopped herself. She wanted to talk first. She let go of him and tried to move away.

He ignored her and carried on kissing her. She pulled away from him, turning her head to the side. 'I want to tell you something,' she said.

He put his hand on the side of her face and pushed it back to where it had been. Polly resisted against his hand: she really wanted to talk. He paid her no attention and carried on kissing her cheek before his tongue made its way into her ear.

'I was thinking...' she started. She stifled a giggle as he tickled her ear. 'I was thinking, maybe we could go somewhere else.'

He stopped, pulling back to look at her. He had a serious look on his face. She suddenly wished she hadn't said anything.

After a moment, a smile broke across his face.

Relief.

'Like last time, in the corridor.' He moved in close again, reaching for the back of her neck with his hand. 'Did you like the people walking by as we fucked? Sure, we can do that again, but let's finish up here first.'

'No, no, that's not what I mean,' she said, stopping him with her hands on his stomach. He had on a flimsy cotton T-shirt; she could feel sculpted muscle underneath. 'Maybe we could go to a hotel, or maybe...'

She stopped talking when his face suddenly changed.

'Or maybe what?' he asked.

She knew not to answer.

'My place? "Or maybe your place"? Is that what you were going to say?' He had a hint of sarcasm in his voice.

Polly looked back sheepishly then slowly nodded.

He sighed heavily. 'I've already explained what's going on here, right?'

They both stayed silent, him eyeing her angrily, Polly with her head bowed.

Eventually she dared to look up at him. He was still staring at her, but his brow had started to smooth out. 'Look,' he said, placing his hand on her cheek and then running it down to cup her chin, 'I love hooking up with you, but, if you think this is something more than it is, we'll have to stop.' He dropped his hand and shrugged, resigning himself to the notion.

Polly panicked. 'No, no, don't do that. I get it, I totally understand what this is.' She grabbed his hand and put it back on her cheek. She held it there.

He didn't do anything for several seconds then he stroked her face with his fingertips. She responded immediately, moving in closer to him. The warmth of his hand on her skin penetrated every part of her.

'You're a very sexy woman,' he said.

No one ever called her a woman, she was always referred to as a girl – Oliver, her dad, James, even the tramp had called her girly – but not *him*.

'I feel a connection with you,' he continued.

He felt it too.

'And I love watching you with the others.'

'You watch?' Polly was taken aback.

'Of course. @44oro, right? I know exactly where you are and who you're with.'

The thought made her ache even more.

'I love watching your face when they touch you.' He pushed his body into hers.

Polly's breath caught in the back of her throat.

'You try so hard to keep it all in, don't you? Try so hard to hide it from everyone around you.' His hands ran down between their bodies to the tops of her thighs. 'But I know. I see it in your eyes, I see it in the way you move your mouth. I can tell exactly what they're doing to you.' He put his hand flat against her crotch and began slowly moving it up and down.

She exhaled loudly, feeling as if she could fall down right behind the breath.

'I know you. I know what you want.' He suddenly stopped and let his fingers slowly tiptoe up to her belly button. 'Even if you don't, I know exactly what you need.' His fingers continued up until they reached the buttons on her dress. He slowly began undoing each one in turn. 'Do you want me to show you?' He looked deep into her eyes.

She stared back, completely lost in him. 'Yes,' she replied.

'But you need to trust me. You do trust me?'

'I trust you.'

He leant in to kiss her.

'What's your name?' she asked, right before his lips touched hers.

'No names,' he replied as his hands slipped into her dress.

'I want to tell you my name,' she said, her eyes closing as she dropped back against the panel.

'No names,' he said.

The train rattled through the sprawl of Greater London, emerging from the tunnel just as the sun was setting.

Seventeen

As she set off to the next meeting Polly felt eager to please. The thought that *he* might be watching was enough.

When she saw her partner, though, she felt a little disappointed. The man was much older than anyone she'd met before, in his sixties. He didn't seem like the kind of guy who'd be into tubing. He looked soft and cuddly, more like someone's grandad. He'd been waiting beside the door. She'd glanced at him as the train was pulling up, but hadn't for a second thought it was him. There was something vaguely familiar about him; she felt she'd seen him before, but couldn't place him. It unsettled her and she immediately turned to leave. She wasn't going to do it this time.

But he was on her before she had a chance to go anywhere. The text message had said to wear a pink top and skirt with no knickers, so he knew who she was straight away.

He made it very clear what he wanted. He grabbed her from behind and pushed her through the crowded carriage to the corner. Several commuters tutted as they banged into them. Polly smiled apologetically, embarrassed. Once in the corner, he shoved her against the empty corner seat. He ripped up her skirt and tried to push himself into her from behind.

Polly was horrified. She tried to push him back, but he leant over her, grabbing her wrists and pinning her down with his body weight. He thrust himself at her, trying to force his way inside. Sweat started beading down her forehead as panic set in. She tried to buck her body backwards to make him stop, but it didn't make any difference, he was too strong.

She couldn't believe what was happening to her. He had her trapped. Then it suddenly dawned on her where she was. Why the hell was she putting up with this? She opened her mouth to speak, but stopped. She looked around; several people were looking over to see what the commotion was but only their faces were visible, they couldn't see what he was doing to her hidden under the sea of bodies around them. How would she explain herself? They'd think she was being raped by a stranger; how could she possibly admit that she'd gone into the situation willingly? The police would be called, and then the man would show them the online messages…

She turned her head back towards him. 'No,' she whispered. 'I don't want to do this.'

He ignored her.

'Stop it,' she said a little louder.

He grunted as he let go of one of her wrists and pushed into her harder.

'If you don't stop right now, I'll scream this fucking place down,' she said just loud enough for the couple to their left to hear.

He let go of her immediately. She felt him fumble his flies closed behind her. He leant in close to her ear. 'Frigid cunt,' he spat. His breath was caustic.

She waited until the doors opened and shut again. Only when she was sure he was gone did she allow herself to move, and the second she did she began to shake uncontrollably. She steadied herself, reaching out for the small bench seat in front. When she felt in control again, she turned round and sat on the seat, taking slow, deep breaths.

She could feel the couple next to her staring. As much as she didn't want to, she turned to look at them. The girl smiled at her, 'You all right?' she mouthed.

Polly forced a smile while her insides crumbled.

She managed to keep her composure all the way home. It was only when she reached her road that tears broke.

As she walked up the stairs to the flat she could hear voices. There was a sudden burst of haughty laughter. She recognised it instantly. It was Charlotte. She leant against the stairwell wall and closed her eyes. If she had anywhere else in the world to go right now ...

After a couple of minutes of telling herself that everything was OK, she managed to calm down. She forced a smile on to her face and slipped her key into the lock. Once inside, she dropped her handbag next to the front door and threw her keys on top of it.

Oliver heard her immediately.

'Pol,' his voice came booming from the lounge. 'Look who's here.'

Charlotte poked her head round the door.

'Hi,' said Polly softly as she made her way into the room.

'Hello,' said Charlotte curtly.

'We've been waiting for you. Charlotte thought we could all go out for a drink. Bit late now, though,' Oliver continued. He shook his hand until his watch fell down over his wrist so he could see the time. 'I thought you'd be home straight after work.'

'Oh,' said Polly. They both continued to stare at her. 'Sorry, I had to stay late,' she answered.

Oliver came over and put his arm around her. 'On a Friday? I thought you office bods were all in the pub by four o'clock on a Friday. I'll have to have a word with that boss of yours.'

'No, don't do that,' she said, her voice rising.

'I'm only joking,' he said smiling. 'Are you OK? You look as if you've been crying.'

'Hay fever,' Polly lied.

She sat down on the sofa next to Charlotte. Oliver made banal conversation about the hot weather and the roadworks that had started just outside the flat. Neither Charlotte nor Polly spoke. Polly was so wrapped up in her own thoughts that it took a couple of minutes to notice that Charlotte was silent. She was usually the one in charge of the conversation. She turned to look at her. Oliver's sister was staring straight at her.

Charlotte held the stem of her wine glass between her fingertips. It was half full of red wine. She lifted it to her mouth and drained it in one. 'Can I have a refill, Oliver?' she asked without taking her eyes off Polly. 'And perhaps Polly would like one too. She hasn't had a drink yet.'

Oliver jumped up, 'Of course, of course.' He bumbled his way into the kitchen.

As soon as he was out of earshot, Charlotte turned to her. 'Is something wrong, Polly?'

'Why?'

'You look upset.'

'Hay fever, like I said.'

'Hmm,' she pondered. 'You weren't very well the last time I saw you, either.'

Polly didn't need this. She wanted to be on her own, not getting the third degree from Charlotte.

'It's nothing, really.'

'Oliver tells me you've been very busy lately, says he's not seen very much of you.'

'Really?' Polly was surprised he'd noticed. She'd thought she'd been doing a pretty good job of hiding her absences.

'Yes, says you're out and about a lot these days. He had words with me about keeping you out so late last time we met up for dinner.'

Polly's heart started pounding in her chest.

'Funny thing is,' Charlotte said, crossing her legs then smoothing her skirt, 'as far as I can remember, you were gone by half-ten – something about stomach pains.' She looked up, a smile dancing on her lips. 'But he tells me you didn't get in until two in the morning. I can't imagine what you were up to until then.'

At that moment, Oliver came back into the room carrying two glasses of wine.

'Red for you, Charlotte, and rosé for Polly.'

Charlotte let out a snort as Polly took her glass.

'What are my two favourite girls talking about, then?' he said as he sat back down in his seat.

'You,' Charlotte replied, letting out a giggle. 'You're all we ever talk about, Olliepops.'

Polly held her breath. It felt as if the blood were draining from her body.

Once she'd said her piece, Charlotte was back to her usual gregarious self and Polly was forgotten into the background. Charlotte was chatting about someone Oliver knew from back home. Charlotte had bumped into him when she was out with a friend. She talked excitedly, becoming animated as Oliver egged her on. She was telling him about how the guy had sidled up to her when she was at the bar. He'd given her a line about having fantasised about her when they were kids.

'What did you say?' Oliver asked.

'I told him I had no idea who he was.'

Oliver laughed.

'I'm not about to get involved with a prick like him, honestly.'

'Be careful, Charlotte, *you don't want to end up a lonely old spinster*.' He said the last bit in a posh lady's voice. Polly guessed it must be an impression of their mother.

'Don't you start.'

Sister and brother were both smiling at one another, locked in their private joke, then Charlotte turned and looked Polly up and down as if she'd forgotten she was there, her smile disappearing. 'Anyway, I'd better get going.'

'You don't have to. Why don't you stay over? I'll open another bottle.' He got up and started making his way to the kitchen.

Charlotte paused for a moment, contemplating the idea, then stopped herself. 'No, no, I really must go.' She got her things together, ready to leave. She gave Oliver a kiss on each cheek, leaving faint lipstick marks behind. Polly was still seated; she moved to get up but Charlotte insisted she stay put. She leant down and air-kissed her right cheek, then moved to the left, but instead of kissing her she whispered, 'Be careful, Polly, you're playing a very dangerous game.' As she pulled away, she couldn't hide the smug grin on her face.

Polly remained bolt upright while Oliver left the room to see Charlotte out. What the hell was she talking about? For a split second it crossed her mind that she knew about *him*, about the tubing, but how was that possible?

'Well, that was nice of Charlotte, wasn't it?' Oliver said when he came back into the room. He plonked himself down beside her on the sofa.

'What?' replied Polly, propping herself up and slipping her hands under each thigh to hide their shaking.

'She stuck around all this time waiting for you to get home. It's great to see you two getting on so well.'

Polly was in a state of flux. What was Charlotte playing at? Clearly she hadn't said anything about her leaving dinner early that night, but why not? She couldn't imagine Charlotte doing her any favours, especially where *Olliepops* was concerned.

Polly's back was already up when Oliver reached over to put his arm around her. She flinched and tried to move away. He leant forward, his arm chasing her.

'Get off,' she said, the words out of her mouth before she had a chance to think. After what had happened on the train, she couldn't bear the thought of anyone touching her right now. Oliver tutted, but continued anyway.

Did no one listen to her? She remembered the guy on the train pinning her hands down to the seat in front.

'Fuck off,' she shouted jumping up from the sofa. 'Are you deaf? When I say no, I mean no.'

'Polly!' he said, shocked. 'What is your problem? You're like a sullen teenager these days.'

To her relief, he pulled away and got up off the sofa. Her fingers were immediately on her lip, searching for any loose bits of skin to pick at. She remembered the gnat bite she had on her leg. Her hand went to it immediately, her nails tearing at the edges of the scab.

He busied himself clearing up his and Charlotte's wine glasses. 'I never know where I am with you at the moment,' he continued. 'When you come home, I don't know whether you're going to be in floods of tears or skipping through the front door.'

She sat quietly, concentrating on the scab. Once she had a nail under the edge she ripped it off in one go, letting out a sigh as blood seeped under her fingernail. He took her silence as an invitation to keep going.

Just then Polly heard her phone. Oliver was still talking, but she paid him no attention and went to the hallway to get her handbag.

'Where are you going?' he asked, despairing.

She took no notice.

'Polly, I'm talking to you.' He started following her out of the room, but then thought better of it and turned back.

She reached into her handbag and pulled out her phone. The screen lit up her face in the darkened hallway, it said:

I saw what happened. can we meet tomorrow?

It was *him*. He'd been there and seen it all. She messaged straight back. He replied with a time and place.

When she went back into the lounge Oliver was sat on the leather chesterfield by the window, legs crossed and staring into space.

She stood in the doorway. 'I'm sorry,' she said.

He wasn't impressed, and turned his head to the side to let her know. She went over and sat on the arm of the chair.

'I don't know what got into me,' she continued.

'This is exactly what I'm talking about,' Oliver said. 'You've waltzed back in here as if…as if nothing just happened…and now… What's going *on*, Polly?'

His voice was pleading and she felt sorry for him. He was a good guy; he didn't deserve this. But what could she do? She was seeing *him* tomorrow.

'Nothing,' she said. 'I'm just tired, and I think I'm getting my period.'

That put a stop to the conversation.

Eighteen

The next morning, Oliver was up early and whistling. Polly rolled over in bed to check the time on her alarm clock. It was 7.19 a.m.

'What the ... ?' she muttered. It was a Saturday morning and he was up being useful, ironing his shirts for the week and tending to the houseplants.

At times she found him infuriating. He was always so content and happy. She tried to imagine what it felt like to breathe his air – clean, refreshing, like washing dried outside on the line. She hadn't met a single person who had a bad word to say about him. When they had first met she'd been in awe of his good nature; she hadn't been able to believe people like him actually existed, he was so kind and gentle. Right now, it just pissed her off.

At nine-thirty Oliver marched into the room and playfully whipped the duvet off her. She fought to get it back, but in her groggy state lost the battle instantly.

'Come on, Pol, up you get,' he said. 'I need to get these sheets in the wash, and you need to start getting ready.'

Polly rubbed her face roughly with the palms of her hands. 'What?' she asked, her face screwed up like a piece of waste paper. 'Why?' She had been intending to spend the entire day in bed.

'It's Lord's today.'

Polly's face scrunched up tighter.

'The cricket. You haven't forgotten, have you?'

She had. They were supposed to be watching a one-day international.

'Do I have to go?' Her voice whiney.

'Of course you have to go, everyone's expecting you.' By everyone, Oliver meant his friends.

'Can't you just say I'm ill or something?'

'Last time it was a migraine – what do you want me to say this time? They'll begin to think you don't like them, Polly.'

Going to the cricket scuppered her plans. Being out all day meant she couldn't take her time getting ready for later; she had to get everything together before they left. After much deliberation in front of the open wardrobe, she pulled out a short, cap-sleeved floral dress and a pair of flip-flops. In her bag she hid her jute belt, red satin stiletto heels and lots of make-up.

She hung back a few metres behind Oliver all the way to the cricket ground. If he was going to make her go, she was going to make sure he knew how pissed off she was about it. He didn't seem bothered, and marched on ahead of her.

Once there, she was quickly relegated to the 'wives and girlfriends' benches directly behind the men. She was relieved to see Charlotte wasn't there. At times Charlotte felt like their shadow. Polly couldn't understand why she chose to hang around with her brother the whole time. Admittedly Polly didn't have any siblings of her own to compare her with, but from what she could gather most people were quite happy to get away from their brothers and sisters when they left home, whereas, when Oliver had moved to London, Charlotte had moved to be within walking distance of him.

Polly sat down right at the end of the bench. A couple of the women tried to draw her into conversation, asking about her job and where she got her pretty dress from, but she could see through their bullshit questions and didn't give more than one-word answers. There was no common ground between them; they had at least ten years and three stone on her. After a while, Polly put on her shades and started playing with her phone.

Lunch was a cobbled-together picnic. Everyone had brought along a dish – everyone except Polly. She vaguely remembered Oliver mentioning something about it a couple of weeks ago. He shot her an angry look as everyone started getting out their Tupperware. They laid down a banquet of stuffed olives, dolmades, goujons, Greek salad, sliced meats, cheeses and flatbreads.

Polly used an old trick she'd learnt at the clinic: she filled most of her plate with leaves, making it look as if she had a full meal. The bits of feta that did make it on were quickly disposed of in her napkin. She didn't want to eat. She didn't need to. She was beginning to feel like herself again – weightless, her limbs buoyant and her mind floating. At times like this, she felt as if her body could sustain itself, hunger feeding hunger.

She took a large gulp, draining the contents of her plastic wine glass. It immediately went to her head. She sat back and watched the others stuff mezze into their already bulging cheeks. She felt sorry for them: this was as exciting as it got for them. If only they knew, she thought, a giggle escaping her lips.

'What are you laughing at?' Oliver asked as he threw a handful of olives into his mouth and chomped down on them. She could hear the squelching as his teeth mushed the food in his mouth. She wanted to jump on the table and tell them all what she'd been doing. She would have loved to see their reaction, jaws dropping to the floor, choking on bits of pitta.

In the end she just said, 'Nothing,' and went back to playing with her phone.

When the match finished, they all moved to the beer garden of a pub across from the ground. Polly cursed herself when she saw how red and blotchy she was in the mirror of the ladies toilets. She hadn't brought any sun cream with her and, despite her best efforts to keep in the shade, she had burnt across her shoulders and the bridge of her nose. She tried to cover it with foundation and concealer. It took some of the redness down but not all of it. She made up the rest of her face in heavy, bold colours to compensate.

She'd spent most of the day worrying about how to get away, but by eight p.m. everyone was slaughtered. Once she was done with her make-up, she just slipped out of the pub unnoticed.

On the tube she changed her shoes and put on her belt. She pulled the waist of her dress up over the belt so the hem hung just below her buttocks. Next she took down her ponytail and used her fingers to tousle her hair as best she could. She checked herself out in the blackened tube train window. She looked pretty hot, even if her drunken self did say so.

She changed trains a couple of times to get to the Piccadilly Line to meet him. He hadn't specified a station, just that she should get on and he'd find her. The train took her north, further out of London than she'd been before. As her journey continued, the time between stops got longer and fewer passengers boarded. She was beginning to get impatient.

He didn't board until the train was almost at the end of the line. As soon as she saw him she wanted to rush over and throw her arms around him. But she stopped herself. He did not look pleased to see her.

'What went wrong?' he asked, striding up to her. 'Last night, what the hell were you playing at?'

Polly was completely taken aback. 'I…I…don't know…He was just…you know…you saw, right?'

'Yes, I saw. I saw you making a scene in front of a train full of people with a very powerful man.'

Polly couldn't speak. She couldn't believe what he was saying.

He moved closer and lowered his voice, although he didn't really need to; there was only one other person in the carriage, and he was over the other side with his headphones on.

'Do you have any idea who that guy was?'

'No,' replied Polly, her lip starting to tremble. She'd vaguely recognised him, but wasn't sure where from. Now she thought about it, she might have seen him in the business pages of a couple of newspapers. She wanted to say that she didn't care who he was – he tried to rape her – he deserved whatever he got. But she stayed quiet.

'I thought you understood what this was all about. You could have exposed him with your little outburst.' He sighed heavily and started rubbing his temple with the heel of his hand. 'You're making this very difficult for me.' He looked up at her. 'I don't think we can do this any more.'

Polly swallowed hard. A gulping sound escaped from her throat, it couldn't have been more exaggerated if she did it a hundred times over.

Suddenly a voice came over the tannoy announcing that they were approaching the final stop. He didn't acknowledge it. He remained still, studying her face.

She willed herself to find her voice. Say something. Anything.

The train pulled into the last station. The same computerised voice instructed everyone to disembark.

The guy down the end of the carriage got off, but *he* didn't move, so neither did Polly.

After about thirty seconds, all the lights in the carriage went off and the doors closed. The tube station was above ground so she could still just about make out his face in the moonlight. He was still watching her.

Suddenly the train's engine jolted back into life and it pulled out of the station. They travelled back along the line until they were underground again. In the tunnel it was so dark that her eyes played tricks on her; tiny green dots flashed in front of them. She reached for him. She found his hand; he squeezed back.

After a few minutes, the train stopped in a disused station. The platform was only dimly lit and there were none of the usual signs on the walls to say where they were.

The train's lights came back on making Polly jump.

'It's OK,' he said. 'They leave some of the trains in these old stations for maintenance work.'

Polly heard a door slam then the driver's footsteps echoing down the empty platform as he walked along looking in each window to check the train was empty.

'Get down,' *he* said.

They knelt down below the window. He pushed her close up under the sill so they were completely hidden from view. She could feel his breath on the back of her neck, then he leant forward and kissed her. She closed her eyes taking in a deep breath, inhaling him.

When all was quiet, she turned to look at him, 'I shouldn't have made a scene last night,' she said. 'I got scared. I felt like the guy was pushing me too fast.'

He stood up, then reached down to take each of her hands, gently pulling her to her feet.

'You need to relax.' He moved his feet wider apart and pulled her into him. Her body melted into his. 'Let yourself go.'

His hands ran up the flimsy cotton of her dress then slowly undid the four flower-shaped buttons fastening the back. The relief she felt at his touch was overwhelming. He pulled the sleeves of her dress down over her arms, then pulled back to undo her belt. He let it drop to the floor along with her dress. He took a step back and looked her up and down. She was standing in just her underwear. His eyes came to rest on her face. She stared back at him. Their connection was undeniable; it brooded in the space between them.

Without saying a word, he took both her hands and led her over to the row of seats that lined the carriage. Once there, he turned her round and placed each of her hands on an armrest so she was bent over. He stood behind her. He ran his hands roughly over her back, making her body sway from side to side. Then he flicked the clasp of her bra open. She watched as it fell down on to the seat below her. She felt his hands slide down either side of her body until they reached the top of her knickers. He slipped them inside and brought them with his hands as they pushed on down her legs. She lifted each foot so he could take them off altogether.

He knelt down by her feet and kissed each of her toes in turn, then his tongue began working its way up her left ankle and on to her calf. She bent her head down so she could watch him. He didn't look at her; he was too busy working his way up her thigh and between her legs. She took a sharp inhale of breath when he reached her soft, fleshy inner folds. His tongue flicked and teeth nibbled.

He used his tongue to explore her, slowly moving back until he was between her buttocks. Polly moaned with pleasure. He very slowly pushed his tongue inside before inserting his finger. It didn't burn the way it had before. He was much gentler, waiting for her to get used to it before pushing further. Polly allowed herself to move back and forth a little at a time. He stayed still, letting her do as she pleased.

After a minute or so, he got up and undid his trousers. He pulled her buttocks apart then pushed his way in. She jerked away, but he grabbed her round the waist and pulled her back into him.

'Let yourself go,' he whispered gently.

She tried to relax, but the sensation as he entered caught in the back of her throat and made her flinch. Once inside, he stopped, allowing her to get her breath back before moving very slowly back and forth. He pushed a little further each time. Her breath was mechanical as she got used to the intensity. He kept his arm firmly around her waist so she couldn't move away. His other hand slipped round to the front and started rubbing her. Slowly the burning dissipated and every part of her body was flooded with pleasure.

She lifted her head up. She could see him in the reflection of the darkened tube window. He was concentrating hard, his eyes open.

She closed her eyes and let her head drop down again. The feeling inside her grew and grew until every part of her body was tingling and filled with sensation.

Nineteen

They made their way out of the abandoned tube station together. He knew the way.

They left the train through the emergency door at the back of the carriage. He took her hands and helped her on to the tracks. Gravel crunched beneath her feet as she jumped down. He used the light on his mobile phone to guide them to the platform edge.

Suddenly they heard voices approaching. A group of maintenance men were making their way down the platform. He grabbed her hand and quickly pulled her into the mouth of the tunnel, where they waited until the men disappeared down to the far end. Polly's heart was in her mouth; she was terrified they'd be caught. After a couple of minutes, he hoisted himself up on to the platform then turned back to help her. Her dress caught on a cable hook jutting out just below the lip of the platform. She ended up flailing awkwardly over the edge with her dress pulled up around her waist. Her cheeks burnt with embarrassment. He didn't notice.

When he was sure the coast was clear, they tiptoed across the platform. Once in the stairwell, they ran up the stairs two at a time. The old station was a labyrinth of crumbling tunnels and passageways. Polly had no idea where she was.

She held on to his hand tight as he guided her up to the old ticket hall.

'How do you know this place?' she whispered.

'I have my sources,' he replied with a mischievous grin.

They made their way to a set of metal shutters that would have once been the station entrance. Next to it was a wooden green door. He tried the handle; it wouldn't open. He reached up to the top of the doorframe and picked up a key. He put it in the lock. Just before he opened the door, he pulled her close and said, 'I just can't get enough of you,' then kissed her deeply on the lips, not with his tongue; he opened his mouth slightly and took a deep breath, breathing her in. Then they were out of the door and he was gone.

She was on a night bus home when she spotted Oliver walking down Hammersmith Road towards the flat. She got off at the next stop and ran all the way to the flat to get back before him. She felt as though she was flying, her body light and giddy. Once home, she quickly scrubbed her face, stripped off and jumped into bed. He arrived moments later. She heard him open the bedroom door and turn the light on.

'Hey,' she protested from beneath the sheets.

'Oh, sorry, Pol, I didn't realise you were home. Everything OK?'

'Too much sun and booze, I feel rotten,' she said in her croakiest voice.

'You poor thing,' he replied. 'Is there anything I can get you?'

'No, just need sleep.'

'OK. Goodnight,' he said closing the door as quietly as he could.

She snuggled back into the duvet. She almost felt sorry for him.

She couldn't believe it when a message turned up the next afternoon.

need another fix. meet me tonight

Oliver was out that afternoon with friends watching rugby at a bar in town. He wasn't sure what time he'd be home. He'd told her not to wait up as he went in for a kiss just before he left. She managed to dodge his lips so he ended up kissing the side of her head.

She spent the afternoon getting ready. She exfoliated using a salt body scrub before lying in a bath scented with lemon balm oil for half an hour. She then got in the shower to wash off the oil and scrubbed her hair before applying a leave-in conditioner. She wrapped her hair in a towel and slathered her body in a coconut-scented moisturiser.

Once she was done in the bathroom she put on some music. Oliver hated it when she put on her music. He said her taste was childish so they always ended up listening to his acoustic tracks. Alone, however, she went for it, spinning from room to room, ending up in front of the bedroom mirror doing a striptease with her towel. She stopped when the idea suddenly hit her. She quickly went to the wardrobe and dug out her beige mac and red stiletto heels.

They met at Shepherd's Bush tube station. It was a little close to home, but she figured it would be OK.

She got on the train at 9.13 p.m. It was Sunday so there was hardly anyone on board. She saw him immediately. He was seated at the far end of the carriage, reading a newspaper.

There were only two other people near him, an old black lady with a red headscarf on and her eyes firmly shut, and a young guy buried in a book. *He* had the paper lifted high up in front of his face. He lowered it slightly when she got on, then lifted it straight back up again to hide his face. He was playing too.

She nonchalantly made her way over, carefully placing one stilettoed foot in front of the other as though she were walking a tightrope. She kept her head down, watching her pointed toes follow the invisible line. She knew he was watching her; she could feel his eyes on her.

She stopped in the vestibule just before his row of seats. She glanced up and caught him peeking around his newspaper. Her cool, sexy demeanour was momentarily lost when a smile broke out on her face; she couldn't help it. With a little shake of her head she regained her composure, then lifted her hands high above her head to stretch. The hem of her mac lifted, revealing her naked thighs. She saw his eyes light up. He pulled the paper close to his face, so only one eye was exposed, and waited for more.

She nervously glanced at the other two passengers. Neither had noticed her. She took out her train pass from her pocket and waved it at him. She turned around and dropped it on the floor. In a rush of nerves, it went a little further than she'd hoped. She had to take a step forward to get herself in the right place, then, keeping her legs and back perfectly straight, she pivoted forward from her hips to pick it up. She felt the material of her mac rise up the backs of her legs and over her buttocks. She lingered there for several seconds, then stood up and snapped round to face him.

As the train came to a halt in the next station, he got up with his paper still in his hand and went over to the corner of the carriage, where he sat in the side seat near the door. She followed, but stopped just before she reached him. She was enjoying herself too much; she wasn't done playing yet. She leant against one of the handrails and started toying with the leather belt of her mac. She teased the bow slowly, allowing the loop to slip through until there was only a very loose knot holding it together. She ran her hands over the lapels of the jacket, drawing it open millimetre by millimetre until the bottom curve of each breast was revealed, then the smooth skin between her ribs, and finally her belly button – all the time watching him watch her.

'Pol?'

The voice came from behind her just as the train was pulling away. She recognised it immediately.

'Pol. What are you doing?'

She grabbed the belt and fastened her mac shut before swinging round.

It was Oliver.

'Hello,' she said, near-hysterical.

'What are you doing?' he asked again.

'I'm on my way home,' she replied.

'Oh,' he said eyeing her suspiciously. 'You do realise you're heading into town, not back home.'

'Am I?' She looked up at the tube map just above her head, feigning confusion. 'I must have got on at the wrong platform.' She laughed nervously. She could feel her cheeks flushing and tiny droplets of sweat gathering above her lip.

Oliver wasn't looking much better. His face was pale and clammy, not his usual rosy self.

'Wait,' she said suddenly. 'What are *you* doing here? I thought you were already in town watching the rugby.'

'Yeah, I was,' he said, before pausing to clear his throat. 'But I got a message from a friend who said he needed my help. No idea what's going on with him, he's been sending me all kinds of cryptic messages about where to meet.'

It was her turn, 'Oh,' she said.

They both stood looking at one another.

'You're sweating,' she said to him, more to distract from her own appearance than anything else.

He lifted his hand to wipe his brow then brought it down in front of his eyes to inspect it.

'So I am. It's hot out tonight, right? You must be boiling in that mac,' he finished with a weak laugh.

They travelled to the next station together in an awkward silence. Polly kept her back to *him*. She desperately wanted to turn round and explain what had just happened, but she couldn't risk it. Instead she stayed facing Oliver, trying not to look directly at him, pretending to read the ads running along the top of the carriage.

They got off at the next stop together. Oliver said he couldn't be bothered to carry on chasing round town to meet his friend and that he'd just go back with her. As she stepped down on to the platform, Polly glanced back. *He* was still in the same place, leaning against one of the side seats, his paper held up, covering his face. He dropped his paper slightly so he was peering over the top. She gave him a weak smile, trying to convey as much information as possible. She hoped the look said, *Sorry, my boyfriend's just turned up so I have to go, I'd much rather be with you right now*. He raised an eyebrow at her, then lifted his paper back up.

Once the train had pulled away, Oliver took hold of her hand and led her to the correct platform. She was worried that he'd ask her where she had been going or why she was dressed in a mac and stilettos, but he didn't. He looked lost in his own thoughts. They sat on an empty bench in the middle of the platform, waiting for a train home. Polly stared at the LED board in front of her. She didn't read what it said, she just watched the shapes of text running over and over. The message read, *There is currently a good service on all London Underground lines.*

Twenty

For the next two days Polly couldn't concentrate on anything, and moped around, not really knowing what to do with herself. All she could think about was the way he'd looked at her as she got off the train with Oliver. What did the raised eyebrow mean? She prayed that it was some kind of acknowledgement, but what if she was wrong? What if he hadn't clicked that Oliver was her boyfriend? What if he had no idea what happened? Maybe he thought she was a prick-tease and had just been playing with him.

She considered texting *him*. He contacted her from a different mobile phone number each time, but she had them saved. She scrolled down the numbers, trying to figure out which one to use. In the end she didn't. From looking back at Twitter, she'd been able to work out which username he'd used for the meeting with Mousey. It was @can852ran. She thought if she searched for it she could find his other meetings and try to see him again that way. But all she found was a totally blank profile that had only been used once to set up that particular meeting.

At work, James was on her back constantly. He kept dropping by unexpectedly, leaving her to-do Post-it notes if she wasn't at her desk. So far she'd managed to cross off only one of his fifty-nine items, the one that said, *Clear up your bloody desk*. With the rest she was seeing how many she could fit on to the edges of her screen before obscuring it altogether. Not even Alicia's witty replies to Ron's dyslexic emails could cheer her up.

She avoided going home as much as possible. Oliver seemed to be around all the time. She still felt so annoyed with him for turning up like that and ruining everything with *him*. Whenever he put his arm around her or reached out to kiss her, her shoulders were instantly up round her ears.

On Tuesday evening she went shopping after work on Oxford Street, but it didn't last long. Nothing seemed to fit right. She was sure she'd lost weight, but all the trousers she tried on made her hips look big, and the fabric felt as if it was pinching around her bum and tummy. She tried on armloads of clothes just to make sure, but she hated all of them. When she was in the changing room of one shop, the assistant told her the skinny jeans she had on looked as if they'd been made for her. Polly bought them even though she was sure they made her legs look like carrots.

She was glad her first purchase was over and done with. It was usually the way that as soon as she bought one thing she'd be on a roll and there'd be no stopping her. She desperately needed that to happen tonight. But when she took her second purchase to the counter, a tight black jumper with bronze sequins around the shoulders and a peephole fastening at the back, her card was declined. The shop assistant tried it again out of courtesy. Polly stood back, pulling her best confused yet slightly annoyed face. She told the assistant she'd have to call her bank and would be back in to collect the jumper later. She didn't go back for it. She didn't need to call the bank.

By Wednesday she decided to set up a meeting for herself on Twitter. She hoped maybe he'd see and meet her.

Female looking to hook up with male. Charing Cross. Northern Line northbound. Second carriage. Tomorrow 7 p. m. #TubingCharingCross

She didn't bother to tell Oliver she was going out after work; he had cricket practice on Thursday evenings so there was no need. She hung around the office until six before making her way to Charing Cross tube station. That morning she'd dressed for work with her tubing meeting in mind. She wore a skin-tight black Lycra dress with no bra underneath. Over the dress she wore a sheer olive-green shirt that made her look business-like, but was easy to take off on her way to her meeting. She wore zebra-print ballet pumps on her feet, but carried her red satin stiletto heels in her bag.

He found her straight away. He was in his thirties, good-looking, with close-cropped blond hair. He wore a slim-fitting linen suit and a pair of metal-framed glasses. He kept his jacket on despite the heat in the carriage.

He sidled up beside her and began touching her from behind. His fingers crept up the back of her thigh and under her dress. They remained in the packed vestibule amongst the crush of commuters throughout the encounter. Polly lost herself in his touch. He kept his hands on the outside of her underwear. He didn't need to do any more than that. She stared blankly in front of her while he worked his way over her body. Even when she began to shudder all over she still managed to remain focused, her eyes fixed dead ahead.

The commuters around them were oblivious. They pushed past them as they got on and off the train, going about their business. It was as if Polly and her partner were frozen – hustle and bustle all around, while they barely moved in its wake.

He asked for nothing in return. Once she was finished, he pushed her hair back and planted a kiss on the soft skin behind her ear. She didn't turn to watch him leave; she couldn't rouse herself from her dream-like haze until the next stop.

She got off at Euston station. Just as she stepped on to the platform, she spotted *him*. He was standing right in the corner of the train, next to the doors. He looked at her between the heads of a couple chatting. She tried to scramble back on to the train, but the doors had already started closing. He was smiling at her. As the train pulled away, he blew her a kiss.

Twenty-one

She did her best to get home before Oliver. She wanted to have a quick shower and get to bed before he got back from cricket practice. When she looked up at the lounge window from the road she could see the flat was in darkness. 'Yes,' she whispered pumping her arm in the air at the same time.

She slammed the front door shut and dropped her bag in the hallway. She went straight to the bathroom, kicking off her heels and flicking on the bathroom light. She leant over the bath and turned the shower on hot. Steam instantly filled the room. She quickly unbuttoned her shirt, and pulled her dress off over her head and threw it on the floor. She was standing in just her knickers, taking her earrings out, when she felt someone watching her.

She turned to face the bathroom door. Oliver was there. She let out a little yelp in surprise and her hand instantly went to her heart as it leapt out of her chest.

'Oliver,' she said. 'I didn't realise you were in.'

She didn't know what time it was, but guessed it was about nine o'clock. She could see the streetlights and headlamps brushing through the lounge window. Oliver was leaning against the doorway. The light from the bathroom illuminated only part of his face, leaving his left eye hollow and his lip-line protruding.

He didn't say anything. She reached for a towel to wrap round herself, suddenly self-conscious. His silence was making her nervous. After a couple of seconds she said, 'I'm going to get in the shower now,' and pushed the bathroom door shut with the flat of her hand.

He stopped the door with his foot just before it hit him, kicking back gently, and said, 'Come into the lounge. We need to talk.'

She swallowed hard. Did he know? She panicked. Regardless, she wasn't going to talk right now.

'Later,' she said, pushing the bathroom door harder.

'No, we need to talk now.'

'I'm just about to get in the shower. It's a bit inconvenient right now. You'll have to wait.'

He caught the bathroom door in his hand and held on to it. She used all her strength to push against it. It wouldn't budge. 'Oliver, tsstt!' She was getting frustrated.

'Please, Polly, let's go into the lounge and talk.'

He only ever called her Polly when he was serious about something.

'I'm having a shower,' she said very slowly, as if he was slow or foreign and couldn't understand her. 'You'll have to wait,' she continued.

'No,' he said.

She started pushing at the door again. Her towel was coming loose, so she had to stop to pull it up round herself.

'Oh, just leave me alone, will you,' she finally shouted, red-faced and panting from the exertion.

He stared at her in silence for a few seconds longer and then said, 'Your dad died earlier today.'

Her towel dropped to the floor, then she fell on to it.

*

At 4.44 that afternoon, Polly's dad had had a massive heart attack and died. He was making a cup of tea in the kitchen. Polly's mother was in her bedroom at the time. She didn't find her husband until he'd been dead for over two hours.

She had tried to call Polly from the hospital several times that evening, but Polly was underground with no signal. In the end she'd called the flat, and caught Oliver just as he was leaving for cricket practice.

After she managed to pick herself up off the floor, Polly refused to believe him. She was sure he'd got it mixed up and that her mother was dead, not her dad. Her mother was the one who was always in and out of hospital. Oliver assured her that he'd spoken to her mother and it was definitely her dad.

'Why him?' she cried.

'I'm so sorry,' Oliver said as he pulled her into him.

She kept her arms by her sides while he squeezed her tightly into his chest. 'Why not her?' she continued, but he didn't hear her muffled words.

She spoke to her mother briefly over the phone an hour later. Neither said they were sorry, neither felt they deserved the sympathy. To her surprise, her mother wanted her to come home straight away. Then it dawned on her that she needed a new carer now her dad was gone. Polly made an excuse about not being able to get a train home that late at night. Oliver tried to butt in, offering to drive her. She ignored him. She told her she'd get a train in the morning. She needed some time to get her head straight.

That night, Oliver held her until she fell asleep. She wanted to pull away, but she needed his warmth and comfort.

She arrived at her parents' house just before lunch the next day. Oliver wanted to go with her, but she asked him not to. She said she'd be in touch to let him know the funeral arrangements.

On the train journey home, Polly could think of nothing but her mother. She invaded her thoughts, not letting up for a moment. The familiar landscape triggered memories she'd managed to ignore since moving to London. She tried her best to block them, but every time she tried to think about anything else she ended up back in her mother's bedroom, sitting beside the eight school exercise books strewn on the floor.

In her mother's paranoid world, Polly was the enemy. According to her rants, Polly had ruined everything in her mother's life, from her body to her relationship with her husband. It was clear that she hadn't wanted children, but had been persuaded by Polly's father. Polly had never been able to fathom her parents' relationship. All she knew was that they'd met at some church function when her mother was twenty-one and her dad forty-two. Her dad was a practising Catholic and had been active in his local church since moving from Ireland to England in the late sixties. They'd married a year after they met, and a year later Polly was born.

She recorded in great detail everything she loathed about Polly. From the moment Polly was born, her mother was convinced that there was something wrong with her, something wicked. She wrote about wanting to hurt Polly, detailed fantasies about smothering her or drowning her in the bath. As Polly got older, her mother's focus changed and she started to believe that Polly was wantonly trying to steal her husband away from her. The language she used was vile. She described innocent events with such perversion, Polly could barely read them. She went into great detail about how Polly would use her sexuality, parading around naked when her husband came home from work – she'd been five and it was bathtime. As Polly approached her teenage years and her body started to develop, her mother's descriptions became more vicious, and she had started to imagine that Polly was trying to engineer an incestuous relationship with her husband. She didn't believe her husband had any part to play in it all; he was the innocent victim.

Polly had never told anybody about what she read, not even her dad. At first it was because she didn't want her mother to find out that she'd been through her things, but later because she felt ashamed and embarrassed. How could anyone think such things about their own daughter? Maybe there *was* something wrong with her.

These thoughts had consumed Polly. She had found it difficult to focus on anything else. Being at home was a nightmare. She tried to stay out of her parents' way as much as possible, she didn't want to give her mother any more ammunition, and as a result practically lived in her bedroom. She became moody and difficult to be around, and saw less and less of her friends. Her predicted high grades were forgotten as she barely scraped through her exams. Everything in her life was crumbling and there was nothing she could do to stop it or make things right again.

It wasn't long before all that negative emotion turned into self-loathing and weight started to drop off her. She'd never been a fat child, she was as average as they came, but the more pounds she lost, the more food and hunger consumed her, blocking out any thoughts of what her mother had written. She'd found a coping mechanism and managed to get some degree of control over her mind again and, in the process, was making herself disappear. Soon she became totally numb.

Her dad put her behaviour down to typical teenage tantrums. But to Polly it felt as if even he didn't care what was happening to her. It wasn't until she was sixteen and her weight had plummeted to below five and a half stone that he noticed. She'd been in her room with the door ajar. She was doing her homework on her bed. The oversized woolly jumper she was wearing had been scratching all day. She sat up and started to pull it up over her head, and it caught with her T-shirt and rode up to reveal her protruding ribcage. Her dad had just got in from work and was popping up to her room to say hello. She looked up to see him standing in the doorway, then tears started streaming down his face. No doubt her mother had noticed long ago, but hadn't said anything. Polly was marched down to the doctor, who took one look at her and got her admitted to the local hospital. From there she went to a psychiatric unit, then to a clinic that specialised in eating disorders. She had the feeding peg inserted into her stomach after she'd pulled the feeding tube out of her nose for the third time.

The clinic was fifty miles from home. Her mother didn't visit, she said it was too far for her to travel being so ill, but her dad came every day. He did everything he could to aid her recovery, although their conversations about why she'd been starving herself never amounted to much. Polly couldn't bring herself to tell him; she just couldn't say the words out loud.

She let herself in using the front door key still on her key ring. As she slipped it in the lock, she wondered if she'd ever use it again after this visit.

She went straight into the kitchen. It smelt of clean washing and baking. Nothing had changed since she was a child. The cupboards had the same shiny orange fronts, the drawers white, the worktop mottled faux marble stained with tea cup rings and burns; even the totally impractical hot and cold taps remained. Her dad had been the home-maker. He had done all the cooking, cleaning, washing and other household chores. She turned to look at the kitchen door. His *Kiss the chef* apron was hung on the back of the door where he always left it. She could almost see the imprint of his huge belly in it. Tears immediately started splashing down her cheeks.

'Oh, you're here.'

Polly turned to see her mother at the door. She was in her wheelchair, a scowl on her face. She looked painfully thin. When she put her arms down on to the wheels to move forward, Polly could see skin hanging loosely around the bone.

'I didn't hear you come in,' she continued as she wheeled herself round to the sink. She put the brake on, then hoisted herself up using the worktop.

Polly stood watching her, suppressing the urge to scream. Why was she still pretending? There was no one here any more to see.

'Glad you finally made it,' she said sarcastically. 'Would have been nice if you could have come when he was still here – better late than never, I suppose.'

Her mother turned to face her, using the worktop for support. She looked totally out of place. Polly had very few memories of her being in this room. It was usually just Polly and her dad eating dinner together in here. Her mother mostly took her meals in her bed, unless she'd stopped eating altogether. It seemed odd her being in the kitchen now, even though it was her house and Polly hadn't lived there for years.

'You got nothing to say?' her mother said bitterly.

Polly remained silent.

'Are those tears? Why have you been crying, Polly?'

Polly hated her. She was evil, pure evil.

'I didn't think you'd be bothered, you never were when he was alive.'

That was it. Polly jumped towards her, knocking the kitchen table as she went. She didn't know what she was going to do, whether she'd slap her or spit in her face. But her mother stopped her dead by grabbing her wrist.

'Careful, Polly, you're standing right where your father took his final breath.'

Polly jumped back immediately.

'Don't worry, he'll understand. You walked all over him in life; why would he mind you doing it now he's dead?'

Polly turned and ran out of the room. She went straight along the corridor into her old bedroom, slammed the door shut, then threw herself on the bed and sobbed.

She woke up an hour later. At first she couldn't work out where she was. Then she rolled over and saw the poster on the back wall. It was of a white fluffy kitten hanging from a tree by only one paw. The caption below read, *Hang on in there, baby*. Her dad had bought it and put it up for her for when she'd got back from the clinic. She had loved it the instant she saw it. Her dad had stood at her bedroom door, watching her.

'What do you think?' he'd asked.

She had smiled sheepishly.

Then her mother had appeared in the doorway and looked at the poster over his shoulder. 'Pathetic,' she'd said.

Suddenly Polly was crying again, reliving the memory. She tried to picture her father standing in the doorway smiling at her, but the harder she tried, the more tenuous and blurry the image became, until it felt as if she'd never seen him in the first place.

Twenty-two

The funeral was scheduled for a week later. Polly stayed at her parents' house until then.

She saw very little of her mother. She spent most of her time in her room, leaving Polly to organise the funeral. They had plenty of visitors; her dad had been popular in the village. She recognised only a few faces, but they all knew who she was. 'He talked about you all the time, he was so proud of his little girl.' The words cut right through her. Her mother made herself scarce whenever there was a knock at the door. There were lots of gentle nods and pursed lips in sympathy for the terrible grief her mother must be suffering. Polly nodded along, out of respect for him, not her.

On the fifth day at her parents' house Polly received a text message. It was for a meeting that night. Her heart sank when she read it – it was from *him*. She considered sneaking out and jumping on a train to London. She was desperate to disappear into tubing again, pretend all this wasn't happening. But it was a logistical nightmare. The train station was a ten-minute car ride from her parents' house – she had no car. To walk it would probably take over an hour along overgrown, narrow country lanes. Even if she could make it to London, she wouldn't be able to get a train back again after the meeting at that time of night.

Then there was her mother to contend with. Despite hardly seeing her, she appeared to know Polly's movements like she had her on radar.

But mostly she didn't go out of respect for her dad. It was as if, now he was dead, he'd know everything. She imagined him looking down on her from a cloud in the sky, shaking his head in disappointment. She knew it was a childish thing to think – he was at the funeral director's, in one of their fridges – but she couldn't shake the notion.

Her next dilemma was how to reply to the message. She agonised over it for hours. She knew the rules: no personal details, so she could hardly say what had happened. As the meeting loomed closer she paced anxiously in her bedroom. She decided the best thing to do was to just be honest, but light with it, reply with something like, *Not in town, but I'll be back next week, let's hook up then.*

She'd just started composing the message when there was a knock at the door.

'Polly. Door,' her mother shouted.

Polly ignored her and carried on with her text.

'Polly!' her mother shouted louder.

She knew she didn't have a choice. She threw her phone down on the bed and ran to answer it.

It was the priest. He'd come round to discuss the funeral service for Friday.

Polly and her mother disagreed on everything, from the running order of the service to the hymns he'd have wanted. The priest sat patiently waiting for them to come to some kind of agreement. In the end, her mother won out with the line, 'You've hardly seen him lately; you have no idea what his wishes were.' It wasn't her mother's words that persuaded her to drop it, it was the sudden realisation that he was dead now anyway. He wasn't going to be at the funeral, not in a living sense. It didn't really matter.

Oliver came down on the morning of the funeral. Her mother instantly perked up when she saw him. He looked different, the way people did when they were put into well-worn, but unfamiliar settings. The bungalow seemed too small for him and sullied his expensive clothes and shoes. Polly didn't want him there. Not just because of what had been going on in London, but because she'd spent most of their relationship trying to hide all this – the white plastic cladding, the seventies wallpaper, the unkempt garden … her mother.

Polly cried from the moment she saw the coffin until they laid it in the ground. She couldn't grieve silently, didn't understand those who could. She felt as if she was being crushed from the inside – she had to let it out somehow. She let Oliver comfort her. They were awkward in one another's arms. Her mother glared at her over the coffin – she wouldn't even let her alone in her grief.

Everyone went back to the house afterwards. Neither Polly nor her mother had considered this eventuality. There was no food in the cupboards, so they could only offer tea. Oliver, being ever resourceful, drove to the local supermarket and picked up a selection of biscuits and cakes and the spread wasn't bad in the end. He played host for the afternoon. The ladies were charmed by his public school accent and manners. When they discovered he was a surgeon, a hush of admiration rippled round the room. Polly spent most of her time in the kitchen making tea. She found a bottle of brandy in one of the cupboards. She took a quick sip every time she had to put on another brew.

They'd been back at the house for about an hour when Polly noticed her mother had disappeared.

She barged straight into her bedroom without knocking.

Her mother was by the window, staring into space.

'What are you doing?' asked Polly.

Her mother turned, mouth agape, a look of disbelief on her face. 'What the hell do you think I'm doing?'

Maybe it was the alcohol, or maybe Polly had reached her limits. 'I've no idea. Looks to me like you're doing what you've always done: hiding in your bedroom so you don't actually have to face the world.'

'How dare you?' she said, turning to her. 'I've just lost my husband.'

'Your nursemaid, you mean.'

'What?'

From the look on her face, Polly knew she'd gone too far. 'Nothing.'

'No, say it again.'

She'd been trying to pick a fight with her ever since she arrived. 'Fine. I said, "You've lost your nursemaid."'

Her mother slowly started shaking her head. 'Who the fuck do you think you are, Polly? You never bothered with him; I can't even remember the last time you saw him.'

'I saw him a couple of weeks ago, actually. He came to London to visit me.'

Her mother's face dropped. She had no idea he'd been going to London to see her.

'Yeah, he came quite often. Did he not mention it?' Smug satisfaction poured out of Polly's drunken mouth.

'Why?'

'Why what?'

'Why did he come to visit you?' she asked suspiciously.

'Why do you think? I'm his daughter, he wanted to see...' Polly paused, realising what her mother's sick head was getting at. 'You're perverse, you know that.'

'What are you talking about?'

'You and your paranoid delusions. I've read your stupid books,' said Polly, suddenly feeling brave enough to say the words she'd believed unspeakable all these years.

'What books?'

'The ones hidden in the back of your wardrobe,' Polly answered, striding across the room towards it.

Her mother immediately started wheeling herself forward to block her. 'Don't you dare touch my things,' she hissed.

'It should have been you, not him,' Polly blurted out.

'I beg your pardon?' replied her mother, as if she were some kind of innocent in all this.

'You – you ruined my life, you ruined his life...'

'*I* ruined *his* life?' she said incredulously. 'I sacrificed everything for that man.'

'What are you talking about? What sacrifice have you ever made?'

'You. I gave him you.'

Polly just stared at her.

'I never wanted you, Polly. I never wanted any children. But he did, and I did it for him.'

Polly couldn't quite believe what she was hearing. This wasn't news to her, she'd already read how her mother felt, but to hear her say the words out loud... It was against nature, her existence undermined.

'And I've suffered as a result of that decision since the day you were born,' her mother continued.

Polly started to tremble. She hated her; she'd never thought it was possible to hate someone as much.

'Well, you're fucked now, aren't you?' she shouted.

'What? What are you talking about?' she asked, confused.

'He's gone, and there's no one to look after you any more, not that you've ever really needed anyone.'

'How dare you? You have no idea what I've been through.'

'It's all bullshit! There's nothing wrong with you, never has been. I can prove it.' Polly marched over to her. 'Get up,' she shouted.

'What?' Her mother looked genuinely scared.

'You're gonna have to get up. I'm not going to stay and look after you.' Polly grabbed hold of the handles on the back of her wheelchair and started tipping it forward. 'Get up, I said!'

'Don't. Get off!' her mother said, turning, trying to bat her away as she started sliding out of the chair. As Polly had anticipated, her mother put her feet on the floor and started to step to the side.

'You lying bitch, you can stand...' she started.

But the bedroom door suddenly banged open. 'Polly, what's going on? Everyone can hear you in the...' Oliver trailed off, his eyes growing wide with shock as he took in what was happening. He raced across the room. 'Let go of her,' he shouted at Polly, then grabbed hold of her hands and pulled them off the handles of the wheelchair and held on to them tightly. The chair thumped back down. Her mother fell awkwardly back into the seat.

'What the hell are you doing?' He didn't look at Polly's mother, he just stared at Polly in utter dismay.

Polly stared back. Why was he looking at her like that? Hadn't he seen her mother standing? Then it dawned on her. She looked at her mother: she had her hand on her forehead, trembling, breathing deeply. The victim back in her chair, Polly the evil, crazed daughter bearing down on her. She'd played it out just the way she did each time for her husband. Oliver had seen what she wanted him to see.

Polly felt as if she was going to explode. 'Aarrgh,' she shouted, then wriggled free. She ran out of the room and straight to the front door. She didn't stop until she reached the park at the end of the road. Once there, she collapsed on to her knees, taking in huge lungfuls of air. Her entire body was shaking violently; she'd never felt such anger in her life. But not just with her mother, with her dad for putting up with it, with Oliver for being here, with *him* for sending the text two nights ago, with herself for not replying.

Twenty-three

Polly loitered in the park until she saw the last of the mourners leave the house. She didn't have any shoes on. She carefully walked back up the pavement, avoiding any big stones and gravelly areas.

The front door was still open. She went straight to her room and threw all her things in her bag.

Once she had finished packing, she went to the kitchen, where Oliver was clearing up, and ushered him out of the front door by the elbow. He protested and insisted they say goodbye to her mother first. Polly told him he could do what he liked; she'd be in the car.

Once on the road, she pulled her mobile out of her bag to check it. No messages. She swore under her breath.

'What?' asked Oliver looking over at her from the driver's seat.

'Nothing.'

She wished he'd put the radio on; the silence was painful. She reached forward to switch it on. He grabbed her hand as soon as she moved towards the console.

'We should talk,' he said, his tone soft and warm.

Polly stared out through the windscreen.

'Polly, I just want to say that I'm here for you.' He pursed his lips together, pleased with his opening. 'It's going to be hard for you now your dad's gone, but there's someone else who's going to be struggling more than you, and she doesn't have anyone now.'

'Who?' Polly asked, turning towards him, genuinely at a loss as to who he was talking about.

'Well…your mother,' Oliver replied, looking at her as if she was mad.

She wanted to wrench the handbrake up as hard as she could, to make the car crash and explode into a million pieces.

'We had a chat and—'

'When did you have a chat?' Polly jumped in.

'When you disappeared this afternoon.'

Polly exhaled loudly through her nose.

'So, we had a chat,' Oliver continued. 'She's lost a lot. She's worried she won't be able to cope on her own.'

He paused, waiting for Polly to say something. She didn't. There was no point. She'd already filled his head with lies.

'I wish you'd told me how ill she's been. I could have helped.' Again he waited for her input. 'Anyway, that's by the by. I know a specialist at the hospital who deals with cases like your mother's, ones that end up doing the usual round of referrals and getting nowhere. I'm going to give him a call when we get back and arrange an appointment. I've told your mother she can stay with us while he assesses…'

'Shut up,' Polly said, her teeth gritted so tightly they could have shattered.

He stopped abruptly. 'Polly,' he said, letting each letter hang in the air in disbelief.

Every muscle in her body clenched, trying to keep herself under control. She couldn't believe she'd been foolish enough to leave them in the house alone together.

He was quiet for a few moments, then sighed heavily. 'She said you might react like this. You two need to sort out your differences.' He reached out to take her hand. She held it tightly against her leg, refusing to let him hold it. 'I'm here for you, Polly. She told me about what happened when you were younger. She thinks you may be having a relapse, you're looking very thin, and I'm inclined to agree.' He started talking fast, back in the swing of his speech, 'But you don't have to worry, I'm going to look after you, get you fighting fit again. I'm due some time off from work so we can start spending more—'

'Shut up!' Polly screamed.

Oliver visibly jumped when her high-pitched squeal pierced the air.

She put her hands over her face and started crying. She just wanted to get back to London, to *him* – fuck everything else.

Twenty-four

Eleven days after getting back to London, Polly hadn't received a single message. She was pretty certain she'd blown it. The longest time between messages in the past had never been more than a week. Why hadn't she just replied to the message that came when she was at her parents' house? The *should've*s, *could've*s, *if only*s taunted her relentlessly.

Out of desperation, she had replied to the message four days after returning to London. She'd written, *I'm back and ready for action*. It sounded corny, but she didn't care. She'd got no reply. A couple of times her thumb had hovered dangerously close to the call button of the numbers he'd texted her from. But she could never go through with it – she knew the rules. If she called, it would be over for sure.

She tried posting on Twitter. She used her fake handle, @44oro, and wrote:

Woman looking to meet man. Northern Line.
Leicester Square southbound. Second carriage.
6 p.m. tonight. #TubingLeicesterSquare

It was at Leicester Square that she'd seen Mousey and *him*, so she was hopeful that he would search the hashtag and find it. Also, he knew her handle, maybe he was still

173

keeping an eye on it. She didn't have to wait long; half an hour later someone left a reply. It said:

timewaster. no show

He had found it; the reply came from the Twitter handle @can852ran. She was at her desk at work when she checked her phone and saw it. She put her head in her hands. She felt as if she had nothing, there was just nothing. Lionel walked past her desk several seconds later. He stopped and put his hand on her back. She looked up at him, bleary-eyed.

'I think you've come back too soon,' he said.

At first she had no idea what he was talking about, then it dawned on her: he was referring to her dad.

'No, no, I'm OK,' she replied, cringing inside, she felt like such a fraud. 'I just need a moment.'

'If you're sure. I'm happy for you to take more time off if you need it.' He looked so concerned.

She smiled awkwardly and turned back to her desk, willing him to go away.

Oliver, true to his word, was there to force-feed her dinner every night. He managed to swap his surgeries around so he could be home before she got back from work. He sat across from her, carefully watching as each forkful passed her lips. But he didn't stop there: he'd wait patiently until he saw her throat bob, swallowing it down – her mother had obviously filled him in on the protocol. There was no getting away from him. She soon learnt that the quicker she ate, the sooner she could get the bath running and get rid of it.

She spent a lot of time in the bath – it was the only place she could be alone. She'd lie in the piping hot water, letting her limbs float to the surface and her mind drift away. For those precious minutes she just hung there, existing. No thoughts crossed her mind, darkness behind her closed lids, no sound with her ears dipped just below the water, no sensation in her body except for the cushioning warmth of the water. But it didn't last. The water would start to go cold or her skin would wrinkle up so much that it no longer felt like her own, and her hands and feet would get itchy and hot and irritated.

Sometimes in her dazed state *he* would come to her. She couldn't stop herself from tilting her head up ready to kiss him, reaching her hand out to touch his chest and run down his ribs. But just as suddenly she'd realise where she was, open her eyes and see that she was in Oliver's cold, windowless bathroom. She'd plunge herself under the water, holding her breath until her lungs were clawing up her throat for air. A couple of times she left it too long and the world started to go fuzzy.

Her mother had been in contact – not with her, with Oliver. Polly came home one evening to find him pandering to her on the phone. The second she walked in and saw him on his mobile she knew it was her. She stood in the doorway and stared at him until he noticed her. He was sitting on the chesterfield. He had a holiday brochure resting like the roof of a house on his crossed legs – he'd decided it would do her good to have a little break away somewhere. The brass globe floor lamp dangled above his head, illuminating the start of a bald spot.

'It's your mother,' he mouthed when he noticed her.

She left the room and went straight to the bathroom. She ran the bath while she vomited in the toilet and cried like a baby.

She was beginning to give up all hope. But then, quite by accident, she found him again.

She was on her way home from work. The Central Line was closed due to a signal failure – the Underground was in chaos. She attempted to get the Piccadilly Line to South Kensington but it was totally rammed. In the end she walked to Euston Square, where she got on the Hammersmith and City Line.

It was 6.02 p.m., rush hour. A seemingly impossible number of passengers piled in at every stop. Although summer was fading, the heat of the day underground was trapped in the unventilated carriage. She found herself pushed up against a businessman in the main vestibule. He didn't seem capable of breathing through his nose so had his mouth open, blowing each exhalation directly in Polly's face. His breath smelt like cow shit. Polly managed to turn away slightly, but then he lifted his hand up and gripped on to the rail above. The smell from the dark sweat patch on the armpit of his shirt forced her to turn away from him altogether. No one around her was particularly happy about it, but she just couldn't stand it. In her new position she grabbed on to the rail above and let herself hang. She closed her eyes and pretended she wasn't there. It wasn't long before she was thinking of *him* – that first time, how he'd looked at her then moved forward and kissed her, running his hands down her back. Her stomach knotted up. She started to rock ever so slightly, soothing herself.

When she opened her eyes again, *he* was standing at the far end of the carriage. At first her eyes brushed straight past him, he was standing just as she had imagined in her daydream, but then her brain caught up and she snapped back in a double-take. When she realised it really was *him* she physically jumped – much to the annoyance of several passengers.

He hadn't seen her – there were too many people in the way and he was looking down rather than straight ahead. A spotlight lit him from above. She'd never seen anyone so perfect. Among the sea of faces around him, he didn't look real. The other commuters were flustered and red, struggling with the heat, but he looked totally unfazed, completely cool, perfect.

She immediately started making her way towards him. It was nearly impossible to get through the crowd, but she ploughed ahead as best she could. There were lots of grunts and groans followed by quick 'sorry's from Polly's lips. He was quite far down towards the end of the carriage. She tried to move quickly before the train reached the next stop and he got off or she lost him, but she kept getting bogged down in the other passengers. She was forced to stop altogether, halfway down the carriage, where the crowd was so densely packed there was no getting through. A French family were taking up most of the room. She said, 'Excuse me,' several times, but they were too busy arguing over the flimsy tube map being snatched from hand to hand to notice.

After a couple of seconds, Polly decided she couldn't wait any longer and pushed through them. She didn't see the enormous black suitcase at their feet and walked straight into it. Everyone turned as she clawed on to the people around her to try to stop herself from falling. It made little difference. She fell awkwardly on to her shoulder then straight on to the side of her face. A woman close by helped her up. The French family just stared at her in disbelief.

Once back on her feet, her only option was to stay put until the next stop, when she'd be able to hop out and then get back on through the doors closest to him. She felt a ripple of excitement run through her. He'd be so surprised to see her. She thought she'd play it cool, sidle up to him without letting on, then slip in behind him and go straight for his crotch.

She was in a far worse position now than she had been before. It was difficult to keep an eye on him amongst the newspapers and heads bobbing in front of her. After a lot of ducking and diving she finally managed to get herself into a good spot with a decent view. But then out of nowhere a girl's head appeared. Polly couldn't believe it. The girl positioned herself directly in front of him, totally obscuring her view.

'Get out of the fucking way,' Polly said under her breath.

The girl had her back to her at first, but then turned so she was facing front. She had a glazed expression on her face, as if she was in some kind of trance. It took several seconds for Polly to realise what was happening. And, when she did, everything drained away – everything except the girl. She was with *him*.

She was beautiful – long, straight blonde hair with a heavy blunt-cut fringe, full, pouting, luscious lips, long, slender limbs – as untouchably beautiful as he was. Jealousy punched Polly repeatedly in the stomach. She swallowed hard as his face slowly came into view, nuzzling into her neck. She continued to watch as the girl's eyes closed when his mouth moved across her neck to bite down on her earlobe. Polly could imagine what was going on down below where she couldn't see. She knew the intimate places he'd be touching her and how it would make her feel.

Polly's eyes narrowed, projecting every ounce of hatred on to her. 'Die, bitch, *die*,' she muttered through gritted teeth.

Suddenly the girl jolted. Her eyes flicked wide open and her entire body went rigid, then collapsed forward as if every muscle had just given out. There was something horribly awkward about her movement. Polly was immediately up on tiptoe trying to see what was going on, but she couldn't see her any more; he'd caught her and swung her round so she was now hidden behind him.

The train's tannoy system announced the next stop, Baker Street. She saw him start moving towards the doors. He hauled the girl along with him. It was as if she had absolutely no control over her body any more; she was barely conscious. Once at the door, he paused for a moment to reach into his pocket. He took out a baseball cap and put it on his head with his free hand. He pulled the peak down low over his face.

Polly pushed her way to the nearest doors so she could follow. Something told her that whatever had just happened was bad. Very bad.

Once off the train, she watched as he half walked, half dragged the girl down the busy platform. Polly sped up to get a better look. The girl seemed to have regained some level of consciousness. Her eyes opened and closed as if waking from a deep sleep, but her arms and legs lolled as if she had no control over them. He stopped when they reached the bottom of the platform near the tunnel entrance. He moved close to the wall and propped her up against it as though she was a mannequin. He looped his arms under her armpits then put his hands flat against the tiles to support her. He looked around cautiously, checking to see if anyone was watching.

Polly hid behind a large group of tourists. From where she stood it looked as if he was talking to her. She wasn't responding; occasionally she'd lift her head up to look at him, but mostly it was flopped down to her chest as if she had no strength in her neck. Polly desperately wanted to hear what he was saying, but knew she wouldn't be able to get close enough without being spotted.

The platform was busy. It was a narrow platform so several rows of people began forming along the edge, waiting for the next train. His eyes kept flicking up to the LCD board. As soon as it said the next train was approaching, he put his arm around the girl's waist and pushed his way into the front row of commuters. Polly followed, keeping a safe distance away from where they stood. She watched as he steered her round so she was facing forward and he was holding her from behind. He had his hands firmly around her waist, but her feet were dangling precariously close to the edge of the platform. She seemed to be coming round a bit more. She was looking left to right, trying to figure out where she was. Her eyes were small and squinting, as though she couldn't see properly.

Polly was suddenly aware of the sound of the train thundering towards the platform. She looked across towards the tunnel. Her hair lifted in a rush of wind to her face. She could see headlights cutting through the darkness. She looked back at him. His face was taut with concentration. The girl was now so close to the edge of the platform that her hair and dress blew up, caught in the warm gust, making her appear more vital than she was. Polly stared in disbelief – was he really about to do this? She started making her way towards them, reaching her arms out in anticipation, unable to stop herself, getting dangerously close.

As the train sped into the station he let go of her. Polly stopped dead, transfixed as the girl fell in front of the train. The driver hadn't yet started to apply his brakes, so he struck her at full speed. She exploded like a watermelon hitting the floor.

Suddenly the station was filled with the sound of squealing brakes. No one moved. No one took a breath. When the train finally came to a halt, silence engulfed the crowd. It was as if the entire scene had been paused.

The girl standing next to Polly was the first to make a noise. She lifted her hands to her face and cupped the scream between her palms. She went up an octave when she realised the damp, sticky fluid on her face was the girl's blood. Polly felt something on her lip, and her tongue instinctively flicked out to lick it. The taste of hot metal filled her mouth.

Chaos broke out. Everyone around her was malfunctioning, bouncing into one another, unable to take one step in front of the other. Screams whooshed past her like aeroplanes taking off. She stood in the midst of it, a hot ache of fear starting in her toes and rising up through her entire body until she was deafened by it.

An announcement came over the tannoy instructing all passengers to make their way to the nearest exit. A man bashed into Polly in his confused state, nearly knocking her off her feet. The buzzing in her ears was suddenly gone and she was wrenched back into reality. The girl next to her had gone from screaming to crying and was being helped off the floor by a couple of guys in rolled-up shirtsleeves. She could hear bewildered voices further down the platform asking what had just happened.

'One under,' a voice replied.

Then someone further down shouted, 'What's under?'

Followed by, 'A bomb. There's a bomb under the train!'

A tsunami of panic worked its way down the platform until, by the time it got to the bottom, word was that a bomb had gone off under the train. People started screaming and pushing to get to the nearest exit.

Polly looked to her left. *He* was still standing there, exactly where he'd been when he let go of the girl. But he wasn't concentrating hard or staring forward any more. He was looking straight at Polly. His eyes were wide, surprised to see her, but they quickly narrowed when he realised she'd seen what he'd just done.

Twenty-five

He started moving towards her. For a second she couldn't move. Her brain couldn't quite get to grips with what had just happened or what she should do about it. When she finally did turn to run, she didn't get very far. The crowds of people around her were like treacle, clinging to her in their disarray. She shook most of them off, but was soon caught behind a bottleneck heading for the stairs. She looked behind her. He was gaining on her, eyes on her, gliding through the crowd as if there was no one else there.

'Please move,' Polly shouted, but no one listened. She shoved the people in front with her shoulder, trying to force her way through.

'Hey,' said the man ahead of her without turning round. 'We're all trying to get out. A little patience, my dear.'

'I have to get out, now,' Polly said breathlessly, fear making her voice rise and fall in all the wrong places.

'It's all right, we'll be out of here soon,' he continued in his polite but firm manner.

'You don't understand!' She was verging on hysteria, half sobbing, half screaming. 'Please let me through,' she screeched.

The man turned to look at her. He flinched, taken aback by her appearance. The splatters on her face had mixed with her tears and were now streaming down her face as if she was crying blood. He was an older man, in his late sixties, but tall and well built enough to easily assert his authority. He grabbed the top of her arm and started making a path for her.

'Excuse me,' he said to the mass of people in front.

'Join the queue, mate,' said a fat, balding guy ahead of them.

'This young lady is very distressed and needs to get out, so kindly move.'

The fat guy turned back to look at her. He quickly moved out of the way when he saw the state she was in.

Once she got to the stairs, things got moving again. Adrenalin coursed through her body, giving her a hit of energy. She wriggled free of the man's grip and pushed her way through the crowd up towards the bridge over the tracks. On the bridge she broke stride momentarily to look behind her to see how close *he* was, but she couldn't see him, he was nowhere in sight. She figured he was probably still stuck on the platform or at the bottom of the stairwell.

She let out a long, shaky breath and leant against the wall. What was going on? Had she really just seen him push her under the train? It couldn't be real. It suddenly occurred to her that no one had jumped up after him – was she the only one who'd seen? Impossible – someone must have seen what he did. Her head hurt; she didn't want to think any more. All she knew was that she needed to get out of the tube station as quickly as possible. She wanted to be home.

She pushed her way up the second, short set of steps towards the concourse, ready to go through the gates. She could see the exit to the street just beyond them.

But there *he* was, waiting for her.

She hadn't noticed him running up the parallel staircase; she'd been too busy searching for him on the platform below. She yelped, then turned to run back across the bridge away from him, but it was rammed full of people. She tried to push her way back, but the crowd was unforgiving in their panic to get out. She was jostled and prodded with outstretched hands and elbows until she had no option but to face front again. The crowd moved slowly forward, presenting her up to him like a sacrifice. There was nothing she could do, nowhere she could go – only straight towards him.

He stood smirking at her. She didn't have to move her feet to get off; the press of panicking people delivered her straight into his arms. He grabbed her wrists and yanked her away from the crowd pooling at the exit gates. She fought back, pulling away from him, but he had her so tightly that every time she moved the skin on her wrists would twist and burn.

The chaos from the platform was now filling up the foyer of the tube station. People were clambering on top of one another to get out of the station.

'Help,' Polly shouted. 'Someone help me.'

But no one listened. Her voice was drowned out by all the other cries for help as everyone tried to get away from the suspected bomb blast.

He started to move forward, dragging her behind him. Suddenly, she felt a hand on her shoulder, pulling her back. They both turned to see the older man from the platform.

'Are you all right,' he asked.

Her guardian angel.

'No,' she replied, pulling away from *him* and moving closer to the old man. 'Please help me: he pushed—'

'Come on, now, Polly, I know you've had a nasty shock,' *he* said.

Polly turned to look at him, dumbstruck. How did he know her name? He hadn't let her tell him her name.

He tried to grab her back, latching on to the top of her arm. 'She'll be OK,' he said to the man. 'I just need to get her home.'

'Well, if you're all right,' the man said to Polly, turning to leave.

'No, I'm not all right,' Polly said, grabbing on to his shirtsleeve, not letting him go. 'I don't know him. Please help me.'

The old guy looked from Polly to *him* and then back to Polly.

'Honestly,' *he* said. 'I can take care of her. She just saw that girl jump under the train. I think she's in shock.'

The old man was eyeing him with suspicion now. 'What exactly are you to this young lady?' he asked.

'I'm her boyfriend,' he replied without breaking eye contact.

'No, he's not,' Polly protested. 'I don't know him.'

Polly felt the older man's hand return to her shoulder.

'I think it might be best if I escort this young lady out of the station,' he said. 'She's clearly distressed, probably in shock, as you said. If you don't mind,' he continued, moving his head to the side to indicate the vice-like grip *he* had around the top of her arm.

He thought for a moment then relented with a forced smile and a nod. 'You're right,' he said, then turned to Polly. 'I'll catch up with you later, Polly,' enunciating the syllables of her name. He curtly turned and started making his way to the nearest exit.

The older man wanted to take her all the way home, but she insisted he only take her as far as the bus stop. She was numb. He asked her several questions, but she barely heard him. Even if she had, she wouldn't have been able to string a sentence together to answer him. Once at the bus stop they waited in silence until the next bus came. She didn't care where it went – as soon as the doors opened, she got on and tentatively set herself down on a seat near the back. She didn't thank her guardian angel or wave him goodbye as he stood and watched until she was safely on her way.

The bus went north. It wasn't until it terminated at Hackney that she realised she was miles away from home. She'd spent most of the journey staring out the window, wide-eyed and mouth agape. The image of *him* letting go of the girl and watching her slowly fall into the train's path played over and over in her mind. It was like a bad dream. She kept shaking her head to try and wake herself up.

She didn't notice the bus enter the depot or the other passengers getting off. The driver sat in his cab, watching her in the rear-view mirror.

'Hey, lady,' he shouted. 'You gotta get off.'

She didn't hear him.

He heaved his rotund body out of his seat and trundled down to where she was sitting at the back.

'Lady, time to get off.'

Still no response. He tapped her roughly on the shoulder.

Polly turned to look at him. 'Where am I?' she said, her eyes filling with tears.

'Oh, shit,' said the bus driver, rolling his eyes. His shift might have ended, but he wasn't going anywhere right now.

She was still crying when she got back to the flat. The bus driver had bundled her on to a bus heading back to central London and swiftly left her to it. She had wept the whole way. It felt as though every conceivable emotion was flooding out of her. She felt stupid and betrayed and scared, but mostly she felt totally bewildered.

Oliver was sitting on the sofa watching TV when she finally got home. She dropped her bags and launched herself at him, head-butting him in the stomach as she fell. He responded immediately, wrapping his arms around her and cradling her like a baby.

It took a full fifteen minutes for her to get herself under control long enough to get a sentence out.

'I...I...saw...' hiccup '...her...' she swallowed loudly '...her...' She looked up at him. 'She was killed.' She was overcome by tears again and dropped her head down into his lap.

'You what?' Oliver asked, pulling her up so they were facing one another, panic etched all over his face.

Polly's breathing was stop-start as she choked through her tears. She was finding it hard to breathe at all – her throat was coated with gloopy saliva and her nose was completely blocked.

'What did you see, Polly?' he asked, cupping her face firmly between his palms. He was looking at her intently, waiting for an answer.

She suddenly felt the most crushing guilt. What had she got herself involved in? How could she have done this to him? The way he looked at her made her heart break.

He could see she was really struggling, so he went to the kitchen to get her a glass of water and some tissues.

Once she'd taken a sip and blown her nose, he continued. 'What happened?'

Polly was sat upright now. He took hold of her soggy hand.

'I was on the tube and...' She stopped. What should she say? She could hardly tell him the truth – that she saw the man she was infatuated with on a train with another woman and decided to follow them, only to see him murder her.

She pulled her hand away and looked up at him. 'I'm so sorry, Oliver,' she said.

He straightened a little and pulled back slightly.

'Why?'

'Because you're so good to me and I've been such a bitch to you.'

'All that doesn't matter now,' he said shaking the notion off. 'Tell me what happened. You were on the tube, and...?'

'No, no... I was waiting for a tube and... the girl was...' She trailed off.

'Was what?'

'Pushed.'

'Pushed? What do you mean, pushed?'

Her mind was racing, was now the right time for honesty? Would there ever be a right time to tell him? It didn't take her long to make her decision.

'No, no, not pushed. I mean, she jumped,' she looked up at him nervously. 'She jumped in front of the train.'

'God,' he said.

'I was practically next to her. If I'd moved quicker or made a grab for her, I could have...' She broke off as tears choked her up again.

'Hey, hey,' said Oliver, pulling her close. 'This isn't your fault. You couldn't have done anything to stop her.'

This made her cry even harder. She had seen what was happening – why hadn't she tried to grab her? Stop him? The words she'd muttered on the train made her shudder: 'Die, bitch, *die*'.

Oliver held her while she squeezed her eyes shut, and fat, heavy tears burst from the corners. He patted her back and said soothing words: 'everything will be OK', 'it's not your fault', 'you're safe now'. At first she resisted, but then she let go and absorbed his words. She knew his meaning was different from hers, but she took them at face value and fitted them to her purpose.

That night they had sex for the first time in months. It was awkward and over quickly, but she just needed to connect with him, to be close to somebody. She lay awake all night, wrapped in Oliver's arms. She allowed herself to be completely smothered in his warmth. She didn't let guilt or shame or any other feelings hold her back. She felt calm, as though a tornado had just passed – it had been terrifying and dangerous, but she'd survived, and she was safe now.

Twenty-six

Polly thought long and hard about what to do next. The right thing to do was to go straight to the police – that much was obvious. But, if she did, she'd have to explain how she knew *him*. She couldn't bear the thought of telling people what she'd been up to. What if Oliver found out? She couldn't understand what she'd been thinking or how she'd even managed to get herself involved in the tubing scene in the first place. All she wanted now was to put it behind her and feel safe again.

During the daytime this was easy. She was able to forget what she'd seen by busying herself with menial tasks. At work, she focused on the easy things that didn't require too much effort, like filing and shredding. There was an enormous shredding machine in the photocopying room. She sat in the corner of the room, mesmerised as she fed the large mechanical beast sheet after sheet. It held her attention just enough so that no other thoughts could penetrate. At home, she went on a cleaning spree. She took out every plate, cup, pot, pan, knife, fork and spoon in the kitchen and fastidiously washed, dried and put them away again. She scrubbed every inch of the bathroom, including the plugholes and shower screen. She even ironed all of Oliver's shirts, much to his amusement.

But the nights were torture. In the dark there was nowhere to hide from her thoughts. She'd lie in bed reliving every second. Sometimes her subconscious would add extra excruciating scenes to the memory, like Polly reaching forward and grabbing the girl then being dragged down on to the tracks with her, or *him* grabbing her at the top of the escalator, marching her down to the platform and pushing her under the next train. She always woke up just as the train was about to hit. She was up several times a night, stripping off her sweat-drenched pyjamas. In the end she started sleeping with just a towel wrapped around her.

She knew she couldn't go on like this forever, but she clung to the hope that in time the memory would lessen and start to fade. That was, until she came face to face with the dead girl again.

She was on a bus on her way to work. The tube was a 'no go' area – for the rest of her life, she hoped. She'd woken early. He'd been chasing her up a down escalator that she couldn't conquer no matter how hard she climbed. She woke with a start, the towel stuck to her saturated body. It was 5.30 a.m. She knew there was no way she'd be able to get back to sleep, so she got up and made a start on her list of tedious tasks.

By 7.45 a.m. she was leaving the flat with an armful of clothes that didn't really need to go to the dry cleaner's. Once she'd dropped them off, she stopped in a coffee shop and picked up an extra-hot soya latte. She kept herself occupied by closely scrutinising the barista to make sure her order was made exactly as she'd requested.

The bus was packed. There were no seats available so she made do with a spot in the aisle near the back. The bus might be slow and jerky but she felt safe on it. There was no chance of anything dodgy going on. There were too many windows and too much daylight.

She'd forgotten to pick up a paper on her way to the bus stop so she made do with reading that of the guy next to her. He carefully folded each page, which let her read the back section while he read the front. He seemed to be taking forever, scrutinising every page from cover to cover. Polly preferred to flick through newspapers, rarely stopping to read anything in detail. He seemed to have become stuck on page ten. Polly was beginning to get annoyed and was tapping her foot impatiently. If he didn't turn the page soon, her mind would start wandering again, and she knew there was only one place it would go. But when he finally turned the paper round to move on to the next page, she wished he hadn't.

The page was split into two. The bottom part was taken up with an ad for a sofa company that had just cut its sale prices even further (but only until Sunday). The top half contained just one story. It had three columns of text and two photographs. The first was a picture of a pretty blonde in a graduation hat and gown, smiling straight at the camera. The second was a picture of an older woman holding the same photo, standing outside a court building. The headline read: *Mother disputes transport police suicide verdict*. The photo was of the girl – the one Polly had seen pushed in front of the train.

Without thinking, Polly snatched the paper from the man.

'Hey!' he said. 'I was reading that.'

Polly ignored him and started reading.

'Give me my paper back,' the man said, making a grab for it.

Polly pulled it back and looked at him, her face screwed up, an ugly combination of shock and horror. It was enough to scare him off. He grumbled something about having finished reading it anyway and sloped off towards the front of the bus.

The article gave details of the girl falling in front of the train, but said she'd jumped rather than been pushed. The police were treating her death as a suicide and claimed they had no reason to think otherwise. But the girl's mother didn't agree. Her daughter had moved to London six months ago after landing a graduate job with a corporate bank. She had been living with a couple of girlfriends in a nice part of London and meeting lots of new people. According to everyone who knew her, she had been a happy, intelligent girl who'd had everything to live for. She'd even started seeing some guy.

Her mother had presented all these facts to the police, but they hadn't listened. The case was closed, her death declared a suicide. The girl's mother was demanding an inquest.

Polly read and re-read the story until she got to Holborn. She walked to work in a daze, unable to tear herself away from the girl's picture.

Her name was Sarah. She didn't appear to be the bitch Polly thought she was. Polly had never for one second entertained the idea that she deserved to be pushed under the train, but her defence mechanism had kicked in and her thinking had been along the lines of, if you played with fire, you sometimes got burned. Seeing her graduation photo and reading her mum's story, she realised she wasn't some coke-snorting party girl who probably would have ended up overdosing in a crack den. She was normal, went to work every day, had a boyfriend, hung out with friends. Polly felt ashamed for calling her a bitch, for wishing her dead, for thinking so little of her for tubing and for being with *him*. But mostly she was sickened that she hadn't told anyone about what she saw.

She made the mistake of googling her later that morning at work. The first couple of links took her to news sites covering the story she'd read in the paper. She winced as she flicked through more pictures of Sarah. One of the sites had a link to a Facebook page set up in her memory. She clicked on the link to have a look and instantly regretted it. It was full of messages from her family and friends all with the same sentiment; shock, disbelief, incomprehension. One friend had written, 'My world is a lonely place without you. I miss you, Saucy. I love you.'

Polly suddenly started shaking uncontrollably and had to stop for a minute. All the thoughts she'd been avoiding over the last week were suddenly trampling all over her. She reached for the upturned drawing pin on her desk and pressed her finger into it. She pulled away as soon as she felt it puncture the skin. A red blob quickly formed on the tip of her finger. She put it in her mouth and sucked it. She looked again at the picture of Sarah staring back at her from the crumpled newspaper on her desk. It was as if she had found her now, and wasn't going to let her go until she did something about it.

'Hey, hon.'

Polly looked up. Alicia was standing in front of her desk.

Polly quickly flicked back to her desktop as Alicia leant over to see what she was looking at on her screen. 'What you so engrossed in?'

'Nothing,' she bumbled.

'Fancy gettin' some lunch?'

Polly couldn't remember the last time she'd eaten anything proper. She'd drunk a lot of tea, but had little in the way of food. Her stomach was constantly churning.

'No, I've got stuff to finish off here,' she replied.

'You sure? If you don't mind me saying, you look like you could do with some feedin'.' Alicia smiled at her with so much warmth, it felt as if she'd reached out and stroked Polly's hair.

'I can't.' And she meant it: she didn't think she'd ever feel like eating again.

'Suit yourself.'

She watched Alicia sashay her way out the door.

Polly went back to Google. In the news section she noticed a story had come up as a related link. She clicked to open it. It was a different news story about a young woman who'd committed suicide by throwing herself under a tube train. She'd done it in rush hour on her way home from work. Her friends and family were distraught; none of them could understand why or how it had happened. She was twenty-six and had worked for an ad agency in the City. Polly scrolled down the page until she found a picture. Her hands went up to cover her mouth in horror. It was a picture of Mousey.

Twenty-seven

When she got home that night, Oliver had ordered in Chinese takeaway. He got her favourite – pork with honey and egg-fried rice. She couldn't eat a mouthful, not even to please him. She was sick with nerves about what she had to do in the morning. She had no choice but to tell the police. Even if Oliver did find out, it was a risk she'd just have to take.

Oliver wolfed his food down, using his chopsticks as a shovel rather than as the delicate pincers intended. Polly pushed the food around her plate. She tried to hide what she hadn't eaten by burying the pork under the rice. But Oliver was watching closely. He gave her plate a disapproving look as he cleared it away. When she went into the kitchen after him, she found him filling up a Tupperware box with her leftovers. He put it in the fridge so she could take it to work for lunch tomorrow.

When the alarm went off the next morning she felt lost in her own personal purgatory. She was relieved that the night was finally over and she no longer had to lie in the dark with just her thoughts, but the day had arrived. Her stomach cramped and grumbled continuously.

Her plan was to get to work early and make the call first thing. As soon as she got in, she dumped her bags on her desk and went straight to the kitchen to make herself a cup of camomile tea. When she got back, Lionel was there waiting for her.

'Prayers, Polly,' he barked, then turned on his heels and went back into his office.

Polly had managed to avoid the weekly 'prayers' meeting for the last couple of months. On the mornings she remembered there was a meeting she'd call in sick; otherwise she'd make up important appointments she had to attend, or just not bother turning up at all. She'd completely forgotten about the early morning meeting he'd arranged. Of all the fucking days to come in early, she berated herself.

Lionel's tiny office was already rammed. The only free seat was right at the front, practically nose to nose with him. She reluctantly sat down. She'd brought a notebook and pen so busied herself, pretending to take notes as soon as the meeting got under way, but it didn't take long for her to drift off.

She stared at the phone on Lionel's desk while unconsciously doodling on the page, a series of interlocking stars and triangles. She needed to make the call to the police, get it over and done with. Maybe she would make the call from Lionel's office when he popped out for lunch – that way she could have a bit of privacy. She had no intention of giving her name, so using her mobile was out. But then it occurred to her that it wouldn't take a genius to work out who made the call from the office: she and Alicia were the only women in today. Suddenly calling from work seemed like a stupid idea. If she made the call from a phone box she could remain anonymous. She couldn't believe she hadn't thought of it before. The more she thought, the harder she pressed, until she ripped through the sheet of paper to the page below. She was so consumed, she didn't notice the office had gone quiet and all eyes were on her.

'Polly!' Lionel shouted.

Her head snapped up.

'If you're quite finished,' he said, tipping his head towards her scribblings.

She quickly placed the notebook face down on her lap.

'Your update, please. What's going on with legal?' he said, picking up his fountain pen and taking out a clean sheet of paper ready to make notes. He had a large black stain on the inside of his right index finger from the leaky pen.

Polly had nothing to offer. There was a pile of unopened letters and bits of paper on her desk that she hadn't touched for months, not to mention her bulging email inbox.

'I'm sorry, Lionel, I didn't have time to prepare for this morning's meeting so I don't have an update for you.' She tried to sound firm and in control. Her fingers were crossed under her notepad.

'Well, just give us a brief run-down, off the top of your head if you like. We don't need anything in detail right now.'

She couldn't even do that.

Lionel looked up from his empty page. 'Can you give us *anything*, Polly?' he sighed. He looked at her as if he'd resigned himself to the fact that she'd fall short even before she opened her mouth.

She didn't answer.

'Right, well, let's not waste any more time.'

He moved straight on to Ron – the only staff journalist. Lionel was suddenly back to his jovial self, cracking jokes with Ron and having a laugh with everyone in the room – everyone except Polly; his gaze kept flicking over her as if she were invisible.

When the meeting was over, Polly was first up. She was almost out the door when Lionel said, 'Polly, a word please.'

She stopped and let the others out from behind her.

'Shut the door,' he said when everyone had gone.

She did as she was told.

'Sit down.'

She sat down.

'We need to talk about what you've been up to over the last couple of months.' He clasped his hands together on the desk and looked at her solemnly.

Polly was perched on the edge of her seat legs crossed, nervously picking at her lip.

'I know things have been tough for you recently, with your dad passing, but that really can't excuse the work you've let drop. James and I have had several chats about it and things simply can't carry on this way.'

She was surprised. She thought she'd done a pretty good job of hiding her lack of work. The fact that they'd been having little chats about her behind her back made her feel defensive.

'How can James possibly know what's going on? He's never around,' she said, a little too aggressively.

'Well, this is the thing, Polly: recently he's been in and out of the office several times a week, and you're the one who's never here.' He was shaking his head at her with his lips pursed.

She really had no argument. She could feel her face starting to crumple, ready for tears to come.

Lionel suddenly softened and reached his hand across the desk.

'If you're struggling with things, you need to let me or James know.'

She couldn't answer. She desperately didn't want to cry in front of him. She was scared that if she started she might never stop. They sat in silence, Lionel like a therapist waiting for his patient to open up. She didn't; she couldn't.

Eventually he spoke.

'Why don't you take some time off? Get that surgeon of yours to take you somewhere nice for a few days. How is Oliver?'

Oliver's parents were good friends with Lionel; they were the reason she'd got the job in the first place.

'Fine,' she murmured.

'I hear he's thinking about moving into paediatrics.'

It was news to Polly. She nodded non-committally.

That was the extent of his small talk. When it became clear things weren't going to progress any further, Lionel let her go. She said she'd think about taking some time off and let him know.

By lunchtime she'd plucked up enough courage to leave work and make the call. She was jittery with nerves as she walked over the road to the phone box across from her building. She hoped she'd faint or collapse on the pavement before she got there so she wouldn't have to go through with it – but no such luck.

The phone box was a modern affair, not an old-style red box. It was made almost entirely of glass except for the black metal frame that ran around the edges. Inside, several cards had been stuck on the back board where the phone was attached: women in various states of indecency were 'waiting for your call'. It felt as if she'd just opened an oven when she yanked open the door. It was a sunny day, about twenty-five degrees Celsius, but it must have been about forty degrees inside the box. She held the door open for a few moments to let the hot air escape. She was tempted to linger longer, but stopped herself. The sooner she got on with it, the sooner it would be over.

She put her hand on the receiver and took several deep breaths before finally lifting it up. Her last hope was that it wasn't working, but when she put it to her ear she heard a healthy dial tone. She dialled the first 9, then the second. She was just about to press it for a third time when something caught her eye. Someone was waving at her from across the street outside her office block. She couldn't make out who it was at first. She moved her head forward, accidentally banging into the glass. She moved back a little and focused her eyes.

It was *him*.

She immediately slammed down the phone and ducked down to hide. She kept still, holding her breath for several seconds. What the hell was he doing there? Had he followed her?

Suddenly there was a rap at the door. She turned to see a young Indian man shaking a dead mobile phone at her through the glass. Polly stared back, unable to move a muscle. Eventually he opened the door.

'You finished?' he asked.

Her eyes remained wide and blank.

'Hello,' he said, waving his hand in front of her face as if she was blind.

'Is there a man standing across the road?' she whispered.

'What?' the man asked. Her voice was so thin it was barely audible.

'You see the white building across the road,' she said a little louder.

He craned his neck round the phone box door to look across the road. 'Yep, I see it.'

'Is there a man standing outside it?'

He narrowed his eyes and jerked his head forward to look.

'No, there is no one there.' He turned back to her. 'Now, if you please,' he said, pointing to the phone.

Polly very carefully inched her way out of the phone box, her head peeping round the door then darting back to safety again. The man watched her, eyes narrowed, as though she was insane. When her foot finally crossed the threshold, he impatiently pushed his way past and pulled the phone box door shut behind him. She looked across the road to where *he'd* been standing – there was no one there. Despite the heat, she hugged her arms around herself and shivered.

When she got back to the office she was in tears. What the hell was going on? He couldn't possibly know where she worked – she'd not told him a single thing about herself. He'd insisted, no personal details. Maybe she'd just imagined him standing there. No, he had definitely been there. He already knew her name, where she worked – what else did he know?

She could feel everyone in the office watching her as she tried to subtly mop up her tears. It didn't take long for word to reach Alicia. She came rushing over, arms outstretched. 'Hon, what's the matter?'

Polly couldn't speak.

'Come on,' she said, taking her hand and guiding her to the toilets. A hush rippled round as they made their way through.

Once inside, Alicia locked the toilet door.

'It's so tough when you lose someone close to you,' she said, walking over to the toilet and putting the seat down so Polly could sit on it. 'When I lost my mum I was a total wreck. I couldn't do nothin', I was crying all the time.'

It took Polly a second to catch on. 'Oh, yeah,' she said, sitting down.

'It gets easier.' Alicia reached out and rubbed the top of Polly's arm. 'But, to be honest, you ain't really got no option but to wait it out. Grief's like that: you can't do nothin' about it.'

Polly sighed.

'You wanna talk about it?' Alicia asked.

'It's not just Dad – there's loads of stuff going on at the moment.'

'Tell me.'

Polly considered for a moment. She was sorely tempted – she certainly couldn't carry on the way she was. She needed help from someone.

Suddenly her mobile vibrated against her hip. She reached into her pocket for it without thinking.

we need to talk. tonight 7.35 kings cross st pancras metropolitan line westbound, first carriage

The phone shook so violently in her hand that she almost dropped it.

'You OK?' asked Alicia, leaning forward to try and get a look at the message Polly had just read.

'It's nothing,' Polly said, stuffing the phone back in her pocket. 'I'd better get back to my desk,' she said, getting to her feet.

'It's all right, everyone knows what you've been through – they'll understand if you need some time out.'

But Polly was already up and unlocking the bathroom door. She let the door slam shut behind her without another word.

Twenty-eight

The message remained on the screen of Polly's phone for the rest of the afternoon. Every time it started to dim ready to turn itself off, she'd brush her thumb over the top to keep it there. She felt as if she was having an out-of-body experience. Her out-of-body self looked down on her from the ceiling, screaming at her to delete the message. How could she even contemplate meeting him after what she'd seen him do? But she didn't. She just sat there staring at the message.

At seven-thirty she found herself walking down the steps of King's Cross St Pancras tube station. A train arrived at exactly 7.35 p.m. She got on. The first carriage was busy, much to her relief. At least if he tried anything, there were plenty of people around.

He was already on the train. As soon as she saw him, Polly was immediately on her guard. She stayed right in the middle of the carriage, close to the double doors. She noticed a red panic lever above her head to the right of the handrail. She moved closer to it. He saw.

'Polly, it's OK,' he said as he moved towards her. 'I'm not going to hurt you. I just want to talk.'

His hands were palm up in front of his chest as if to surrender. He was still as beautiful as ever.

In spite of everything that had happened, her heart skipped a beat.

'I know how bad it must have looked the other day, but I can explain. Will you let me explain?'

She glanced behind him. A burly man with a baseball cap perched on his head was sat on the bay of seats. Close enough. She gave one quick nod of her head.

He took a few too many steps towards her. She flinched, so he stopped immediately.

'The girl you saw me with…'

'Sarah,' said Polly.

'Sarah, was that her name?'

Polly looked at him, dismayed.

'I'm sorry, I didn't know her name,' he said, his head bowed. He exhaled loudly before looking back up to continue. 'She was threatening to expose everything.'

'What?' said Polly.

'Tubing. She said she was going to the police, the press, whoever would listen.' He lifted his hand up to the bridge of his nose and pinched it between his thumb and forefinger. 'She got hold of my phone. She had a list of the phone numbers of everyone involved.'

'What?' said Polly, the pitch of her voice rising.

'I know, I know,' he said. 'It was my fault. I was a total idiot. I had a bad feeling about her from the first moment I met her, but the guy who introduced us said she was cool.' He took his hand away from his face and looked up at Polly. 'She was a journalist, working undercover.'

Polly was taken aback. It took a couple of seconds to collect her thoughts and get back on track. 'But in the paper it said she was an investment banker.'

'I guess they're trying to cover it up.'

'But they interviewed her mum in the paper…'

'I'm sure they did.'

She stared at him, waiting for further explanation. He stared back. After a couple of seconds he shrugged his shoulders, unable to offer anything more.

'Why would they do that? Go to all the trouble of covering it up and putting in a fake interview with her mum?'

'I really don't know, Polly.'

Her name – it jarred. How did he know her name?

'None of this makes sense,' she said, shaking her head. 'How do you know my—' she started.

Suddenly he lost patience. He slammed his fist against the metal frame next to her, making her jump. His cool demeanour was replaced by a flushed, pinched, mean-looking face. 'What do you want me to say? I did what I had to. I didn't mean to kill her; she struggled and it just sort of happened,' he said, lowering his voice and moving in closer, as if suddenly remembering where he was.

Struggle? There was no struggle, Polly thought. She opened her mouth to say so, but he cut her off.

'Can you imagine what would have happened? You have no idea how many people are involved in this – some of them in government, in the media … you … me.' He ran his fingers through his hair to smooth it down. 'I had to stop her. I did it to protect everyone involved.' He reached out and touched her face. 'To protect you.'

'But you killed her,' Polly said matter-of-factly.

'I know, and I have to live with it for the rest of my life.' He dropped his hand away.

Polly thought she could see tears welling up in his eyes. She felt the urge to console him, but she didn't; his story wasn't right.

'What about Mousey?'

'Who?'

'The girl I saw you tubing with just after we met.'

'What about her?'

'She's dead too.'

'What?' He sounded genuinely shocked.

'The papers say she committed suicide a couple of weeks ago, under a train, just like Sarah.'

'I had no idea.'

They eyed one another suspiciously.

He was the first to speak. 'You don't think I had anything to do with that, do you, Polly?'

There it was again, her name. Every time he said it, it threw her off course.

'Well…' She paused, suddenly unsure of herself. 'It's a bit of a coincidence.'

'Whoa, whoa.' He was on the defensive, his hands up in front of his chest. 'I had nothing to do with that. I didn't even know about it until you just mentioned it.'

Polly didn't know what to say. Had she got it all wrong? She'd been so sure, but now…

'I hooked up with her a few times,' he continued. 'She wasn't well – depressed, I think. She seemed really destructive, and not just to herself. I stopped seeing her in the end.'

She remembered the way Mousey had pushed him when she'd seen them on the train together. She had seemed really mad. Polly thought it was because he hadn't warned her before ejaculating in her mouth, but maybe it wasn't that – maybe she *had* been unstable.

'Polly.'

There it was again. She looked up, dazed. He smiled his perfect smile.

'The reason I wanted to meet with you was to tell you something.'

'Tell me what?'

'This whole thing has been a total nightmare. I can't believe what's happened. Every time I think about Sarah...' His voice caught in the back of his throat, stopping him from talking.

Polly instinctively reached out for him. She couldn't hold herself back any longer. She put her hand on the back of his neck. He leant forward until their foreheads were touching. His skin felt soft and warm. Her entire body melted into his touch.

'I've had enough of all this. I'm done with tubing and this place. I'm leaving London.' He pulled back to look at her. 'Will you come with me?'

She looked at him, aghast. Was he for real?

The train's tannoy suddenly sprang into life, announcing that they were approaching Baker Street. Their eyes were still locked. He leant forward to kiss her. Polly started to move forward but then stopped – her name – *how did he know her name*?

'How do you know my name?'

He stopped dead.

'And where I work, how do you know where I work?' she continued.

He sucked in his cheek until it left a hollow in the side of his face. Her words hung in the air between them. He quickly turned to check behind him before his hand darted out, grabbing her round the throat.

It happened so fast, she didn't have time to react. The span of his hand almost encircled her entire neck, his fingertips pressing deep into the hollows either side of her spine while the base of his thumb pushed down hard over her voice box. He bore down on her, concentrating every ounce of strength he had.

Within seconds her lungs were scrambling for air, her diaphragm opening and contracting in a desperate bid for breath. She tried to scream, but all that came out was a heavy, rasping sound.

She looked over at the guy still sitting in the bank of seats behind them. His eyes were firmly shut, with the peak of his cap pulled down low.

Polly could feel herself going. Her eyes were filled with black and white blocks. Weakness engulfed her. She didn't have long; she had to do something.

She used every ounce of strength she had to buck her body forward. By sheer fluke her knee caught him square in the groin. His grip loosened as he instinctively bent forward. She let herself drop straight down, kicking her legs out from beneath her and sliding across the floor towards the seats behind. He moved to follow, but stopped when he noticed the man. He was looking over, bleary-eyed, to see what all the commotion was about.

'You stupid cunt, you'll ruin everything,' *he* said through gritted teeth, his face scrunched in pain.

The train doors opened behind him. He took a long, hard look at her and said, 'Life as you know it is over, Polly.'

Then he turned and was gone.

Twenty-nine

The man looked over at Polly for a while debating whether or not to help her up. After a couple of seconds he closed his eyes again and pretended to be asleep. Polly stayed on the floor, breathless, for a few moments before reaching up and pulling herself on to the seat behind her. She couldn't believe what had just happened. Her hand went up to her neck. She tried to swallow, and her throat bobbed several times before she finally managed it; it felt as if it had collapsed in on itself.

The train pulled out of the station and entered the tunnel. She looked across at her reflection in the darkened window. She could see red marks around the side of her throat where his finger had been, and a larger red area at the front. She prayed bruises wouldn't develop.

She sat in the same seat until the train reached the end of the line. She couldn't believe she'd fallen for it. He'd convinced her that she'd got it all wrong; she'd even believed for a moment that he wanted them to leave London together. Stupid, stupid, stupid. She'd stood there listening to his lies while he got ready to pounce – it almost defied belief. She was in no doubt about what he would have done with her. She could almost see the headline: *Woman grieving loss of father throws herself in front of tube train.* No one would have been any the wiser.

By the time she got home her neck was in agony. She didn't know what to do – whether to go to the hospital to get it checked out or just hope for the best. In the end she decided to keep her fingers crossed. There was no way she could explain what had happened without getting the police involved.

As soon as she was through the front door of the flat she went straight to the wardrobe in the bedroom and dug out a chunky wool roll neck jumper. It was still about twenty degrees outside, and she started sweating the instant she put it on.

Oliver noticed the jumper as soon as she walked into the lounge. 'What are you wearing *that* for? You must be boiling.'

He had all the windows wide open; there wasn't even a hint of a breeze.

'I'm fine,' she replied, trying to ignore the sweat beading down her neck and back.

He made room for her to sit next to him on the sofa. She chose to sit on the chesterfield opposite.

He shrugged, turning his attention back to the documentary he was watching on the TV.

The shock that had afforded her some protection earlier slowly started to disappear and she was gradually exposed to the harsh reality of her situation. *His* words rang in her ears. *Life as you know it is over.* The more she thought about it, the harder it was to breathe. It was as if his hand was back round her throat, crushing her windpipe, each breath getting shallower and shallower until she was only able to take tiny snippets of oxygen into her mouth before they were lost. Her nails dug into the soft leather of the seat she was sitting on. All at once, pins and needles were spreading up her limbs before overwhelming her insides until they were spasming. Everything was spinning, and her head felt so heavy she couldn't keep it up any longer. She crumpled forward, falling to the floor with a thud.

'Oh my God, Polly.' Oliver's voice came from a faraway place, then silence.

She woke up in bed. The room was in darkness except for the soft glow from the bedside lamp. Oliver was sitting beside her, holding her hand. She tried to sit up, but felt too weak to move.

'Hey, you're back with us,' said Oliver. The relief on his face was palpable.

'What happened?'

'You fainted.'

She suddenly realised she didn't have her jumper on any more. Her hand shot up to her neck to cover it.

'Don't move, you need to rest. Would you like some water?' he asked.

She was still barely able to swallow, her throat felt so swollen, 'Yes, please,' she said, her voice croaky.

As soon as he was gone, the darkness in the room loomed around her. She reached up to her neck; it still felt tender but there was no swelling on the outside. She prayed it hadn't bruised – how on earth could she explain to Oliver? She felt scared, more scared than she'd ever been in her life. She burrowed deep under the duvet. By the time Oliver came back into the room, only two little eyes were visible from underneath.

'What are you doing under there?' he said as he rounded the bed and put the glass on the bedside table.

She didn't answer.

'What's going on, Polly?'

'What do you mean?'

'You're not right, are you? Tell me what's going on.'

'I guess I'm just still really missing Dad.' She winced as she said it. She couldn't keep using his death to cover this mess up.

'Are you sure there's nothing else?'

'I...don't...' She trailed off.

'Is it something to do with the girl you saw jump under the train?'

He was spot on, but not in the way he thought. Tears were suddenly stinging her eyes. 'Hug me,' she said.

He looked at her as though he was about to ask another question.

'Just please hug me,' she said before he could get the words out.

He pulled back the duvet and curled his body around hers.

'I love you so much, Oliver.'

She desperately needed him to say the same soothing words back to her.

'I love you too, Polly.'

Thirty

They lay wrapped in each other's arms all night. A couple of times Oliver tried to get up, but Polly wouldn't let him, gripping on to him as tight as she could. He said he needed the loo and wanted to brush his teeth, but she couldn't be alone, not even for the few minutes it would take him to use the bathroom. She stared at the alarm clock on her bedside table until three a.m., and after that she couldn't remember anything.

When she opened her eyes it was daylight. Oliver was gone. She could still feel the impression of his body on hers, but it was cold, as if he'd been gone a while. She panicked and called out to him. What if he'd gone out and left her on her own?

'It's OK,' he said coming back into the room with a steaming mug in his hand. 'I was just making you a cuppa.'

He was dressed in a pair of khaki chinos and a blue cotton shirt.

'Why are you dressed? You're not going out are you?' Polly asked.

'I've got to go to work.'

'It's Saturday.'

'I know. I swapped shifts around, remember? I did tell you.'

216

'You can't,' Polly said, suddenly panicked. She couldn't be on her own, she just couldn't be.

'Come here,' he said sitting down on the bed and putting his arms around her. 'You'll be all right. I'll be back before you know it. Why don't you go for a walk to the Green, stop at that pâtisserie you like for a big slice of cake. It's a lovely day.'

There was no way she could leave the flat. What if *he* was watching her? She was desperate to tell Oliver what was going on: her life was in danger, and she knew Oliver of all people would do whatever he could to protect her. But how could she, after what she'd been up to? Then she'd have no one.

'I'd better get going,' he said, kissing the top of her head and getting up.

She had to use all the strength she possessed to hold herself back, not to jump up and grab him, beg and plead with him to stay with her.

Once Oliver was gone, she burrowed down deep into the duvet. Her senses were on high alert; every sound cut into her, making her nerves sting. Their flat was one of three in a converted town house. Polly had never noticed how much noise came from their neighbours before, but now it was all she could hear: floorboards creaking; a door slamming; the low, bassy drone of voices. Suddenly there were footsteps thundering up the communal staircase that ran alongside their bedroom wall. Had they stopped at their front door, or gone on up to the next set of stairs? She strained to listen. Maybe it wasn't one of the neighbours, maybe it was *him*. He knew her name, where she worked – who was to say he didn't know where she lived too. She pulled the duvet over her head and lay as flat as possible pretending she didn't exist. Soon the air under the duvet became hot and sticky and suffocating. She carefully peeled back the cover, her eyes sweeping every corner of the room. Her bladder was painfully swollen; she'd needed the toilet since before going to bed some twelve hours ago. She had to get up.

She made her way silently to the bedroom door, then very carefully opened it. She held her breath as she poked her head out into the hallway. Once she was sure there was no one there, she dived across and into the bathroom.

After she'd used the toilet, she examined her neck in the bathroom mirror. Much to her relief it hadn't bruised, but it still looked a bit red and was still tender to the touch. She then turned around, put her hand on the door handle and braced herself to leave.

Back in the hallway, she picked up Oliver's golfing umbrella that sat below the coat hooks by the front door. She carefully searched the rest of the flat, the umbrella wielded high ready to attack. When she was satisfied there was no one there, she checked all the windows were locked, closed the blinds and double bolted the front door.

She sat on the sofa in silence for the rest of the day. She didn't want to sit in silence, she wanted noise. She'd take any form of company right now, no matter how artificial. But what if she missed something? What if the TV or radio drowned out the sound of him coming up the stairs or trying to break in through the front door? She couldn't risk it. She positioned herself right in the corner of the sofa so she had a clear view of the lounge doorway through into the kitchen. With every sound her head snapped round to chase it.

Without thinking her fingers went to another mosquito bite on her arm. Her nails scratched around the small scab, looking for an edge to work their way in. It hurt, but the sensation translated into relief rather than pain. It wasn't until her fingers felt sticky that she realised how deep she'd gone. She looked down to see blood pooling from the skin around the scab. Her fingernails had dug down through layer upon layer, unchecked. The once small bite was now a deep gash.

Oliver put his key in the lock at half-past six. He struggled with the door, kicking it twice before knocking hard and calling her name. As soon as she heard his voice she went running to unbolt it. She fell into his arms the second he was through the door.

'Whoa,' he said, trying to put down the bags he was carrying and close the door behind him.

When they went into the lounge Oliver started fussing with the blinds, opening them up. Polly started to protest, but knew it was pointless. Oliver liked the blinds pulled up halfway, with the top slats fully open. He was annoyed that she'd had them closed all day.

'Right,' he said, looking her up and down – she was still in her pyjamas, 'are you in the shower first or am I?'

'What?'

He looked at the time on his watch. 'We've got to be there in an hour, need to start getting ready.'

She looked at him blankly.

'Dinner tonight, remember? It's Crispin's birthday.'

Crispin was Oliver's closest friend. They'd gone to medical school together. A group of them were having dinner tonight to celebrate his birthday.

'I can't go,' said Polly, shaking her head.

'Why not?' said Oliver.

'Well, after last night…'

'You fainted is all, no lasting damage,' he said.

She stayed silent.

He walked to the bathroom and turned on the shower, then went into the bedroom. After a few moments she followed him. He was standing in just his shirt and pants, rifling through the wardrobe for a pair of trousers. His boxers were too tight; the fly gaped open at the front.

'Can you just call him and say we're not coming?' she asked.

'What?' he snapped, annoyed at the suggestion.

'Oliver, I still don't feel well. I think I'm coming down with something.'

'Polly, come here,' he said sternly.

She did as she was told. He put his hand on her forehead.

'You seem fine to me. Come on, go get ready.'

'I can't. Please just call him.'

'What is with you? Why are you always doing this? We've a perfectly nice evening arranged with friends and suddenly you don't want to go,' he said, exasperated.

She started to chew her lip.

'Look, if you're really not feeling well, stay here, but I'm going. There's no way I can cancel on my best mate's birthday. OK?'

Polly looked out of the window. It would be dark soon. Spending the next five or six hours alone in the flat just wasn't an option.

They met in a Mexican restaurant in Notting Hill. Polly persuaded Oliver to get a cab even though they were only two stops away on the tube. Despite being safely inside the taxi, she spent the entire journey on high alert. Oliver kept asking if she was OK. She evaded the question. In the end he left her to it, thinking she was in a mood about something or other.

The restaurant was a small, intimate place set over two floors. The ground floor only had enough space for a couple of tables; the basement housed the main part. Polly could see them all sitting at the back of the restaurant as they made their way down the steep steps and through the windowed door to the basement.

They were greeted with cries of 'Polliver' as soon as they walked in. Oliver's friends often referred to them by one name made up of both their names. Polly hated it. It made her feel like a non-person, nothing more than a part of Oliver.

The decor was Mexican tat: fake cacti, fairy lights, sugar skulls, plastic skeletons, and candles burning in empty tequila bottles on every table. It was owned by the son of a rock star and accordingly become the place to hang out. Oliver hadn't made the booking and was struggling to hide his discomfort. He preferred fine dining that he could clearly see on his plate – not food inspired by South American street vendors served in dusk.

Polly was handed a margarita as soon as she got to the table. She promptly downed it in one.

'Thirsty?' Crispin asked. 'Want another?'

She nodded without hesitation.

There were four couples at the table, five including 'Polliver'. There was Crispin and his wife Sophie who had just had a baby; Alex and Millie; Lucas and his Portuguese girlfriend Elena; and Julian and his pregnant wife Lucy. The food came in dribs and drabs as it was ready, a few starters here and a main course there. They decided not to wait for everyone's food to arrive; instead they just tucked in, sharing one another's plates.

As the evening wore on, Polly began to relax a little. Oliver held her hand under the table, encouraging her to become more involved in the conversation. She didn't; she was just happy to be with him.

Halfway through the meal, when all the mains and two-thirds of the starters had been brought out, Polly got up to use the loo. The restaurant housed a series of low-ceilinged corridors that opened up on to one main dining area. She couldn't figure out which one led to the ladies' so had to ask the waiter where to go. He instructed her to turn right just before the front door and follow the corridor to the end. She felt a little drunk as she went down the darkened passageway and through the toilet door at the end.

As she walked in, she caught a glimpse of someone in the mirror above the basin. It made her jump. When she realised it was her own reflection, she laughed and shook her head, 'Get a grip, Polly,' she said aloud.

She went into the last cubicle on the end of the row. She figured it would be the least used toilet. Or maybe not, maybe everyone thought the same.

Once she'd been, she smoothed her dress down and flushed the toilet. The lock on the door clicked loudly as she drew it back. Again she jumped. She washed her hands at the basin and then splashed cold water on her face.

'You're fine, Polly,' she said to her reflection. 'Nothing's going to happen with Oliver around. You're fine.'

She dried off her face, tousled her hair to give it a bit of body, and left.

She was just making her way back to the table, past the front door, when it suddenly opened, knocking into her. An immaculately groomed blonde with pink glossy lips and a string of pearls round her neck tried to push past her. Polly stopped abruptly.

'Darling, be careful, you nearly knocked the poor girl off her feet.'

She recognised the voice instantly. Her heart froze.

A pair of hands went around the girl's shoulders before *his* face slowly came into view from behind the door.

Polly stared back at him in shock. She didn't know what to do. Her instincts told her to run, get away from him as fast as she could, but to where? She glanced back at the table. Crispin was up on his feet, pulling a silly face, doing an impression of someone. Everyone else was laughing, including Oliver. She turned back to face *him*; his eyes had followed hers and he was now looking over at the table, smiling. Her frozen heart suddenly kicked into life and started beating so fast she thought it might explode. The last thing she wanted to do was go back to the table. What if he followed? She looked over again. Oliver had noticed her; he had a confused look on his face, as though he couldn't understand what she was doing hanging about the front door. He waved at her to come back. She had no choice. She slowly made her way over on jelly legs. She had to restrain herself from running back as fast as she could. Keep cool, she told herself.

She shuffled back in next to Oliver without looking back. It wasn't easy – she was shaking so much, she kept tripping over her feet. She had no idea where *he* was, and she didn't want to know. The only thing she could do right now was pretend he wasn't there, pretend everything was fine. He wouldn't do anything with all these people around her in the middle of a busy restaurant, surely? She grabbed on to Oliver's hand under the table and squeezed it tight. He squeezed back.

The conversation continued around her as if nothing had happened. Polly kept her head down and tried to take even, steady breaths, trying to stay as calm as possible. But she could already feel pins and needles in her fingers and crawling up her legs.

'Are you all right, Polly?' Lucy asked from across the table. 'You look really pale.'

Polly looked up. She opened her mouth to say she was fine, but the word dropped silently when she saw *him* striding towards the table. The blonde walked beside him, his outstretched hand on the back of her neck as if he were steering her.

What was he doing? He was looking directly at Polly, coming straight towards her. She tensed everything, preparing for the worst.

'Oh, my God,' said Oliver. 'Sebastian?'

All the men started getting up from the table.

'Seb, so glad you could make it,' said Crispin.

They were all gravitating round him, shaking hands and slapping backs.

'Mate, how you doing?' said Oliver, giving him a big bear hug.

Polly gripped on to the side of the table, trying to keep it all together while the world swung upside down around her.

Everyone started shuffling round to make room for *him* and the blonde girl.

'We can't stay long, just dropped by for a quick drink,' he said.

He chose to sit directly opposite Polly. She couldn't bring herself to look at him. Crispin went round the table checking that everyone had been introduced to *him*. Sebastian. Polly was forced to look up when he reached her.

'And this is Oliver's girlfriend.'

'Ah, yeah,' he said, 'we've met before, haven't we, Polly?'

Polly couldn't speak. She was so overcome no sound would come out.

Crispin suddenly started coughing, choking on his drink. 'Down the wrong hole,' he said in a raspy voice.

'So what you been up to?' asked Oliver.

'Been busy, dividing my time between here and the States. Emmi doesn't like to be left on her own too long, do you, honey?'

He turned and kissed the blonde. His hand was still cupping the back of her neck. He owned her.

'The wedding's only a couple of months away,' she replied in her slow, deliberate American drawl.

Polly suddenly felt jealous, then instantly disgusted with herself. She needed to get out of here, get some air. She couldn't cope with what was happening. She was just about to make her move and negotiate her way out when a waiter appeared with champagne.

'What's all this?' asked Crispin.

'For your birthday, bud,' replied Sebastian.

Several bottles of Moët were popped and glasses filled.

'A toast,' said Sebastian when everyone had a glass. 'To my very good friends. Never take life too seriously: no one gets out of here alive,' he said, looking directly at Polly and smiling.

Everyone laughed then lifted their glasses and clinked them together. Polly could only lift her glass a fraction off the table. With that one look he'd drained every ounce of strength from her.

'Darling,' Emmi said tugging Sebastian's sleeve. 'We gotta go.'

He removed his hand from her neck and looked at his watch. 'Shit, you're right.'

With that they both got up and said their goodbyes. They'd only been at the table less than ten minutes, but to Polly it felt like a lifetime.

'Wow, who was that guy?' asked Elena once they'd gone. 'He's like a whirling wind.'

'Whirlwind,' said Lucas, correcting her English.

'Yes, a whirling wind,' said Elena in her soft, singsong accent.

Polly reached for her glass. She needed a drink to steady her nerves, but pulled her hand back when she saw how much it was shaking.

'Sebastian,' replied Crispin. 'Yeah, he's a bit full-on.'

All the men at the table agreed.

'You know his dad is one of the richest guys ever,' Oliver said, then paused grasping for an example, 'like Sultan of Brunei rich or Bill Gates rich – he's a billionaire.'

'*You* should know,' said Crispin swilling the champagne in his glass. 'You were almost family.'

'Hey, hey, stop. I don't even want to think about that.'

Polly's head started throbbing and her ears buzzed – what the hell was Crispin talking about?

'What do you mean?' asked Elena.

'Oliver's sister, Charlotte, and Sebastian's brother, Ed, were once engaged,' said Crispin.

'Really?' said Elena.

'Long, horrible story,' replied Oliver. 'Not much fun to talk about,' he finished, making it clear that was all he was going to say on the subject.

'Good idea, let's move on, don't want to waste another breath on that fuck-up,' said Lucas, lifting his glass to his mouth.

'You *do* know he bought that champagne you're quaffing,' Crispin retorted.

'What do you mean?' asked Elena interested.

'Sebastian's just a bit of a dick. Thinks he's a really big deal, acting like he's being really fucking funny when actually he's being a total bastard. Doesn't give a shit about anyone,' answered Lucas, ignoring Crispin's comment.

'I've got a theory about Sebastian,' chipped in Alex from the other side of the table.

'Yes?' said Elena encouragingly.

'Think about it: if you've got that much money, why *would* you give a shit about anything or anyone? Remember when we were in the first year, I think it was right at the start of medical school, in the first term, and Sebastian's body disappeared...'

'I am sorry,' said Elena. 'His *what* disappeared?'

Lucas explained. 'In medical school everyone gets assigned a body to practise on and...'

'Practise on?' interrupted Lucy.

'You know – we get to cut up the people who donate their bodies to medical science.'

Lucy shook her head bemused.

'So what happened to Sebastian's body?' asked Elena, trying to get back to the story.

'We turned up to anatomy class one day and it was gone,' continued Alex. 'Dr Crawley and the lab tech guy were flapping about all over the place looking for it. No one knew what to do. It's not every day that a dead body goes walkabout. Anyway, later that day there's all this kerfuffle going on in the halls on campus. Some girl comes screaming out of her room half-naked and runs outside into the middle of the road…'

'Nothing unusual about that,' joked Oliver.

Everyone laughed.

'Quite,' said Alex. 'Anyway, this poor girl had just got back from the showers and sat on her bed to dry her hair. The bed felt kind of lumpy, so she pulled back the sheets to see what was there. Anyone want to take a guess what she found?'

'Sebastian's body?' asked Elena.

'You got it.'

'That's gross,' said Lucy. 'Who would do a thing like that?'

'Sebastian. He'd been trying to get with this girl for weeks. She wasn't having any of it; she had a boyfriend back home. I guess he felt he had to teach her a lesson or something.'

'That's horrible.'

'The thing is, everyone knew it was Sebastian who did it, it was bloody obvious, but nothing happened to him. If you or I did something like that, we'd be kicked out and banned from every medical institution in the country, but not Sebastian. He went home for a week then came back as if nothing had happened. About a month later, the Dean announced that Black Inc., his dad's company, had donated over a million pounds to help fund a new research centre at the university.'

'Oh, my God, that's awful,' said Elena.

'Yeah,' said Lucas. 'Nothing makes people forget faster than a big fat cheque. All a total waste of money, of course: he never did graduate. Daddy's grooming him to take over his media empire. It was a technical exercise, nothing more.'

'Exactly my point,' said Alex. 'If you've spent your whole life doing whatever the fuck you want and getting away with it, where's the incentive to play by the rules? There are no consequences, therefore the normal rules and laws that you and I live by don't apply.'

The conversation danced around Sebastian for a minute or so longer before moving on.

Polly sat in shock. She didn't know what scared her more – the fact that she was being stalked by a psychopath, or the fact that Oliver knew him.

Thirty-one

They left shortly after coffee. Polly was desperate to get out of there and tried to hurry Oliver along, but he was having none of it. He ordered a pudding, then a liqueur, and finally coffee.

They got a black cab back to Shepherd's Bush. Polly sat in the corner, motionless, with her hands scrunched in her lap. She stared out of the window, watching the lights of London whizz by, her mind buzzing with a million questions. She was struggling to comprehend everything that had just happened. Charlotte had been engaged to *his* brother – how was it possible?

Her eyes suddenly started stinging and she realised she hadn't blinked for the last couple of minutes.

After opening and closing her mouth several times, she finally managed to get a word out. 'Oliver,' she said slowly, dragging out his name.

'Yes,' he said absently, lost in his own thoughts.

'What happened between Charlotte and that guy's brother?'

He turned and looked at her. 'Huh?' he replied.

'Sebastian. Sebastian's brother.' Saying his name aloud to Oliver felt so unnatural.

'Why do you ask?'

'I didn't know she was engaged.'

'Yeah, a few years ago now.'

'What happened?'

He looked over at her as if weighing up whether or not to tell. Finally he spoke, 'To be honest, I don't really know. Charlotte won't talk about it, even now. All I know is that they had a massive row a couple of days before the wedding and she called it all off.' He paused for a moment, as if that was all he was going to say, but then he started again. 'We all thought it was a joke at first: Charlotte and Ed were perfect for one another.' He stopped again. From the expression on his face, she could tell it was a painful, horrible memory.

'Go on,' said Polly encouragingly.

'It was awful. She locked herself in her flat and wouldn't let anyone in. We had to break the door down in the end. I hate even thinking about the state we found her in.' He shuddered as he said it.

'What?' Polly asked, her voice barely a whisper.

'I shouldn't really be telling you this…'

'Please,' said Polly.

He mistook her anguish for concern.

'We found her in her wedding dress in a bath of cold, bloody water. I thought she was dead when I first saw her. There were at least four bottles of wine smashed all over the bathroom floor. Her legs and hands were cut to shreds from crawling about all over it. There was vomit everywhere. It was lucky she was in the bath and sitting upright; I hate to think what would have happened if she'd been lying flat on the floor.'

Polly stayed silent.

'I feel really bad about the whole thing, I'm the one who introduced her to Ed. Sebastian and I were good mates at medical school. To this day, I still can't understand what happened. I've asked her about it, and I've asked Ed about it, but neither one of them will talk.'

Polly was too drained to take in any more; she'd zoned out in an attempt to protect herself.

He looked over at her, then slid along the back seat and put his arm around her, pulling her in close. 'Enough about all that. Did you have a nice night?' He breathed his boozy breath all over her as he spoke.

'Yep,' she said quietly.

He snuggled in close, resting the side of his head on top of hers.

Polly thought she was going to be sick. She'd never believed in coincidence – the world was full of such random events that sooner or later you get inexplicable things happening – but this was something else entirely.

Thirty-two

Polly spent the rest of the weekend in a daze.

Monday was August bank holiday so she didn't have to go to work, much to her relief. It was a beautiful sunny day. Oliver wanted them to go out to a park, but she managed to persuade him to stay in and watch a box set with her. It was some American crime drama that she had no interest in watching – too gritty – but she was willing to endure it to avoid leaving the flat.

But it was Tuesday morning before she knew it. The thought of going outside terrified her. She had visions of Sebastian standing right up close to the front door, his nose resting on the shiny black paint, waiting for her to turn the handle so he could jump her. It wasn't an unreasonable thought: she was under no illusions that he probably knew where Oliver lived, therefore he knew where Polly lived.

Oliver left for work half an hour before her. She spent several minutes going back and forth between the lounge and the bedroom windows to scope out the front and back of the flat. Just when she'd finally built up enough courage to leave for work, there was a loud bang from upstairs, a door slamming. That was it – she wasn't going anywhere.

She called in to work sick. Alicia answered the phone. Polly said she had a bladder infection and that Oliver had put her on antibiotics. Alicia started going into great detail about a pelvic infection she'd had a while back and how painful it had been. Polly tried to tell her it wasn't the same thing, different part of the body, but she carried on regardless. In the end Polly said she had to run to the loo and hung up.

But as soon as she was in the silence of the flat again, she regretted calling. Now she'd have to spend the entire day alone. Sebastian was probably on his way to get her right now. At least if she'd gone to work and he'd turned up there'd be people around. In the flat, there would be nobody to hear her scream.

She assumed her usual position on the sofa, right in the corner facing the lounge door so she could see through to the kitchen and into the hallway and front door. At first she just stared into space, but it wasn't long before she started crying. How had all this happened? Everything was such a mess, and she had no idea how to fix any of it. She thought about what Sebastian had said. 'Life as you know it is over, Polly.' He'd been true to his word so far, what else was to come?

She looked over at Oliver's laptop on the dining table. Should she? Did she have any choice? She turned it on and went straight to Google. She typed in 'Sebastian Black'.

Several articles came up about the media corporation Black Inc. They all name-checked Sebastian as a possible successor to his father's empire. His father's name was Robert Black. There was also mention of an older brother, called Ed, who was also in the running as successor. She clicked on a link to an article in *Time* magazine. The cover photo was of an old, balding, saggy-faced man in a sharp suit and glasses. He was looking directly at the camera, the background blurred and brooding. The headline read: *How this one man took over the world's media*. The article gave a run-down of Robert Black's career, starting as an East End barrow boy and ending with him as the most powerful media mogul in the world, owning forty-four per cent of the world's media outlets, from newspapers to TV networks to social media channels. Polly had heard of Black Inc. before, but not realised the extent of the corporation. They had businesses all over the globe, with the focus on Europe and America.

It was all getting a bit heavy, so she clicked on to a link for one of the glossy magazines. It was an exclusive at home, with Robert Black's new wife. Robert only appeared in one photo with his Thai bride, a stock photo taken at some charity event. The rest were pictures of her in various outfits in their Monaco mansion. The lavishness portrayed in each photo was eye-popping – crystal chandeliers in every room, Regency furniture, gold and marble fixtures, a Picasso or Renoir on practically every wall. Further down the page was a picture of Robert as a much younger man, with a beautiful Italian model. Polly recognised her eyes immediately. She had the same brooding black eyes that had caught her that first night. The caption below stated that the picture was of Robert and his first wife Lucia. They had two children together.

She went back to Google and searched Ed Black. Again it just brought up articles about Black Inc. She tried to find some articles or photos specifically about his sons, but there was nothing. It made sense: if he really had that much power over the media, he could easily quash any stories or information that came out about them.

She clicked through to another couple of articles. It seemed that not everyone was happy about Robert Black owning almost half the world's media. Several groups were up in arms about how much control he'd been able to accumulate. There were a number of impassioned pleas to governments to step in and do something about it. But, from what she could gather, Robert had built an impenetrable fortress around his family and his empire; nobody could touch them.

Polly sat back, letting out a long sigh. What the fuck had she got herself involved in? Alex was right: the normal rules and laws of the land didn't apply to these people. She quickly shut the lid of the laptop. She didn't want to know any more.

The thing she couldn't understand was how all their lives – hers, Sebastian's, Oliver's, Charlotte's, Ed's – were intertwined, seemingly by chance. *He* was a stranger on the tube; it defied belief that he'd picked her out at random on the train that first night. She often wondered why he'd chosen her, she had hardly been looking her best – she had been drunk, with smudged make-up and a head full of frizz. No, it just wasn't right – there were too many coincidences. The start of a line of thought was banging round in her brain, but it wouldn't stay still long enough for her to catch it.

She found herself a pen and piece of paper and started writing a chronological list of everything that had happened involving *him*. She had just got to the second meeting, when she'd thought she was with him but had actually been with the old guy, when she stopped and screwed up the piece of paper. It made her feel horrible; writing a list was a stupid idea. She threw the ball of paper on the floor and curled herself up on the sofa.

She woke up several hours later with a start. She could hear a set of keys in the front door. She was immediately up off the sofa and looking for somewhere to hide.

There was a thud at the door, as if someone was trying to force it open.

'Pol?' Oliver's voice came from the other side.

She'd put the bolt on the door right after he left that morning.

'Oliver?' she replied. The sound of her own voice made her jump.

'Pol, can you open the door for me? I can't get my damn key to work.'

She went to the door to open it, but stopped as she reached up for the bolt. None of this was right. What was Oliver's connection? Was he somehow involved?

'Pol? Are you there?'

Oliver had said it himself, that he and Sebastian were good mates at medical school. He must know what Sebastian had been up to – about the whole tubing thing.

She started backing away from the door.

'Pol, can you please open the door?'

She suddenly flashed back to when Oliver had appeared the night she'd met *him* on the tube at Shepherd's Bush. She remembered the way Oliver had appeared in the middle of her striptease. Had it been a set-up? Was Oliver supposed to be going to a meeting, or watching? She knew there'd been something weird going on – he was supposed to be watching the rugby, not running around on the Underground on a Sunday evening.

'Polly,' he suddenly shouted from behind the door.

She felt her back come into contact with the wall on the other side of the hallway.

'No,' she replied in a very small voice.

'What?'

'I said "no".' Louder this time.

Oliver, tubing? The thought was beyond ridiculous. He was one of the least sexually motivated men she'd ever met. But maybe that was why. Maybe he was getting his kicks on the Underground and didn't need anything from Polly.

'Polly, what the hell are you doing? Just open the bloody door.'

'No, what the hell have *you* been doing? You fucking perve,' she screamed.

Suddenly she was hyperventilating. It wasn't long before pins and needles were clawing up her legs and into her guts again. She groped the side of the door to try and steady herself. She hit the ground just as Oliver broke through the front door.

Thirty-three

When she came to, she was lying on the sofa in the lounge. Oliver was in the kitchen. He turned and looked at her.

'Hey, you're awake,' he said coming towards her.

She was immediately on high alert, pulling herself up into the corner of the sofa, bracing herself.

Seemingly unaware, he sat down next to her.

'What's this?' he said, leaning forward to pick up the list she'd screwed up and thrown on the floor.

'Nothing,' she said snatching it out of his hand and stuffing it up her sleeve.

'How are you feeling?' he asked gently.

She didn't answer.

Suddenly he didn't look like Oliver any more. He was a stranger to her. She'd always thought he was such an honest, genuine guy, but now it seemed that everything about him was a lie, right down to the fact that he never lied.

'What are you doing to yourself, Polly?' he said shaking his head.

'What?' she replied, taken off guard.

'I know what you've been up to.' He paused, taking a deep breath, readying himself for what he was about to say next. 'It's time for us to start being honest with one another.'

She just stared at him.

'It's OK,' he said moving in a bit closer.

She immediately flinched.

'I've been there myself.'

She was struggling to follow what he was saying. Was he admitting to it?

'Well, not in the same way as you have, of course. In fact, that's a stupid thing to say – very different for a man, much, much harder for a woman, I think.'

She couldn't believe they were having this conversation. She looked over at the window. The thought occurred to her that, if she ran fast enough, she could dive through the open window before he caught her.

'I understand why you've been doing it. It's totally understandable considering what you've been through.'

She stared at him, mouth agape. Was he forgiving her? Was he expecting her to do the same?

'Your mum warned me something like this might happen.'

Polly shook her head. 'Wait… What? My mum?' What the hell did her mum have to do with this?

'A relapse.'

'A what?'

'When I spoke to your mum, she told me how this happened when you were a teenager, suddenly disappearing, getting really paranoid, not eating.'

Polly closed her eyes and put her head in her hands. Right, she got it now: he thought she was having some kind of breakdown.

He carried on talking. 'Polly, don't worry, I'm going to make everything right. I'm going to make sure you get better.'

She looked up at him in disbelief. 'And what about you, Oliver?' She suddenly felt enraged. 'What about all your lying and cheating?'

'What?' he replied, sounding genuinely shocked.

'Are you having sex with other people behind my back, Oliver?'

The words were out of her mouth before she even knew they were coming.

'I beg your pardon.'

She had no plan as to how this would go. Best just carry on.

'Are you fucking other people?'

'What?' he exclaimed, then shook his head as if it was some kind of a joke.

'You heard,' continued Polly, deadly serious.

'I don't even know… What are you talking about?'

'Just answer the question.'

'Polly…' he said confused, all the features on his face crumpled into the centre.

'Why won't you answer the question? Am I right?'

He didn't say anything, just stared at her.

'Yes or no?' she said raising her voice. Why wouldn't he just give her an answer? As far as she was concerned it could only mean one thing: he was guilty and trying to evade the question.

He reached out to touch her. She flinched, yanking her arm away. 'Why won't you answer me?' she erupted, screaming the words in his face.

Oliver physically jumped back. He looked really hurt.

'Why?' she shouted.

'Because it's such a ridiculous question to ask,' he replied, shrinking away from her.

'Not good enough,' she continued. 'We barely have sex, so you must be getting it from somewhere else.'

'Polly, calm down, just calm down and—'

'Don't tell me to calm down, you patronising twat,' she snapped.

He was looking at her as if he'd never seen her before. He started to get up and move away from her very slowly, as if making any sudden movements might unhinge the beast and bring on an attack.

'You never want to have sex with me,' she continued, her anger defending her against the embarrassment of her words. She got up to follow him. 'Always pushing me away whenever I try to instigate anything. Why is that, Oliver? Is it because you're a dirty perv who gets his sexual kicks elsewhere?'

He'd turned his back on her now and was shaking his head in – what? Disbelief? Or maybe he was mad at being found out? Polly couldn't tell. She was right up behind him now. She reached out both hands and pushed him hard. 'Why do you do it, you bastard?' she shouted.

The push was a step too far. He swung round and pinned her up against the lounge wall. His face was bright red and he was shaking with rage. *I'm right*, she thought, *this is Oliver, this is the real Oliver.*

'Just admit it,' she said.

But suddenly his grip loosened and his face softened. 'I don't know what you're talking about, Polly. You're the one always pushing me away. I can't think of a single time I've refused.'

'I can,' she replied defiantly, 'The morning after I…'

She stopped herself. She was thinking of the morning after she'd met Sebastian. She couldn't believe she'd nearly said it.

She pulled away from him. Everything was so muddled in her brain, she couldn't quite get a grip on what was Oliver and what was tubing.

She turned and faced the wall. Maybe if she focused solely on the white space in front of her she could get some perspective. It was no good. After a few seconds tears began rolling down her cheeks. She slowly started tapping her forehead against the hard, cold brick.

'Stop that,' said Oliver gently.

She ignored him and started hitting her head harder.

'Stop it,' he said, pulling her away and guiding her back to the sofa. Once she'd sat down, he knelt before her and took both her hands. 'We'll get through this.'

He looked at her with nothing but love. But she'd seen that look before. Sebastian had looked at her the same way, right after he'd asked her to run away with him, just before he'd tried to strangle her.

She pulled away from him and got up. 'I'm going to bed,' she said.

'But it's not even six-thirty,' she heard Oliver say as she slammed the bedroom door.

Thirty-four

Polly called into work sick again the next day.

She had a brainwave in the middle of the night and the next morning got on to Oliver's laptop as soon as he left for work. She went straight to his Facebook page. She hadn't looked at it in a while. His profile picture was the same: Oliver playing the fool, his stethoscope in one hand and a pint of bitter in the other. When they'd first met, Polly had trawled through his page, reading every comment, looking at all his photos. At the time, none of the people had meant very much to her, she hadn't recognised any of them, but she did now.

There were several photos of Sebastian. She couldn't believe she hadn't remembered seeing him before. Charlotte also featured heavily. Ed appeared in a couple of them. As soon as she saw his face, her heart sank and her head dropped to the table. She recognised him immediately. He was the last guy she'd been tubing with. She slowly lifted her head up to look at him again. He looked nothing like his brother, much more like his father. He had the same close-cropped blond hair and wore glasses.

She'd just been a piece of meat for Sebastian to pass round to everyone he knew, for them to fuck.

She scrolled down Oliver's list of friends. *He* was there. She clicked on to his page, but it was closed access so she couldn't see anything other than his profile picture. It was a self-portrait, probably taken using his mobile. His black eyes glared at her down the lens. She would do anything to get into his page.

Then she had a thought. She logged out of her Facebook account and put in Oliver's username instead. Password, she thought, what would he use as his password? She typed in 'password', clicked OK and was in.

She went straight to Sebastian's page. There was hardly anything in it. There was the odd comment from other people and a couple of photos that had been tagged to him, but nothing else.

She went back to Oliver's page. He was also friends with Ed. She clicked on his name. There was very little content there either. She scrolled down a bit and was about to give up when she noticed several messages of congratulations on 12th March five years ago. She couldn't work it out at first; they weren't birthday wishes. Then it dawned on her. She clicked back to Oliver's page to look for Charlotte. She found her and went straight to her page. The same messages of congratulations appeared. It was the date they'd announced their engagement. Charlotte had updated her Facebook status from 'in a relationship' to 'engaged'.

From then on there were endless comments on Charlotte's page; it was a public diary of her wedding plans. Polly couldn't help wincing as she read each post. There were pictures of various styles of wedding dress she liked, as well as details of the venue, the menu for the wedding breakfast, a YouTube video of the band who'd be playing at the reception. The last few posts were a running commentary of her feelings as she counted down to the big day. The last one read, 'Tomorrow I become Mrs Black'. Two hundred and thirty people had liked the comment and there were loads of messages wishing her luck. After that, there was nothing; the page had been totally abandoned.

Polly sat back, letting out a long breath. What happened between them? She got up and made herself a cup of tea, unable to look any more at the mausoleum that was Charlotte's Facebook page.

Her phone suddenly vibrated into life on the dining room table where she'd left it next to the laptop. She let out a little yelp in surprise. She went over to get it, hand over heart, trying to stop it racing. She looked to see who it was before answering. It was James. 'Shit,' she said aloud. She immediately put it back down on the table and paced around until it stopped ringing. Once it was quiet again, she returned to the kitchen to finish making her tea. She heard a loud electronic chime to signal that James had left a voicemail. She chose to ignore it.

She went back to the laptop and straight to Gmail. She didn't have an account there, but Oliver did. She typed in his email address and 'password'.

His email account was very neat. He only kept messages that were strictly relevant. Polly's email account was bulging with bits of spam and junk; she could never be bothered to delete anything. She scrolled down his list of messages. Lionel was right: he had applied for a couple of paediatric positions. There was nothing else of much interest. The odd email from Crispin arranging his birthday bash, a couple of viral messages and several from online bookshops – he'd bought a lot of medical books over the last few months.

She was scrolling further down his list of messages when one in particular caught her eye. The email address was *reservations@oxo.co.uk*. It was a table booking for the

OXO tower restaurant. Oliver had taken Polly there on their first date. They had a table right by the window with views over the South Bank across the Thames and into central London. Polly was impressed beyond words. The email confirmed a booking for two people on 14th June. He left instructions with the booking: 'We'll be celebrating a very special occasion, so if possible can we have a table by the window and champagne ready for when we arrive? Thanks in advance. Oliver.' She knew the date – their anniversary. 'What the … ?' Polly said aloud.

She went back to his inbox and carried on looking down his list of emails. A couple of messages later there was one from Tiffany & Co. She opened it with a sense of trepidation. It said, 'Dear Dr Elliot-Smith, we wanted to let you know that the engagement ring you ordered has been resized and is ready for you to collect.'

There was more to the message, but Polly didn't bother to read it. She clicked straight on the words 'engagement ring'. It took her to a page on the Tiffany & Co. website. It was a stark white page with a picture of a sapphire and diamond engagement ring. It was beautiful.

Thirty-five

On Friday Polly had to go to work. She'd listened to James's message. He wished her well, but made it very clear that he needed her back in the office as soon as possible.

She was still reeling from having read Oliver's emails. He'd made all those plans so that he could propose on their anniversary. She'd seen all his missed calls that night but chosen to ignore them. She had visions of Oliver sitting in the restaurant, a bunch of roses on the table, champagne on ice, an engagement ring burning a hole in his pocket, while she had been drunk on a train having it off with a stranger – well, someone she'd thought was a stranger. It was painful to think about.

But then, did it really change anything? Asking her to marry him didn't necessarily mean anything. Sebastian was engaged and it hadn't stopped him tubing. Emmi. She hadn't thought about her since meeting her on Saturday night. Maybe she should tell her what he'd been up to. But she immediately dismissed the thought. God only knew what he'd do to her if she did something like that.

Then it occurred to her. Was tubing the reason Charlotte and Ed had split up? Had she found out what he was up to and called the wedding off?

*

She was running late when she left the house. She'd spent far too long going back and forth between the bedroom and the lounge window. She took a deep breath as she pulled open the front door, bracing herself for the worst. There was no one there.

She'd intended to get the bus, but if she did she'd be at least half an hour late. James had said he wanted her in at nine sharp so she was forced to get the tube. On board, she couldn't help looking around nervously; she was like a little bird, her head darting mechanically this way and that.

She'd barely sat down at her desk when James appeared and said he needed a word. They used Lionel's office – he was out for the morning. She could tell by the way he shut the door that he hadn't invited her in to discuss her prospects of promotion or give her a bonus.

'I'm going to get straight to the point, Polly,' he said as soon as he sat down in Lionel's chair. The leather creaked as he leant forward and placed his hands flat on the desk. 'Court proceedings have been started against the paper because of our T&Cs.'

Polly's fingers immediately went to her lip and started picking.

'You told me you'd changed that document, Polly, but it's becoming abundantly clear that you didn't.'

Her fingernails dug in deep, but she didn't feel any pain. There was a long silence

'Do you have anything to say for yourself?' he asked, annoyed that she hadn't spoken.

'I'm sorry,' she said meekly.

James considered her for a few moments, 'Do you even care, Polly?'

She didn't answer.

'I've lost count of the number of times you've called in sick over the last couple of months. Do you have some sort of illness you need to tell me about?'

Silence.

'No, I didn't think so. In that case, Polly, you've left me no option. I'm going to have to let you go.'

She'd known the words were coming. Her head dropped down on to the desk in front of her, and she pulled her arms up around her ears and started to sob.

James didn't seem to know what to do. He went over to her and patted her on the back. When that wouldn't stop her heaving shoulders, he went to the door to try and signal to someone. There was no one about. He danced around the office, unsure what to do with himself.

Eventually Polly lifted her head up for air. Her face was hot and clammy; she could barely get a breath in for all the snot and saliva that was clogging her airways. James offered her the handkerchief he kept in his top pocket. Polly had always thought it was for decoration. She blew her nose loudly and squinted up at him.

'I'm so sorry, James,' she said. 'I just can't believe all this is happening.'

'What *is* happening, Polly?' he asked softly. 'It's clear something's wrong. You've always been so conscientious, but over the last few months...well, you've been like a different person.'

Polly thought for a few moments – then she told him everything. She told him about seeing the girl pushed under the train, about Sebastian chasing her, following her, about the attack, everything – except about tubing.

James listened carefully. He didn't react to anything she said; he waited until she'd finished.

The first thing he did was smile at her. Then he said, 'I wish you'd come to me sooner.'

'I couldn't,' said Polly. 'I couldn't go to anyone. He tried to kill me. You're the first person I've told.'

'Well, we're going to have to do something about it.'

'Please don't tell me to go to the police. I tried that, but he came out of nowhere; he knew exactly what I was doing. If he finds out…' She trailed off at the thought.

'OK, OK,' said James. He thought for a moment then said, 'I know someone in the Met who owes me a favour. I'll talk to them about it, see what they can do.'

'No, no, please don't,' said Polly, reaching up to him, imploring.

He knelt down in front of her.

'It's all right, I'll keep it off the record. I'll explain the situation. No one will approach this Sebastian guy until you're happy for them to. OK?'

She slowly nodded her head, tears trickling down her cheeks again.

He took her hand. 'You don't have to worry any more. We'll get it sorted.'

Once she'd cleaned her face, James told her to go back to her desk and get on with some work. He called his friend at the Met from Lionel's office. A few minutes later he went over to Polly's desk and leant down close to her, his knees clicking as he knelt down.

'I've set up a meeting for this evening at my house.' He handed her a piece of paper. 'Here's my address. It's set up for seven p.m., but feel free to come earlier if you want to; I'll be in from about five.' He pushed back the sleeve of his shirt to reveal a solid gold watch. 'I'm due in court later this morning to sort out the T&Cs mess, so I really need to go. Will you be OK?'

She wanted to hug him, tell him how sorry she was for the entire mess. But she didn't; she just nodded awkwardly and he rushed off.

Thirty-six

She took James up on his offer and turned up at his house just after half-past five. He was pleased to see her, if a little flustered. It dawned on her that the 'drop round earlier' bit had been more of a gesture than anything. She apologised profusely and tried to slope off again, but he wouldn't hear of it and dragged her in through the front door.

James lived in a three-storey town house off Sloane Square. A large hallway led to high-ceilinged, impeccably decorated rooms. They went into the living room. There was a formal three-piece suite in the centre of the room that looked anything but comfortable. In the corner were two beaten-up old leather chairs with a small coffee table between them facing an open cabinet containing a flatscreen TV.

He told her to make herself comfortable in the corner while he got them some tea. She lingered around the sideboard looking at his photos for a while before sitting down. One man featured prominently in the pictures. He was in his thirties, Oriental-looking, maybe Cambodian or Vietnamese. They looked good together, even though James must have been at least fifteen years older. Polly was happy for him.

James returned with a teapot and two matching cups and saucers. They were white bone china with blue and yellow polka dots. She could barely believe this was the same unassuming guy she'd worked with in the office over the last year. She felt guilty that she'd never had any time for him before now. She was always civil, but had never really bothered to get to know him. But here he was doing everything he could to make her feel at ease, letting her hide out in his home.

They talked for a bit about nothing very much, then James excused himself so he could finish off some bits of work. He left Polly with the remote control for the TV. She must have fallen asleep soon after he left the room. She remembered flicking through a couple of channels; the next thing she knew James was standing over her, trying to wake her.

'Polly,' James said gently. 'DS Watson is here, my friend from the Met I was telling you about.'

Polly opened her eyes. A woman in her late forties was standing next to him. She was surprised: she'd expected a fat, balding middle-aged man with coffee breath and BO, not this slim, sharply dressed lady in front of her. She looked good for her age despite the lines on her face and the puffiness under her eyes.

'Hello, Polly,' she said, putting out her hand for Polly to shake. Polly rubbed her face with her palms and straightened up before taking her hand.

DC Watson, who insisted she call her Gin, sat on the chair opposite. James grabbed a hard-backed chair from the dining room.

Gin rifled through her bag then placed a notebook and pen on the small coffee table.

'OK, Polly,' she said. 'James has filled me in on a few bits, but I'd like to hear the whole story from you, if you're up to it.'

Polly hesitated momentarily. Now was the time to tell the truth, to tell her about tubing. But she didn't. She told her the edited version of the truth. She didn't lie, just omitted things. She started at the point where she'd seen Sebastian push Sarah under the train and how he'd chased her out of the station. She told her about him suddenly appearing outside her office when she'd tried to call the police. It was difficult to explain the attack on the train – she could hardly say she went willingly to meet him – so instead she said he followed her. The part about Oliver and Sebastian knowing one another was patchy, but she needed to explain how he knew her name. She went on to tell the detective sergeant that she was pretty sure he'd also killed 'Mousey', although she instantly regretted mentioning that bit.

Gin listened in silence. She didn't make any notes in her notebook, even though it lay open on the table.

When Polly had finished she said, 'Sounds like you've had quite a time of it.' She said it with no inflection in her voice. Her face remained emotionless and her body language gave nothing away. Polly wasn't sure what to make of her.

'I have a couple of questions I'd like to ask, if that's OK with you, Polly,' Gin said. Polly didn't like the way she kept tagging 'if you're up to it' or 'if that's OK with you' on to her sentences. The way she said it was like an afterthought, like something she'd just remembered from her training at police school, a nicety to put people at ease then catch them out.

'OK,' said Polly.

'How did Sebastian know where to find you?'

'What do you mean?'

'When you tried to call the police from outside work and then later when you were going home on the tube?'

'He must have been following me.'

255

'Right,' said Gin. 'And where were you going when he attacked you on the tube?'

'Home,' said Polly without thinking.

'This was straight after work.'

'Umm, well, no,' Polly said suddenly remembering how late it had been. 'I'd been working late. I think it was half-seven or eight.'

'OK, and you were on your way home?'

'Yeah.'

'Where were you exactly when he attacked you?'

'Just coming into Baker Street.'

'Isn't that the same station where you saw him push Sarah under the train?'

Polly couldn't believe she hadn't made the connection before. 'Yes,' she replied.

'OK,' Gin said in her slow, protracted manner, mulling it over. 'What tube line do you usually get home from work, Polly?'

'Central Line.' Shit, Polly thought the second the words were out. She knew exactly what was coming next.

'But Baker Street isn't on the Central Line.'

She was right, of course. Polly thought about saying that she had been going to meet a friend or something, but no doubt Gin would want to know who they were and every other minuscule detail about their life.

'I like to mix it up sometimes,' she said. 'The journey gets a bit boring if you get the same lie … line all the time. Gives me a chance to see other parts of London and—' She'd started babbling inanely.

'But you're on a tube train underground.'

Polly let out a nervous snort, 'Yeah, it's funny really, isn't it? I know lots of people who do it though, especially if—'

'OK, OK,' said Gin, raising her hand to stop her.

Polly took a deep, shaky breath, suddenly wondering why she'd started all this.

Gin resumed her questioning. 'When did you try to call the police from the phone box?'

'A week ago.' Polly thought for a moment. 'It was last Friday.'

'And when did you see him push Sarah under the train?'

'On the Tuesday.'

'Three days before?'

Polly knew where this was going. 'No, the Tuesday before that.'

Gin paused, cocking her head back, confused. 'Why did you wait ten days to contact the police?'

This was all going horribly wrong. She should have worked all this out beforehand. 'I don't know. I was scared,' she replied weakly.

Silence. Gin didn't say anything. She just looked at Polly intently, as if she was trying to read her mind. Eventually she spoke.

'It's quite a coincidence that Oliver and Sebastian went to medical school together, don't you think?'

'Well…' Polly struggled for words. 'Yes…I guess it is.'

'And you'd never met Sebastian before you saw him push the girl under the train?'

Polly could feel her face burning; she prayed it didn't show. At least she had the darkness of the room on her side. The sun was setting outside and James hadn't switched any lights on in the room yet.

'No,' said Polly firmly. She tried to sound as definite as possible.

'Not even at a social event?'

Polly was starting to get annoyed. Gin was asking all the wrong questions. 'I don't really see what all this has to do with what I saw, or the fact that I'm being stalked by a psychopath.'

'I'm just trying to get all the facts, Polly. There's no need to get upset.'

'I'm not getting upset,' she said, clearly getting upset.

'It's OK, Polly,' interrupted James. 'We only want to help. Gin's going to have to pick Sebastian up and interview him. She just needs to make sure she's got everything straight first.'

'OK,' said Polly, calming down.

Gin was watching her carefully, her posture straight and upright. 'I've one last question for you, Polly. and then we're finished.'

Polly waited, expecting the worst.

'Why do you think he's responsible for the murder of the other women, the one with the mousey hair? You only saw him push *Sarah* under the train, right?'

'Right,' replied Polly.

'So what makes you think he killed this other girl?'

Polly knew mentioning Mousey had been a bad idea. It was proving very difficult to tell a truthful, coherent story when so much had to be left out.

'Well...' She was willing herself to think of something. 'I saw it in a news story online and it seemed like a similar type of thing.'

'I don't understand. Other people have committed suicide on the Underground in the past couple of months. Why do you think he killed that particular girl? Do you know her?'

'No,' said Polly a little too quickly. 'But I mean, it's obvious, isn't it? I read in the paper that she had no reason to kill herself – just like Sarah,' she added as an afterthought.

Both women stared at one another. Polly desperately wanted to look away, but was too scared – liars always looked away first.

After an eternity, Gin inhaled sharply and picked up her notebook and pen from the coffee table.

'OK, so what'll happen now is I'll get some uniforms to pick up Sebastian tomorrow morning,' she started, then changed tack, reacting to the panic suddenly etched all over Polly's face. 'Don't worry, they'll arrive unannounced and take him straight in for questioning. You'll be perfectly safe, I give you my word on that. I'll also start looking into the other girl's death.'

She put her notebook and pen in her handbag then closed the buckle making sure it was securely fastened.

'Try to get some rest, Polly, you look like you need it.' She suddenly broke into an unexpectedly warm smile. 'Don't worry,' she said, reaching out and patting her arm.

James started walking her to the door. They were almost out of the room when Gin suddenly stopped and turned back, 'There's nothing else I should know is there, Polly?'

Now is the time, Polly's brain screamed, *tell her, tell her everything*. But she couldn't.

'No, there's nothing else.'

'Good,' Gin said before turning to leave the room.

Polly slumped back in her chair. She tried to tell herself that she'd done the right thing, that it would soon all be over, but unease niggled and prodded at her, refusing to let her alone.

Thirty-seven

Polly didn't leave the flat all weekend. Oliver was playing cricket on both the Saturday and Sunday so she barely saw him. She'd thought she would have heard from James or Gin, but no one called. She tried desperately not to think about Sebastian and what was happening to him, but the harder she tried, the worse it got. Had the police taken him in yet? Had he confessed? Been arrested? Would she need to give evidence against him in court? She paced the flat constantly, drinking mug of tea after mug of tea. She couldn't remember the last time she'd eaten – and even that thought didn't make her feel any better.

When she got to work on Monday morning James was already at his desk. She smiled as soon as she saw him. He didn't smile back.

'Everything OK?' she asked as she put her bag down.

He glared, his eyes levelled straight at her. Clearly everything was not OK. 'We need to go to the police station.'

'What? Now? But I've only just got in.'

He didn't answer. He got up from his desk, picked up his briefcase and gently tucked his chair under his desk.

'I'd better tell Lionel first,' she continued, flustered. She didn't want him thinking she'd skived off for another day.

'It's OK, I've already spoken to him and he's fine with it.'

As if by magic, Lionel appeared at his office door with a mug of something hot in his hand. She could see steam rising from his cup in the sun's rays through the windows behind him. He took a long slow sip as he carefully watched her.

She smiled at him. He didn't smile back.

'You didn't tell him did you?' Polly asked, suddenly panicked. Lionel knew Oliver's parents; she didn't want word getting back to them or Oliver. She'd thought she could trust James; now she wasn't so sure.

'Just pick up your bag and let's go.'

'I'm not sure I should. Sebastian might still be following me. If he sees me going into a police station … well … I don't know what he'll do.'

James turned and looked at her. 'Drop the act, Polly.'

'What?' said Polly in disbelief, but he was already halfway down the corridor.

He held the lift for her until she arrived. They went down to the ground floor in silence. Polly was lost for words. Her mind was racing: what the hell was going on? They left the building by the main door and went to where James's car was parked. Polly nervously followed, constantly checking behind her for any sign of Sebastian.

James's car was a sleek black Jaguar. The interior was padded white leather. It still had that 'new car' smell. Radio 4 blasted out of the stereo as soon as James started the engine. His hand leapt up to turn it off. She asked him again what was going on, but he carried on as if she hadn't said a word.

They arrived at the West End Central Police Station on Savile Row fifteen minutes later. James parked down a side street. He turned to look at Polly as if he was going to say something, but stopped himself and just frowned instead. He got out of the car. Polly followed.

At the custody desk, James asked for DS Watson. They were directed through reception and down a corridor to an interview room. Gin and a uniformed officer were waiting for them. It was a grimy room with off-white walls and no windows. A naked strip light in the centre of the ceiling was all that lit it. There was a metal table with two uncomfortable looking hard-backed chairs on each side. Gin and her officer were on one side, a pile of typed notes between them, James and Polly sat on the other. A laptop was set up in the middle of the table.

The room was silent, all eyes on Polly. The tension in the room was suffocating. Polly found herself taking short, sharp breaths, in need of air.

Eventually Gin spoke. 'Polly, thank you for coming in to see us.'

Polly wanted to say that she hadn't had much choice in the matter, but instead mumbled, 'It's OK.'

Gin introduced the officer sitting next to her as Inspector Phillips. He nodded at her, his face serious. Then said, 'Do you mind if we record this interview?'

'Why?' asked Polly.

'We just need to go over your statement again. We need to keep a record of it.'

'OK,' muttered Polly.

Gin signalled to the wall behind Polly and James. Polly turned round to see a large mirror behind them. It was on the same wall as the door, so she hadn't noticed it when they first walked in. Whoever was behind it did as they were told and a red light appeared just above the mirror. Gin got on with the formalities, stating the date, time and case number, and listing who was present in the room.

'We've asked you to come back in today, Polly, because we've uncovered a few inconsistencies with your story that we'd like to clear up.'

Who the hell is 'we'? thought Polly. When she'd met with Gin and James before the weekend it had been kindly 'I's; now it was 'we'. She turned to look at the glass screen behind her again. Why was she in an interview room, being taped and watched by God knew who? This was all wrong.

'What's going on?' asked Polly. 'Have you spoken to him?'

'I assume by "him" you mean Mr Sebastian Black,' Gin said, staring straight at her, her posture perfect, her hands clasped together resting in front of her on the table. 'Yes, we interviewed him over the weekend.'

'Well, what did he say?'

'He tells a very different story from you, Polly.'

'What do you mean?'

'He claims that you were stalking him, not the other way round.'

Polly was floored. She couldn't believe what she was hearing. 'That's insane,' she said. 'Why on earth would I be stalking him?'

Gin looked down at her notes. 'When we last spoke you told me that you'd never met Mr Black before the evening you saw him push Sarah Wilson under the train, is that right?'

'Yes, that's what I said.'

'I know that's what you said, Polly, but is it true?'

Polly hesitated for a moment. 'Yes.'

Gin took a deep inhalation flaring her nostrils, looked straight at James, then back at her notes again.

'We asked Mr Black about the evening in question, the evening you allege he murdered Sarah Wilson. He doesn't know anything about it. He says he was working from home, didn't leave his flat all day.'

'He's lying,' Polly said. 'I saw him there. I saw him push her under the train.'

'His fiancée has corroborated his story.'

She would, thought Polly. 'She's lying.'

Gin paused to look at her notes again.

'We had a look at the tube station's CCTV of the incident.' She paused, holding Polly's gaze for several seconds.

'Well?' asked Polly impatiently.

'We didn't see him on the footage.'

'But he was there, right next to her – you must have seen him.'

'We saw you, but not him.'

Polly suddenly remembered the baseball cap he put on as he got off the train. 'He was wearing a baseball cap. Did you see anyone wearing a baseball cap standing next to her?'

Gin just stared at her.

Polly turned to James for support, but he was looking straight ahead, still not acknowledging her.

'Mr Black claims you made the whole thing up, Polly.'

'Why would I do that?'

'He claims that you did it to get back at him.'

'For what?'

'Mr Black says that you two were having an affair. When he ended the relationship you started stalking him and made up the story about him pushing Sarah Wilson under the train.'

'What?' Polly couldn't believe what she was hearing. 'That's bullshit.'

Silence.

'So you weren't having an affair with Mr Black?'

'No!'

'Now is the time to tell me the truth, Polly.'

'I was not having an affair with him,' she replied belligerently.

'OK.' Gin reached over and opened up the laptop sat in the middle of the table. 'Polly, I'd like to show you something.'

She switched on the computer. She tapped a couple of keys then turned the laptop round so it was facing her and James.

The screen was poised at the start of a video. A large *Play* button throbbed in the middle of the screen, waiting to be clicked on. Gin leant over and used the mouse at the bottom of the keyboard to start the video.

Polly couldn't make out what was going on at first. The picture was dark and she could hear lots of rustling, as if someone had their hand over the camera's microphone. This went on for several seconds until the camera began to pan back. She recognised the blue and red surroundings instantly: it was the inside of a tube train carriage. The picture moved round to show the back of someone's head. It was a head she knew – not one she saw very often, but one she knew well. The camerawork was jerky and the picture was moving all over the place – it soon became clear why.

She could tell that it had been taken using a camera on a mobile phone. She watched in horror as the camera slowly moved down until the top of two milky white buttocks filled the screen. She desperately wanted to turn away, but she couldn't. The camera continued on until she could see the penis thrusting. She heard a gasp, a familiar voice. The camera stayed put, recording the intimate act. The detail was so graphic it was animalistic.

Polly looked round at James. He wasn't looking at the screen; he was still staring straight ahead past Gin at the dirty wall in front of him.

She looked back at the screen to see the camera slowly pan back until it had a full shot of the person in front. Just above in the glazed window of the train a reflection of the faces of both people were clearly visible. It was Polly and Sebastian.

Polly's heart dropped as if it had just fallen out of her body. She remembered that moment. She'd had no idea he was filming, she couldn't fathom how he'd managed it without her noticing. She stared back at the girl on the screen, the girl from six weeks ago. It seemed as though a lifetime had passed. She couldn't even begin to explain.

The room was silent. Polly prayed that no one would speak, no one would ever ask her to give a reason for what was on the screen. For a few seconds no one did, but the stay of execution didn't last long.

'So now you understand our problem with your story, Polly.'

Her face burned with shame.

'Let me ask you again. Had you ever met Mr Black before you saw him allegedly push Sarah Wilson under the train?'

'Yes,' said Polly. The evidence was indisputable.

'Did you have an affair with Mr Black?'

'Yes.' She put her head in her hands. How the hell was she going to explain?

'You know, Polly, we're well within our rights to charge you with wasting police time.'

Polly lifted her head, dragging her hands down over her face to look at her. 'But I did see him push the girl under the train.'

'Did you? Did you really?'

'Yes, I swear it.'

'The problem is, we can see you on the CCTV footage of that day, but not Mr Black. All the evidence *we* have suggests that he was at home when Sarah Wilson committed suicide.'

'He's lying! He was there!'

Gin exhaled loudly. 'James tells me that you've been under a lot of pressure recently, I was sorry to hear about your father passing away. I'm going to let this drop. We won't be pressing charges against you.'

'Against me? I didn't do anything.' Polly stood up abruptly sending the chair she was sat on flying behind her. 'He killed her. I was there, I saw him.'

'Sit down, please,' commanded Gin.

'This is insane. He's twisted everything.'

'I said sit down.'

The uniformed officer, DI Phillips, got up ready to grab her.

'For Christ's sake sit down, Polly,' shouted James. They were the first words he'd uttered in the room.

Polly picked up the chair from behind her and sat down. She was shaking uncontrollably, every ounce of her body trembling with frustration. The laptop was still turned on. Her face filled the screen. She put her head on the table and started to cry.

After a few moments she heard chair legs dragging across the squeaky vinyl floor. She looked up to see everyone standing up and getting their things together. James was at the door, briefcase in hand.

'Wait,' said Polly desperately. 'What am I going to do?'

He took measure of her, contempt written all over his face.

'I suggest you go to the office and clear out your desk.'

Thirty-eight

Polly didn't go back to the office. She had no intention of ever going there again. She went back to the flat – the only place she felt any semblance of safety. She resumed her usual position on the sofa.

What now? He'd managed to prove his innocence and humiliate her all in one fell swoop, but she knew that wasn't it. After what she'd put him through at the weekend, there was no doubt he had a whole lot more in store for her.

It didn't take long before her fears were confirmed. A text message arrived half an hour after she got home:

big mistake, polly
you can't hide at home forever

The phone fell from her hand on to the floor. There was a loud crack as it hit the ground face down.

She immediately jumped up and ran around the flat checking the windows were locked and closing every blind and curtain. As she reached up for the bolt on the front door, she stopped herself. What was she doing? Was she going to barricade herself inside this flat for the rest of her life?

With her back against the door, she slowly slid all the way down until she hit the floor. She slumped down lower and lower until her chin was touching her chest.

She wanted to cry, but she couldn't even do that; she had no tears left. She sat there, numb. It felt as if her body was shrinking into itself. Maybe that was the best thing that could happen; maybe she could just make herself disappear, die even.

She held her breath, but after about forty seconds her lungs involuntarily opened and forced her to inhale.

'You won't even let me do that, will you?' she said to no one in particular.

There were no options left for her. He held all the cards, knew everything about her. She couldn't stay locked in the flat forever. But then the second she walked through the door... She couldn't trust Oliver, couldn't go to the police, her dad was... Even if there was something she could do, Sebastian could easily put a stop to it. He'd got away with murder at least twice as far as she knew, but that was probably just the tip of the iceberg. He could buy off the entire world, or so it seemed. There was no one and nothing.

Out of sheer despair she shouted, 'Fuck you.' Then, barely a whisper, 'Fuck you, Sebastian Black.'

His words went round and round in her head – *Life as you know it is over, Polly.*

He was right: it was. It really was.

She must have fallen asleep. When she came to, she was still slumped up against the front door. Her neck ached from craning over so long. For a few moments she was blissfully ignorant of her predicament, then it came flooding back to her, battering her entire body. She hurt everywhere, physically and mentally.

She got up and went into the bedroom. Maybe she could go back to sleep again. Perhaps unconsciousness was the way forward. She fell down on to the bed that Oliver had made neatly before going to work. But her eyes wouldn't shut, choosing instead to remain fixed on Oliver's bedside table. She might as well just get it over with, call Sebastian up and tell him to just come and get her. But she couldn't even do that; every text he sent came from a different mobile number.

She had a thought and immediately sat up. Oliver must have an address or number or something for him. She wrenched open the drawer of his bedside table, pulling it right off its runners and spilling the contents on to the floor. Torch, mobile phone charger, official-looking letters, a couple of paperbacks … but no address book.

She went into the lounge and ransacked the bookshelves. Nothing. She went back to the bedroom and went through his chest of drawers, even his shelves in the wardrobe.

'You must have something, you're supposed to be mates,' she cried out in frustration.

Then she stopped. She knew exactly how to find him – tubing. She could set up a meeting. He knew her Twitter handle; she was in no doubt he would see. That way she could get it over with, get whatever he had in store for her done.

And then it occurred to her that the reverse was also true, she could track him down through the tubing scene, without giving herself away.

She got on to Oliver's laptop and set up another fake Twitter account, @win44ty. She didn't really have a plan, but figured her best form of attack was to surprise him, somehow engineer a meeting without him knowing. She had no idea what she'd do if she did track him down, but at least she was doing something; she wasn't helplessly waiting.

Maybe if she could catch him in the act or a compromising situation, or have it out with him and get a recording of a confession … He'd already admitted to killing Sarah to her, so it wasn't beyond the realms of possibility.

She went to his Twitter handle, @can852ran. She could only find a record of the meeting he set up with Mousey and the reply he'd left on Polly's message; the rest was blank. She ran a Google search too, but couldn't find anything else.

She then went on to search #Tubing for various tube stations. Maybe if she went along to enough meetings she'd find him, eventually. From what she could gather, the meetings were tweeted on the day or a day in advance, none of them planned any further ahead than that. She decided to target all the stations at which she'd met him or where she knew he'd watched. She didn't need to make a list, she knew them off by heart.

After an hour or so of searching, it was all beginning to feel a bit futile. Direct action was called for. Using @win44ty, she tweeted:

Female hook up with male. Central Line. Oxford Circus eastbound. Third carriage. 11 p.m. tonight. #TubingOxfordCircus

She drummed her fingers nervously on the table, waiting for a like or a reply. She was worried. He seemed to know her every move, she wouldn't be surprised if he somehow knew about this new account too, impossible as that seemed. After fifteen minutes she got a like from @thr12356ty. She clicked on the profile; as expected, it was blank.

Thirty-nine

Her next dilemma was how to get out of the flat without Sebastian following her. For all she knew, he might be camped out in one of the flats across the road, doing a proper surveillance job on her. She wouldn't put anything past him.

Backing on to the bedroom of their flat was a roof terrace, of sorts. It was essentially the rear end of a mini-mart that fronted on to the road to the other side of them. There was a small courtyard behind, which was mostly filled with old bits of junk and rotting rubbish. If the wind was blowing the wrong way on a sunny day the smell of 'bin juice' was unbearable. At the back of the terrace was a rickety old fire ladder that should have been ripped down and replaced years ago. Outside on the terrace, Polly stood over the ladder and gave it a good shake. She heard a chime as one of the screws holding it together came loose and fell on to the floor below. But it seemed secure still; if she could climb down it to the courtyard, she could cut through the alley next to the shop and get out on to the road on the other side.

Oliver was due home at eight p.m. that night. She made sure she was ready and gone by seven-thirty.

Once out of the front door of the flat, she went down the stairs to the half-landing where the door to the roof terrace was and climbed out on to it. The nights had started drawing in, but it wasn't quite full dark as she tiptoed across the terrace to the ladder. She didn't dare risk shaking it again in case more screws came loose. She put her bag over her shoulder and fastened her jacket, then climbed on to the first step. The ladder instantly made a loud creaking sound and dropped down a couple of centimetres. Polly yelped, then tried to stay very still while it settled itself into its new position. Once she was sure it was steady, she slowly began to climb down.

What she hadn't realised from looking at the ladder from above was that it didn't go all the way to the ground. It stopped about six feet short. There was a large industrial bin to her left, and she stretched out her leg to try to reach it, but couldn't quite get there. 'Bollocks,' she muttered. Her only other option was to let herself drop. She continued climbing down the ladder until she was crouched on to the last rung, then slowly let her feet come away so only her hands were holding on. She thought she almost had it until her arms gave out just as she got her legs a quarter of the way down. At least there were plenty of rubbish bags to break her fall. She just wished one of them hadn't exploded when she landed on it.

She stood up and brushed herself off as best she could. She had just turned to start down the alley when she had a thought. She went over to the large industrial bin and pushed it closer to the ladder: she might need this as an exit again.

Once out on the main road, she was suddenly nervous; it felt all wrong being outside. She checked all around her, but she didn't see him. She checked the time on her phone: it was just after 7.45 p.m. She knew Oliver would be coming back through Shepherd's Bush tube station, so she went in the opposite direction to Hammersmith. She caught the Hammersmith and City Line, changing at Baker Street to get the Bakerloo Line to Oxford Circus.

It was as she was getting off at Baker Street that she suddenly stopped. This was where the whole mess started, where she saw him push Sarah under the train. She found herself walking to the westbound platform. She could pinpoint the exact spot where it had happened. She stared at the spot, reliving the moment in her mind. She could have stopped him; she had seen what he was doing, slowly inching Sarah closer and closer to the edge of the platform. Why hadn't she stopped him? Had she been that deluded, so infatuated with him that she had passively stood by while he murdered another human being? She fought hard to stop tears from coming.

It was then that she noticed the tracks. She moved closer to get a better look at them. They were flat on the ground, not raised like they usually were. She'd never noticed it before. As far as she could remember, tube stations had raised tracks. She suddenly had a thought. Sarah had been killed at this station, and this was the station they had been pulling into when he attacked her. She went up to the ticket hall. A craggy-faced man in his fifties, dressed in a blue uniform and peaked cap, was slumped over the baggage gate.

Polly went over to him. He begrudgingly stood up straight and motioned to open the barrier for her.

'It's OK, I'm not going out,' she said. 'I just wanted to ask a question.'

He slammed the gate shut, annoyed at her for disturbing his slump.

'Go on, then,' he said, sighing. He had a thick yellow-tinged moustache that had grown down over his lips, making it look as though his moustache was speaking to her, not his mouth.

She put on her best, most polite voice. 'I've noticed that the train tracks in this station run along the ground, and I just wanted to know why?'

'You what?' He looked at her as if she was mad.

She replayed what she'd just said in her mind and realised how nonsensical it sounded. 'The train tracks,' she started again. 'They're usually raised with a big gap underneath them, but in this station they're not.'

'Oh,' he said nodding his head, 'I get ya. Not all stations had suicide pits dug out in them. Most stations on the Circle and Hammersmith and City Lines don't have 'em.'

'Suicide pits?' repeated Polly.

'Yeah, during the Depression in the 1930s, every bugger was killing themselves by jumping under trains. Trenches were dug out under the tracks to try and stop 'em, like so if they did jump they'd fall below the track underneath the train. That or to help with drainage, whichever you prefer.' He shrugged.

'Oh,' said Polly.

'Works as long as the idiot don't touch the third rail, mind, otherwise they light up like a flippin' Christmas tree.'

'Oh,' said Polly again, her mind far, far away.

'Bloody nightmare when some poor bugger does himself in at this station,' he continued. 'Makes one hell of a mess; they got absolutely no chance.'

That was why Sebastian had used this station. Polly turned and walked away in a daze. A large tube map hung on the wall opposite. She stopped and took a closer look. Mousey had been killed at King's Cross St Pancras – it was on the same line.

'Hey, you better not be thinking about doing anything stupid,' he said after her. 'I don't like that look you got on your face.'

Polly barely heard him.

'Hey, girl, my shift's ending in half an hour and I don't wanna be spending it scraping you up off the tracks,' he shouted after her. 'Hey, you listening to me?'

Polly got to Oxford Circus just before nine p.m. She left the station and went out on to Oxford Street. It felt safer being around people, even if they were strangers.

She went to a coffee shop and ordered a soya latte. She was still shaken as she sat down at a table at the back of the café. She couldn't believe how logical and ordered he was, using a particular tube line to kill them so there was no chance they would survive. It was difficult to reconcile her feelings: she'd been besotted with him, but he was a murderer. How could her judgement have been so off? Part of her felt relieved to have survived the affair, but the other side was horrified, repulsed even.

At half-past ten, she went to the ladies to get herself ready. Once her make-up was done, she took a long, hard look at herself in the mirror. She had no idea what she was doing. She just knew she had to do something.

She went back to the station at 10.55. She was wearing a skin-tight black Lycra dress and her red satin stiletto heels. Her hair was slicked back into a tight ponytail and her eyes were made-up with thick kohl liner and false lashes, her lips cherry-red. She looked like a silhouette.

She spotted the guy on the platform immediately. She couldn't say how she knew it was him, she just did. At this point, she had every intention of walking away. It wasn't Sebastian, so what was the point in staying? But in spite of everything her heart suddenly started pounding in anticipation, and she followed him on to the train. She wanted him; she wanted to do this. It wasn't about what Sebastian or Oliver or anyone else thought. Alicia suddenly came to mind: 'if something feels good, then it is good'. She allowed herself to focus solely on what she wanted; she went with her gut, her own desires, and she refused to feel bad about it. It didn't matter how all this had come about. For the first time in her life she made her own choice.

He was in his early thirties, handsome, with sandy hair and cool blue eyes. Polly stood at the far end of the carriage and just watched him for a while. He waited patiently, only looking up when the train stopped at a station to see who was getting on.

After a couple of stops he finally noticed her. He smiled at her. She smiled back.

At Liverpool Street a glut of late-night travellers boarded the carriage. There were enough people around for her not to be in any danger. She went to him without further hesitation. He put his hands around her waist and gently guided her through the crowd of passengers to the corner of the carriage. He tried to push her up against the small side seat at the back. She stopped him, gripping on to his forearms, her nails digging deep. He looked confused. She pulled him round and pushed him down on to the seat, then draped her right leg up over his lap. He smiled at her and pushed up against her naked crotch.

Forty

Polly got back to the flat just after midnight. To her relief Oliver was already in bed.

She went straight to the bathroom to take a quick shower. Just as she was getting in, her mobile vibrated into life. It made her jump. She climbed out and went to her handbag, which she'd dropped behind the door. She picked up her phone and took it out, flicking the screen. The message read:

> *oxford circus – u just can't help yourself can u – dirty slut*

She sat down on the edge of the bath and just stared at the message. Her hands started to tremble and she was in danger of losing it. He'd either been following her or seen the tweet and gone to watch the meeting, not realising it was her. She was pretty sure he hadn't followed her; the lengths she'd gone to on leaving the flat made it near impossible. How could she *use* this? There must be something. She sat lost in thought for so long that the water from the shower ran cold. She looked up to see all the steam disappearing from the bathroom. She had a quick, cold strip-wash at the sink then went to bed.

She barely slept that night. Her mind was racing chasing down every possible eventuality, but she just couldn't work it out, it all felt so slippery.

When she did sleep, she had a nightmare about Oliver. Oliver was chasing her through a tube station. She made it to an escalator and started running up it as fast as she could. But no matter how hard she ran she couldn't get away from him. In her dream she didn't realise she was running up the down escalator. Oliver grabbed her round the back of the neck and dragged her to the platform. Sebastian was there waiting for them. Oliver put his arms round her waist and started moving towards the edge of the platform. Polly was totally powerless to do anything, as if she'd been drugged.

Sebastian looked on, sizing up what he was doing. 'Maybe try linking your hands together in front,' he said putting his hands out to demonstrate.

Oliver did as he was told.

'That's it. Maybe hold her a bit higher up. She's less likely to flop forward. You don't want to drop her before the train comes.'

'OK,' replied Oliver, changing his position. 'Yeah, that's much better.' He hung her over the platform edge. He started dropping her slightly then pulling her back so he could practise.

'Are you ready, Oliver? Here comes the train.'

She woke up just as he let go.

'Morning, Pol,' said Oliver cheerfully from the other side of the room.

She immediately shrank back under the duvet. For a second she wasn't sure if she was awake or still dreaming.

They'd barely spoken since their argument. By making herself scarce or going to bed early, she'd managed to avoid seeing him pretty much altogether. She eyed him suspiciously.

'Why are you looking at me like that?' he asked playfully.

She didn't reply.

'It's after eight – you getting up for work?'

He was being nice to her. Why was he being so nice? It was as if the other evening hadn't happened, as if she hadn't accused him of cheating on her, as if he hadn't suggested she was on the edge of some kind of breakdown. She couldn't figure out whether he was just trying to ignore it or was lulling her into a false sense of security – most likely the former, knowing Oliver. All she knew for sure was that she couldn't trust him.

'Earth to Pol,' he said after she still hadn't answered.

'I'm not needed until later,' she finally replied, pulling the duvet over her head and pretending to go back to sleep.

She lay there listening to Oliver moving around the flat getting ready for work. She was braced, ready for him. She wasn't expecting him to attack, exactly; she just knew she should be ready for anything. Her breathing was slow and hot under the duvet.

When she heard the front door slam and Oliver's footsteps on the stairs, she threw the duvet back and sat up, taking big gulps of cool, fresh air.

Once up, she got straight on to Oliver's laptop and logged into her new fake Twitter account. She started going through the hashtags of stations she'd compiled in her mind. A couple of meetings had been set up for that evening. She chose the one that said:

Male hook up with female. Central Line. Oxford Circus eastbound. 18.30 tonight. Third carriage. Red top, no knickers. #TubingOxfordCircus

Forty-one

She dressed the part for her meeting that evening – heels, too much make-up and a red short-sleeved top, as instructed in the tweet.

She boarded the 18.34 train at Oxford Circus. It was packed and, despite the cooler autumn weather, it was stifling inside the carriage. She took off her jacket and found a spot near the single door at the back of the carriage and waited. But her wait was cut unexpectedly short when she saw Crispin through the crowd on the same train. 'Fuck,' she muttered, and quickly turned to face the other way, but it was too late, he'd already spotted her.

He strode up to her, pushing his way through the crowd.

Polly panicked. What if Sebastian turned up? She needed to get rid of him as quickly as possible.

'Polly,' he said as he awkwardly made his way round a large man stood in front refusing to move. 'How are you?'

'Fine,' she replied as they air-kissed each other's cheeks.

'Wow, look at you…' he said, eyeing her up and down. 'I almost didn't recognise you. On your way out somewhere?'

She tugged at the hem of her skirt to try to make it longer. 'Yeah, something like that,' she mumbled.

Suddenly a smarmy smile appeared on his face. 'Your top – it's red,' he said.

Polly looked down at it. What an odd thing to say. 'Yes,' she said as she looked back up again.

He slowly started nodding his head, raising his eyebrow suggestively at the same time, then he leant in close to her ear and said quietly, 'I think you're here to meet me.'

Polly froze.

Once her brain had caught up, she quickly turned to move away. But he stopped her, grabbing hold of her wrist. 'Where are you going?' he said softly into her ear.

'I'm not doing this,' she whispered through gritted teeth, pulling away.

'Why not?'

She looked up at him incredulously. 'Take one guess,' she replied, her face screwed up in disgust, inches from his.

'Oh, I get it. You'll cheat on Oliver with a stranger, but not if it's me.'

'This isn't about cheating. Well … it isn't for me, anyway; it may be for Oliver.'

'What do you mean?'

'Fuck off Crispin, you know what I'm talking about. I know all about what you, Sebastian and Oliver get up to.'

He suddenly threw his head back and started to laugh, a burst of loud, haughty laughter that made several people in the carriage turn and look at him.

She stared at him, not sure what to make of it.

When he'd calmed down a little, he managed to get a few words out between each snort of laughter. 'You think Oliver…' Chuckle. 'Oliver, tubing?' Laugh. 'Are you mad?' he managed to finish.

Polly just continued to stare.

'Oliver doesn't do tubing. Wouldn't fit with his "principles".' He made speech marks in the air.

'What?' said Polly.

'Oh, dear, oh, dear, Polly,' said Crispin, sarcastically shaking his head and leaning into her again. 'You've been shagging about while good ole Oliver's been waiting home for you.'

Polly wanted to gouge his eyes out. She wanted to gouge her own eyes out. Suddenly she couldn't even remember why she'd thought Oliver was involved. What was wrong with her? It was as if she'd been living in some kind of parallel universe.

'You know, I've been hoping to bump into you. I heard you were on the scene.'

'What?' snapped Polly.

'You're such a dirty girl. I bet you haven't even got any knickers on, just like I said in my message.'

He suddenly shoved his hand up her skirt, fumbling for her naked crotch.

'Get off,' she shouted loudly.

Several commuters looked over.

Polly lowered her voice and moved in closer.

'What do you mean, you heard I was on the scene? Who told you?'

'Calm down, Polly,' he said, reaching out to stroke her hair. She flinched. 'Come on, don't make a fuss,' he said condescendingly.

'Tell me,' she demanded through gritted teeth.

'It was a while ago. I think it might have been Charlotte.'

'*Charlotte*?' Polly couldn't hide her shock. 'How does Charlotte know?'

'Enough of all this,' he said, grabbing her by her wrists and pulling her into the corner. 'We've our own business to get on with.'

Polly was repulsed. Crispin had suddenly morphed from Oliver's best friend into this drooling, sweaty perv in front of her. She had to get away from him as quickly as possible.

'Get off me, Crispin,' she said, her voice low and deadly serious.

He ignored her and carried on pulling her into the corner.

'Get the fuck off me!' she exploded.

Everyone in her immediate vicinity turned to look at them.

'This man is a pervert,' she shouted, pointing directly at Crispin.

Crispin's face flushed red.

The train was just pulling into the station. She quickly moved through the commuters to the nearest exit. Crispin tried to follow, but the crowd moved in around him, preventing him.

'Why don't you leave her alone, mate,' she heard someone say.

'Oh, my God,' Crispin said, exasperated. 'She's not serious. I know her. Polly, come back here,' he shouted after her.

The train came to a halt and she was out of the door as soon as it opened.

Forty-two

Polly stumbled on to the platform and made her way to an empty bench. Her head was buzzing; she needed a couple of minutes to try to get things straight. She slumped awkwardly down on to the metal seat, her hip hitting the armrest first. How had she been so wrong about Oliver? He had nothing to do with tubing, yet she'd been so convinced. And Charlotte? How the hell did she know about Polly being on the scene? She stared blankly, not seeing the hordes of people filing out of the platform exit.

'Polly? Hon?'

She didn't hear the voice at first; she was lost in her own confusing world.

She felt a hand touch her shoulder and jumped, looking round to see who it was. Alicia was standing beside her.

'Are you OK, hon?' Alicia asked.

Polly stared at her, eyes glazed. She was still feeling so bewildered, she couldn't answer.

Alicia knelt down in front of her, taking her hand. 'Polly, what's going on?' she asked, concern in her voice. 'I've not seen you in ages. They said you just upped and left at work. Hon, what happened?'

Just then a guy clipped Alicia's back with his briefcase and tutted loudly at her for blocking his path on the busy platform. 'Fuck you, moron,' Alicia shouted at him. He looked at her, startled, then put his head down and quickly went on his way.

'Let's get out of here. Do you want to go for a drink or something?' Alicia asked.

Polly didn't answer, so Alicia looped her arm around her waist and gently guided her along the platform.

They were just approaching the exit when Polly suddenly stopped and turned to her. 'What are you doing here?' she asked. Paranoia was getting the better of her.

'On my way home from work,' Alicia replied.

Polly looked up at the blue and red sign on the platform wall just above the track; she was in Holborn.

They went into a coffee shop next to the station. Alicia pulled out a chair at the first table they came to and pointed for Polly to sit. 'You're shivering,' she said, taking Polly's jacket out of her hands and putting it round her.

The place was almost empty this time of the evening – everyone was too busy fighting their way home from work to stop for coffee. Polly sat back, suddenly feeling much calmer in the ambient-jazz-infused atmosphere.

Alicia got the waitress's attention and ordered two coffees. Two steaming mugs were placed on the table a minute later. Polly immediately started emptying packets of sugar into her drink.

'Right, lady, talk,' Alicia demanded.

Polly looked up absently.

'What is up with you?' Alicia asked exasperated.

Polly didn't answer.

'You are such hard work, hon, always keeping secrets, never telling me nothin'. For once will you just tell me what is going on with you.'

Alicia struck a chord. It was half-truths and omissions that had got Polly into this mess in the first place. If she'd told James and DS Watson the whole story, Sebastian would probably be locked up right now. And if she'd trusted herself, and stuck with the people she knew cared for her, she'd be safe right now. She wanted to cry.

Polly started talking. She talked for an hour non-stop, telling Alicia everything – absolutely everything. Alicia listened silently, engrossed in what Polly was saying. When Polly finally stopped, Alicia let out a long, slow whistle.

'Fuck,' she said shaking her head. 'You have been through it, girl. What you gonna do now?'

'I don't know,' replied Polly. 'I've got to stop him somehow, I can't spend the rest of my life looking over my shoulder.'

'No, but he sounds hardcore. Go back to the police, let them deal with it.'

'Last time I spoke to the police they said they'd do me for wasting their time. There's no way I can go back to them.'

For the first time Alicia was lost for words. She just sat across from Polly, shaking her head; she couldn't offer anything.

But Polly's mind was racing. Telling Alicia had allowed her to reflect on the whole thing from a totally new perspective

'The thing I really don't get is Charlotte,' she said.

'Oliver's sister?'

'Yeah. She keeps cropping up in all this, especially after what Crispin just said.'

'The guy you just met on the train, right?' asked Alicia, trying to keep up with the story.

'Yeah, how could Charlotte possibly know?'

'Maybe she's into tubing too.'

'I doubt it – if you ever saw her you'd know what I mean. Too perfect.'

'No offence, but there's no way I would have thought you would have been into this kind of kinky stuff neither.'

But Polly wasn't listening any more. It suddenly occurred to her that Alicia had probably seen Charlotte.

'Fuck,' said Polly a little too loudly.

The few occupied tables looked round to see who had interrupted the gentle hubbub of their conversation.

'What?' asked Alicia, surprised by her sudden outburst.

'That night,' said Polly, eyes wide and head nodding as if Alicia should know exactly which night she was talking about.

'What night?'

'You know, when we went for a drink after work. Where was it?' Polly paused trying to grasp her thoughts. 'Oh, I can't remember. It was a new place on Chancery Lane.'

'Oh, yeah, I remember.'

'Charlotte was there.'

'What do you mean?'

'When I went to the loo I bumped into her.'

'Was she?' Alicia paused. 'Oh, that skinny white girl you were talking to by the bar. That was Charlotte?'

'That was Charlotte,' Polly repeated far, far away in thought. She was suddenly up on her feet, ready to leave.

'Hey, where you going?' asked Alicia.

'There's something I've got to do.'

'Wait, let me come with,' said Alicia, grabbing her bag.

'No,' said Polly vehemently.

'I'm coming with you,' said Alicia firmly. 'Let me just pay for the coffees.'

The second Alicia's back was turned, Polly was out of the door. She was halfway down the road when she heard Alicia shouting after her. Polly started running. She had no intention of stopping.

Forty-three

Polly had only been to Charlotte's flat once before, but she could still just about remember the way. She got off the tube at Hammersmith. She went under the flyover then down Fulham Palace Road. She pulled her coat around her and put her hood up as the September wind pressed in against her. She knew Charlotte lived close to Charing Cross Hospital so she headed there and prayed she'd recognise her road when she got to it.

It didn't take long to find. She stood outside the large converted town house. It felt imposing in the dark, lumbering down on her. After several deep breaths, she made her way up the small flight of stairs to the front door.

Charlotte lived in the ground-floor flat. Polly pressed the buzzer. Charlotte answered the door straight away, as if she was expecting someone. The broad smile on her face soon disappeared when she saw Polly standing there.

'Oh, Polly,' she said, the smile back on her face, remembering her manners. 'What are you doing here? I thought you were a hoodlum for a moment with that hood up.'

Polly couldn't think of anything to say, so just barged her way in.

'Come in, why don't you?' said Charlotte, stepping aside.

Charlotte's flat was warm. Polly gave an involuntary shudder when the heat hit her. She pulled back her hood and unzipped her jacket. Sharp, spicy smells came from the kitchen. The elegant dining table was set for dinner.

'I've guests coming,' Charlotte said as she led her through the dining room to the lounge. The table was set for six. 'A little dinner party.'

'Sebastian maybe? Or Ed, perhaps?' Polly didn't know why she said it – the names came out without her thinking.

Charlotte stopped and turned sharply to look at her. 'Sorry, I don't understand,' she said sweetly, but her face gave it all away. She pointed to the sofa, indicating that Polly should sit. She didn't. 'Suit yourself,' Charlotte said, walking over to the antique dresser by the fireplace. She took out two wine glasses and filled each with red. She handed one to Polly as she took a deep gulp from the other.

They both stood in silence.

Eventually, Charlotte spoke.

'It's lovely to see you, Polly, but did you come here for any particular reason?'

Polly wanted to laugh. Charlotte knew exactly why she was here.

'What do you think, Charlotte? Why do you *think* I'm here?' she said, unable to keep the sarcasm from her voice.

'I've no idea,' she said, taking another large mouthful from her glass.

'A lot of odd things have been happening to me lately, Charlotte, a lot of weird coincidences.'

'Ri-i-ight,' replied Charlotte slowly, as if Polly were mad. But the air between them had taken on a sudden sharpness.

'I'm not really a believer in coincidences. I believe there's a good reason behind most things,' she continued.

Charlotte was pulling her best confused face. 'I really don't see what—'

Polly ignored her, talking over the top of her. 'The thing is, there's one person in all this whose name keeps coming up.'

She looked straight at Charlotte.

Charlotte's face flushed. 'I have no idea what—'

'*Your* name, Charlotte. Your name keeps coming up.'

Polly noticed that Charlotte's hands had started to tremble. She suddenly looked very small and frail. After a few seconds she put down her glass and looked at her dainty gold wristwatch. 'My guests will be here any minute, so I really must be getting on.'

'No,' said Polly, slamming her glass down on the small nest of tables next to her. The delicate stem broke, spilling red wine all over her hand and on the table. Polly let the drips from her hand dribble down. Charlotte winced as each droplet splashed on to the cream carpet, but she didn't move to clear it up. 'I'm not leaving until you tell me what's going on.'

'I'm very sorry, Polly, but I really don't know what you're talking about.'

She wasn't going to make this easy. 'Tubing. I'm talking about tubing.'

A quick smile snaked on to Charlotte's lips at the mention of the word, then disappeared just as fast. 'Oh,' was all she said.

'What did you do, Charlotte?'

'I didn't do anything.'

'You set me up.'

'Set you up? Set you up? Polly,' she replied, shaking her head. 'I simply gave you the match – you lit the flame. What happened between you and Sebastian was your own doing. I didn't make you *do* anything.'

Polly was floored – she'd admitted it, she'd actually admitted it.

'Why?' Polly asked breathless, the wind knocked out of her. 'Why would you do such a thing?'

'It was a joke,' Charlotte said dismissively.

'A joke? A fucking *joke*?' Polly said, her voice getting louder.

Charlotte looked genuinely scared of her. 'Well, not a joke. I mean…' She broke off.

Polly just stared at her in disbelief.

'I didn't mean it to go so far. I knew what was supposed to be happening the night of your anniversary; Oliver had already shown me the ring. It wasn't right. When I saw you out getting drunk with that horrid girl, I just thought…I don't know…it wasn't right for you to be getting engaged.'

'Not right for me? How the hell do you know what's right for me?'

'Oliver, you and Oliver – you're not right together.'

'Oh, I get it,' said Polly. 'You don't think I'm good enough for him.'

'You said it,' Charlotte replied smugly.

'But how…what…what did you do?'

'I texted Sebastian with a description of what you were wearing and what tube station you'd be at.'

'But…wait a minute…I mean, how did you know where I'd be?'

'It hardly takes a genius to work out which tube line you'd get home.'

'You fucking bitch. You horrible, evil little fucking witch,' Polly knew she wasn't making sense any more and that throwing random swear words at Charlotte would achieve very little, but she didn't care, she was so mad, so incensed by what she had done. 'Do you have any idea what Sebastian's up to? What he's doing to those women?' she managed after gaining a small amount of composure.

'Spare me the details, Polly.'

Polly couldn't believe how unaffected Charlotte was by all this. She almost seemed to be enjoying herself.

She could feel her blood bubbling up through her veins. 'Just because tubing fucked up your relationship, you thought you'd do the same to your brother. Nice.' She spat the last word out.

'What are you talking about?'

Polly had clearly hit a very raw, precise nerve. 'Ed. That's why you and Ed broke up, right?'

'Who told you?' Charlotte's eyes were suddenly wild, the hurt and jealousy still all there.

'It's obvious.' Polly paused for a moment. 'I've been with him.'

'Who? Ed?'

'Yes, Ed. Your fiancé – sorry, your ex-fiancé.'

'You're vile. *This* is why I had to stop Oliver proposing, I couldn't let him marry a cheap little slut like you. Tubing – it's perverse, nothing but frottage.' Speckles of spit flew from Charlotte's mouth, as if she were a rabid dog. Polly half expected her to fly across the room and attack her, but she didn't, she stayed put, although from the way she was trembling it was taking every ounce of energy.

They looked at one another long and hard, then Polly said, 'Well you'd better get used to me, because I'm not going anywhere.' She didn't know if she really meant it, but she knew it would be her choice and hers alone.

'Oh, really?' The snake was back in the room. 'I think once Oliver hears what you've been up to, you won't be hearing wedding bells any time soon.'

'And once he hears who set me up in the first place, I can't imagine you'll be seeing your brother again, ever. I'll make sure of that.'

Charlotte shrank back a little.

'Boyfriends come and go, and yeah, I'd be sad to lose Oliver, but to lose a brother, to lose your *Olliepops* because of what you did – wow, that really would be shit for you.'

Charlotte opened her mouth to speak, but then shut it again.

'Give me Sebastian's number,' Polly demanded.

'What?' asked Charlotte. 'Why?'

'Because I've got to put a stop to all this.'

'I did try to warn you. I told you he was dangerous.'

'A bit too fucking late, though. Just give me his number.'

Charlotte paused for a moment.

'OK. I don't suppose it'll do him any harm. I'm not sure about you, though.'

'Just tell me.'

Charlotte walked over to the coffee table and picked up her phone. She started slowly scrolling through her numbers. Polly didn't have time for this. She marched straight up to her and snatched the phone from her hand. Charlotte flinched, cowering back away from her. Polly copied the number into her phone then threw Charlotte's down on to the floor.

She turned to leave, then stopped. 'Charlotte,' she said, facing her again.

'Yes.'

'Stop bothering me and Oliver. You really get in the way.'

297

With that, she left.

As soon as Polly was through the front door, she sent a text to Sebastian's number.

Lancaster Gate 10.45 tonight. Eastbound platform.

Forty-four

'We have some breaking news just in,' said the newscaster directly to camera. 'Police in London have cordoned off Lancaster Gate tube station after a person was hit by a train late last night. The police have so far refused to comment, but speculation is rife that there may have been a second person involved in the incident and it is being treated as a murder investigation. Our reporter, Sally-Anne Devlin, is live at the scene.'

The picture cut to a busy Bayswater Road. Morning traffic was piled up behind a slim, plain-looking woman with a bobbed haircut in a red jacket. She took up the story.

'Yes, Colin, the police have shut down Lancaster Gate tube station in light of last night's events, causing major disruption to the Central Line. As of yet we have no official word to say what exactly happened here. So far, all we know is that a person was hit by a train on the eastbound line at this station just before 11 p.m. In a statement released by Transport for London ...' Sally-Anne glanced down at a bit of paper in her hand out of shot ' ... a full investigation is under way and Transport for London are co-operating fully with the police. They're unable to comment further at this time. She looked up directly to camera. 'Our sources tell us that a statement will be read out by the Met shortly, but as yet we've had no official word as to what happened, nor has there been any indication as to when the Central Line will be back up to speed. The best way to describe the situation here in this part of London is turmoil. Back to you in the studio, Colin.'

The saucer clattered loudly as Polly put her teacup back down on the table. She'd been sitting totally motionless with the cup poised by her bottom lip throughout the entire report. But now her hands shook so violently that the stone-cold contents of the cup spilt everywhere in huge waves.

She looked around at the other customers in the all-night café. They were mostly taxi drivers in for their morning fry-up. She'd been sat there since two a.m. last night; it was now 6.36 a.m. She was filthy. Her clothes were covered in black soot. She had a nasty gash on her forehead and the tip of her middle finger was crushed almost completely flat with the nail embedded deep in the skin – she hadn't dared look at it yet.

She'd found the café under the railway arches just down from Paddington station. She had gone straight to the ladies' toilet to try to clean herself up, but the bleeding from her forehead wasn't ready to stop and there was very little she could do about the state of her clothes. The man behind the counter was less than pleased to see her, but soon parked her down in the corner with a cup of hot, sweet tea when he saw the shell-shocked state she was in. He'd asked several times if she was OK and whether he could call someone for her; she had just shaken her head and murmured that she was fine.

In the hours she'd been there everything had become numb; even the throbbing in her finger had become slow and rhythmical. She looked back up at the TV above the counter. It had been on all night, but this was the first item she'd seen about what had happened.

When she had seen Sebastian waiting for her on the eastbound platform of Lancaster Gate station, she had started to tremble, but not with fear this time – with pure, unadulterated rage. She'd watched him from the shadow of the stairwell. He was dressed impeccably in a pair of chinos and an expensive wool coat. He walked back and forth nonchalantly while he waited for the train.

Polly's eyes narrowed as they followed him. His life had continued as if nothing had happened; he'd barely broken stride. She'd been a blip, a minor annoyance, a fly that he'd had to swat away. She'd lost so much because of him. She involuntarily clenched her fists hard, until her nails drew blood from each palm. And he was going to be allowed to carry on doing whatever the fuck he liked for the rest of his life. The world was his playground and he could dick around with whoever he liked in it.

The heady drone of the next train thundering down the tracks echoed in her ears. The sound taunted her as it grew louder and louder. Before she knew what she was doing, she was running straight at him. He didn't see her until she was almost touching him. Her hands were outstretched and clawing for his coat. He quickly turned to try to defend himself. She planted both her hands on his chest and pushed him with all her might. Her nails dug deep into his shirt; she could feel them cut into the flesh below. She bit down hard on her tongue as she pushed harder.

He was forced to take a step back. His heels teetered on the edge of the platform. He reacted quickly, grabbing her around the waist to stop himself falling. They wobbled precariously together as if in an embrace. It didn't take much for him to get his balance back – Polly was so weak and thin that it was like batting away a kitten.

Once he'd steadied himself, he looked up to see the train's lights appearing in the distance in the dark tunnel. A wry smile played on his lips. He quickly swung her round so her back was to the tracks. She could hear the train getting closer and closer.

'So nice for you to give me this opportunity to end it all for you, Polly,' he said.

He grabbed her by her shoulders and used the rest of his body to force her over the edge of the platform. She tried to regain her balance and tip her weight forward, but he gave her no room to move. The front of the train appeared at the mouth of the tunnel. The noise was deafening.

It was then that the moment of clarity came. If she was going in front of this train, she was going to take him with her.

She looped both arms inside his coat around his waist, pulled herself tight into him and squeezed her eyes shut.

She could just make out his scream over the noise of the train as she jumped.

Forty-five

Polly's first thought was that she didn't think you could think when you were dead.

She opened her eyes. It was dark, really dark; she could barely see a thing. She used her hands to explore her immediate surroundings. She knew she was lying on her tummy, but couldn't feel anything in front of her. She reached out as far as she could, but there was nothing. She kicked her legs back and shuffled a few inches backwards, but again there was nothing. She reached out either side and immediately hit concrete. From what she could feel, she was in some kind of concrete channel. She reached up above her head and felt hard metal. She quickly pulled her hand away when her brain caught up with the burning in her fingertips. Then it dawned on her. She was underneath the train. She'd fallen into the suicide pit.

Her eyes were slowly adjusting to the darkness. She could just about make out a faint light up ahead. She started crawling underneath the tracks towards it. She stopped dead when she realised she was dangerously close to the electrified third rail. She moved across so she was to the right of the pit, furthest away from it.

As she got closer to the front of the train, she could see some kind of sack on the tracks, out ahead in the light.

The bottom half of it had fallen down into the pit and the rest was hanging over the side of the concrete blocks. She stopped when she recognised the expensive wool coat. His clothes were still completely intact, holding together his shattered, pulverised remains. All that was missing was his head.

Her body lurched back and forth as her guts heaved inside her until she could barely take a breath. She started reversing back under the train. Once she was a safe distance away, she stopped and took in big gulps of air.

Suddenly there was silence. The train's engine had been switched off.

She heard the tube doors open and then voices as bewildered commuters started to get off the train.

The platform was suddenly alive with activity. She could hear footsteps running up and down the tiled floor, and the crackle of walkie-talkies. Then the tannoy system sprang into life.

Will all customers please make their way directly to the nearest exit. There has been an incident in this station. We need to evacuate all platforms and close the station. Please make your way to the nearest exit in a calm, orderly manner.

The babble of voices on the platform began to steadily rise.

She heard a door open then slam shut. The driver had just climbed out of his cabin.

'Oh, God,' he said. 'Oh, Jesus fuckin' Christ.'

More voices as people went to the front of the train to look.

'Move away, please, ladies and gentleman, please make your way to the nearest exit,' said a male voice, moving closer. 'Are you all right, mate?' said the voice, Polly assumed to the driver. The other people on the platform were moving away so Polly could hear them both clearly.

'I don't know what the fuck just happened. They came from … just … outta fuckin' nowhere.'

'They? You mean more than one went under?' he said.

'I don't know, maybe. I thought I saw someone else, but … I don't know. His coat … his coat was all bunched up, it didn't look right.'

'Look don't worry, transport police are on their way, they'll be here any minute.'

Polly heard footsteps moving towards the front of the train. 'Bloody hell,' said the driver, then he retched and the contents of his stomach splattered on the platform.

'Come away from there, don't look. Transport will sort this mess out.'

Polly stayed as still as possible, terrified that she'd give herself away at any moment.

'You're all right, mate, take a couple of deep breaths.'

Suddenly there were several pairs of footsteps running down the platform. Police radios crackled loudly echoing around the station.

'Right,' said a female voice. 'I'm PC Fowler and this is PC Daniels. We got three carriages with people in them still stuck in the tunnel. They've turned off the live rail so we can get down on the track now and get the body cleared. Then we're gonna need to get the train moved forward to get everybody out.'

'Bod-ies,' said the man who'd been speaking to the driver.

'There's more than one?' asked PC Fowler.

'Oh, God, I don't know,' said the driver. 'It all happened so fast, I thought I saw someone else, but I dunno now. Maybe it was just his coat, his coat was bunched up all funny.'

'Are you saying that the train hit more than one person?'

'I don't *know*,' said the driver, exasperated. He sounded as if he were on the verge of tears.

'Right, well, let's get this place cordoned off as a crime scene until we've had a look at the CCTV footage.'

'Good luck with that,' replied the man.

'What? What do you mean?' asked PC Fowler.

'It's been on the blink since Monday.'

'What?'

'I'm not the man in charge around here – not up to me when these things get fixed.'

Polly heard a loud crackle on the radio, then PC Fowler's voice again. 'Sarge, you're not gonna fucking believe this…'

It wouldn't be long before they were down on the tracks. Polly had to get out of there fast.

She tried to turn around so she was facing the other way, but the gap wasn't big enough. She started crawling backwards, slowly at first, then picking up pace when she heard the first thump as someone jumped down on to the tracks. Bits of dirt and gravel ripped up the skin on her palms as she crawled as quickly as she could. Even though the train's engine had been switched off, the heat was unbearable. Beads of sweat trickled down her neck and dripped off the end of her nose.

She was nearly at the back of the train when she heard a loud squeak and something ran across her hand. She jumped up in fright, hitting her forehead on the metal undercarriage above. The pain gave her a few moments' grace before it hit her. It was blinding. She instantly collapsed flat on the floor, warm, sticky blood oozing down her forehead. It hurt so much she couldn't even make a sound to articulate it. She lay there incapacitated for several minutes. She contemplated staying put forever, keeping her eyes closed and just waiting until they moved the train and found her. Maybe now was the time to give up. But then she remembered *him*. She needed to survive because he hadn't. What good was the world if she couldn't exist without him in it?

With a superhuman effort she picked herself up and got going again.

The train went all the way back into the tunnel. Once she was sure she was clear of the undercarriage, she stood up. It was dark. The train obscured most of the light coming from the platform. She turned and looked down into the tunnel. She tried to estimate how long it would take to walk underground to the next station. Queensway was the next one down. When she was on the Central Line it always seemed to take ages between stations until it got to Marble Arch. It was probably at least a mile, maybe two. She debated it for a second before realising it was a stupid idea – what if there were other trains still running on the track? They'd said they were going to switch the power back on soon. She doubted it after what had just happened, but she couldn't be sure.

She turned back to face the train. There was a small gap between the tunnel and the side of the train. She moved in close to size it up. It was tiny, but she reckoned she could just about squeeze down the ten metres or so to the platform. She took a deep breath and slowly eased her way in. She'd only taken a couple of steps when she found herself in front of a lit carriage window. There were several people down the far end, still stuck inside, waiting at the doors. She tried to duck down, but the space was so small it was impossible. She quickly slid back out behind the train before anyone saw.

She lashed out at the tunnel wall with her fist in frustration. What now? She had to get out of there. The police would be moving the train soon. What would they think if they found her down here? She suddenly had an image of a sharp-suited DC Watson giving evidence against her in a packed courtroom. Tears flooded her throat and threatened her eyes. She took a deep breath. Now was not the time to lose it. Once she was out of here she could fall apart into a million pieces if she liked, but until that time she had to keep herself together and focus on getting out.

After a few minutes, she'd calmed down enough to think straight again. There must be a logical way to do this. Her eyes had become more accustomed to the darkness now, so she was better able to stand back and evaluate the shape of the train. She noticed a small space to the side of the wheels. She bent down to take a closer look. The wheels of the train ran along the tracks above but didn't quite run along the concrete edge, they came in slightly. There was a small gap about three feet by three feet between the train's wheels and the tunnel wall.

'You can do this, Polly,' she whispered to herself.

She got down low to take a good long look. If she could make it to the end of the first couple of carriages, she'd be able to climb up through the gap where it joined the next carriage and on to the platform.

She got on her hands and knees and slowly made her way into the gap. She put her arms out ahead of her as a guide, then slowly pulled her body along. She was completely flat, slithering like a snake. She could see the light from the platform getting closer and closer.

'Keep it going, Polly,' she whispered to herself. 'That's it, nice and steady.'

Suddenly the train's engine fired up above her. The vibrations along the track were bone-shattering. She panicked – not knowing whether to try to back up or carry on. But she was so close now. She had to keep going. She grabbed on to the rail above her head and started dragging herself along as fast as she could. Suddenly the train started reversing above her. A set of wheels crunched over the tip of her middle finger, mashing the nail deep into the skin and crushing the bone. The scream was out before she had a chance to stop it.

The train suddenly stopped and the engine cut out. 'Whoa, whoa,' someone was shouting from up ahead. 'We've found the head. Someone just needs to jump down and get it, then we can get moving again.'

It was now or never. Polly pulled herself forward using every ounce of strength she had left. Her hands ripped and tore at the ground beneath her as she tried to get purchase. Moments later she reached the gap between the carriages. She grabbed on to the edge of the platform. She stopped momentarily to pull the hood of her jacket down low over her face and hauled herself halfway up. The exit was directly in front of her. She looked to her left. Police and tube train staff were busy watching the poor sod who had to retrieve the head. She bent forward and slithered on to the platform. She was up on her feet and out of the platform in seconds. She hid in a side tunnel for the next fifteen minutes until the remaining commuters were let off the train, then she calmly walked amongst them to the exit.

The news channel gave regular updates of the story on the hour every hour. It wasn't until 9.15 that the Met finally made their statement. A DCI who looked far too young to have such an important job read from a single sheet of paper.

'At 10.49 p.m. last night a man was his hit by a train on the eastbound platform of Lancaster Gate station. After a full and thorough investigation of the scene, we can confirm that no other parties were involved, despite rumours to the contrary. However, it is unclear whether the man jumped or fell in front of the train. The body has been identified as that of Sebastian Black, son of Robert Black.'

With this last sentence the crowd of waiting journalists went ballistic – a sudden surge forward, camera bulbs flashing, questions flying. The DCI was unable to continue reading his statement; instead he was forced into action, trying to calm the crowd.

After a few moments, the picture cut back to the studio, although with the live footage from the scene still playing in the background.

The newsreader looked shocked. 'As you can see from our live pictures, an announcement has just confirmed the suicide of Sebastian Black, son of the media mogul Robert Black and heir to the Black Inc. empire.'

He continued on struggling to cobble together whatever he was being told through his earpiece, with all hell breaking loose in the media mogul's newsroom.

They had a real story to report now, one that Polly would play no part in.

She gathered herself together and left the café.

Acknowledgements

Special thanks to the innovative women at RedDoor for taking publishing in a direction that allows new authors to emerge, and for their endless enthusiasm and support. To my editor Linda McQueen for her patience and expertise, as well as the time spent scoping out tube stations. Thank you to my teachers at Brunel who supported the novel from day one, especially Matt Thorne, Celia Brayfield and Fay Weldon. Thanks to Kate Ramsay for the author photo in spite of my awkwardness. Lastly and most importantly, to my family and friends: it would all be nothing without you lot around me.

About the Author

photograph | Kate Ramsay

K.A. McKeagney studied psychology in Bristol before completing a Masters degree in creative writing at Brunel. She won the Curtis Brown prize for her dissertation, which formed the basis of her first novel, *Tubing*. She has worked in London as a health editor, writing consumer information, as well as for medical journals. Her writing has been commended by the British Medical Association (BMA) patient information awards. She is currently working on her second novel.